MARKS

CHRISTOPHER KELLY

CHRISTOPHER
KELLY

INVICTUS

Out of the night that covers me,
 Black as the pit from pole to pole,
 I thank whatever gods may be
  For my unconquerable soul.

In the fell clutch of circumstance
 I have not winced nor cried aloud.
Under the bludgeonings of chance
 My head is bloody, but unbowed.

Beyond this place of wrath and tears
 Looms but the Horror of the shade,
 And yet the menace of the years
  Finds and shall find me unafraid.

It matters not how strait the gate,
How charged with punishments the scroll,
 I am the master of my fate,
  I am the captain of my soul.

—William Ernest Henley
Book of Verses, 1888

PART I

OMENS

1
————

NOT AFRAID

The house is small, with barely enough room to section proper living and kitchen areas in between the two basic bedrooms. Half an hour after Mark Simbas was scheduled to leave for his job at Thirsty Creek High School, his 1985 sedan is still parked in the driveway out front.

"Have you seen my ID?" Mark asks his girlfriend, with an anxious quality to his features.

The sun has just broken above the horizon, the light outside still dim. A single bulb in the hood above the worn, nineties-era stove provides light for the search.

"No. Was I supposed to set it out for you?" Reya asks.

Her voice is soft, the irritation subtle. Mark recognizes the irked tone. He's heard it enough to notice when he is grating on someone's nerves. It isn't only Reya who becomes frustrated with him.

"I'm sorry, it's alright," he says with a shake of his head, attempting to avoid a tense interaction. "You have your own job to worry about."

Reya's brows raise. She remains silent, though, neither confirming nor denying. She has learned that it is best this way.

"Did you put the trash can out?" Mark tries.

A change of subject seems wise.

He bumps and bustles around the packed little house as he looks for his badge. Already late, he'll need to find it soon if there is any hope of making it to school in time to teach his class.

"Trash day is tomorrow," Reya says. "You can put the bin out by the curb tonight."

"Right," Mark replies. He walks to his girlfriend and gives her a quick kiss. "You head on to work. I'll find my ID and go to school."

"Please don't get in trouble with the others," Reya says. "We can barely afford to take care of ourselves … and with the baby coming …"

Mark takes a shallow breath and embraces his girlfriend bluntly. "I know," he replies. "I won't get fired."

"It's just that it's the second week of the year, and you're already late," she continues. "Teachers have to be on time. You should know that."

"It's fine," he says. "Go to work. I'll call you later."

He kisses her on the forehead this time, then pats her pregnant belly and guides her gently out the front door. Reluctantly, Reya gets into her own, much nicer car—a gift from her wealthy parents—and drives away.

Free to go about his business without being watched, Mark tears the house apart until finally, he finds the ID in his pants pocket. He'd placed it there while probing the fridge for a breakfast item that didn't reek of rotten eggs. The persistent stink was his fault as well. He'd forgotten to throw a container of egg salad out before he and Reya had left for her cousin's wedding in South Carolina last month. By the time they'd returned home it could've been submitted for study at a college with all the sickly mold pockets in the Tupperware.

What a lovely day, Mark thinks to himself as he slips the lanyard with his ID around his neck and hurries to the door, moving on.

He grabs a stack of textbooks on his way out of the house, then piles them onto the passenger seat of his clunker.

Glancing quickly through the stack, he makes sure the proper books are there. He'd planned to dig deeper into the Pleistocene Epoch with his students that day, and he'd need the supplemental material to reference. Mark loved world history as much as the next guy in his field, but that didn't mean he could teach it from memory. And talking generally about glaciers, Neanderthals, mastodons, and the like wouldn't be enough, especially for his honor students. They'd demand the nitty-gritty details.

The radio blares when he turns the ignition.

"Once Bitten Twice Shy" is immediately recognizable on the rock station, its familiar "my, my, my" lyrics fill the airspace inside Mark's vehicle and harken back to a time when he'd listened to the song as a kid in his father's garage. If he allowed himself to reminisce, he could still smell the grease on his dad's overalls and the gasoline in the spare can that sat next to a red metal toolbox on the workbench.

Things had been better then. His parents had still been alive, for starters. His older sisters had adored him.

And his birthmarks hadn't been so dark. Instead, they had been faint, nearly invisible to the naked eye.

Oh, what he wouldn't give to go back. The entire world had been his oyster then, shiny and full of promise.

But Mark doesn't want to think about any of that now. Not on this day. Not when things are looking up in his life. He is a different man now. He fastens his seatbelt and tells himself once more that it will be a good day.

The new Mark is committed to focusing on the positive. He'd finally heard enough New Age gurus clamor on about the power of positivity that he'd committed to giving the practice an earnest try. Every time he recognizes negative thoughts creeping into his mind, he forces himself to pivot and to think about something else instead.

It is harder than it sounds, but it has worked, thus far. Mark credits positive thinking to helping him snag Reya, who is, admittedly, way out of his league. He also credits the good vibes to helping the couple become pregnant. They hadn't been trying for a baby, but that didn't mean they didn't want one.

Their little one is a blessing. Mark is keenly aware that some people spend their entire adult lives wanting a child of their own. And now, with a little luck that the baby's healthy, he won't end up one of them. Mark will have his own personal legacy in the form of another human, alive and kicking long after he's gone.

He hopes that becoming a father will change his life in all the good ways people talk about. He believes things can only get better from here. Isn't that what every bonafide positive thinker should believe, anyway?

Tires squeal as Mark picks up speed, the ragged

sedan puffing to keep pace with the heaviness of his foot on its accelerator. He rolls down all the windows, letting Great White's song expand into the morning air while relishing the rush of the incoming breeze against his skin. He is a king at this moment, his troubles pushed aside and the carefree spirit he'd known long, long ago still intact, deep down.

He closes his eyes ever so briefly, delighting in the experience like the positivity gurus urge their followers to do. If Mark focuses on feeling good, he'll manifest more things to feel good about, right? That's what the experts claim.

As it turns out, that part of the ride is unremarkable, in the grand scheme of things. Just another morning commute to work on another normal day. Until it isn't.

An old Ford pickup truck running a red light at Spitz Junction almost changes everything.

Mark is obeying traffic laws, technically, when the crash happens. He has the right of way. His light has turned green just as he arrives at the intersection, so he scoots on through without bothering to notice what is happening with the man in the approaching pickup. A large median with dense landscaping obscures Mark's view until he is past the white line. It's too late to brake at the speed he is going.

When the pickup strikes the back corner of Mark's car, the impact is so forceful that it sends the dilapidated sedan spinning like a top. Metal crunches and glass shatters as Mark spins, unable to regain his bearings. Time seems to stand still as he careens out of control, the world spiraling around him like a carnival ride coming off its hinges.

"Oh, God, oh, oh, oh!" Mark yells, his voice

straining under the pressure being exerted on his body. The sounds he makes are more like grunts than yells, really. They're guttural. Primal. Involuntary.

He tries to steer, but the wheel isn't having it. Not even a bodybuilder with pecs and biceps of steel could stop the spin.

Mark had always heard people say that their lives flashed before their very eyes in situations like this. He suspects he might be learning a thing or two about that phenomenon. Whatever power is administering this lesson on his behalf is a cruel teacher who shows no mercy. Mark doesn't like the feeling of being so utterly vulnerable.

All he can think as he sways and shakes inside the metal death trap on wheels is how Reya will be pissed at him if he doesn't make it out alive. She isn't the sort of woman who will grieve well. She'll keep her feelings bottled up until they come out in a rage, no doubt spewing nasty remarks about him to their child. He doesn't want to leave her, and he doesn't want to exit this world without knowing his kid. Not to mention, he and Reya aren't legally married yet, which might make matters of his estate more difficult to resolve. He wills himself to stay alive.

"Just stay alive," Mark repeats under his breath, still attempting to keep a positive mindset. "Stay alive for Reya and the baby." Then, unable to maintain a false front, he shifts into more negative phrasing, "Don't die. Don't die, you insufferable prick! *Do not die!*"

By a stroke of what can only be described as sheer luck, Mark's car screeches to a halt just in time, narrowly missing a giant tractor parked on a gravel road in front of him. The engine in his car dies and the radio turns itself off unceremoniously, leaving behind an eerie silence.

"Thank the heavens," Mark mumbles, his knuckles white against the dash. He isn't a religious man, but after surviving that hell ride, he might be willing to become one. Closing his eyes, he exhales heavily. Perspiration lines his brows. It's a cold sweat. The kind that comes from sheer terror rather than physical exertion. "Reya," he says suddenly, reopening his eyes and fumbling for his phone. "I need to call you."

Before Mark can regain his equilibrium, a thin man in a hoodie is peering into his window.

"Hey, buddy, you okay in there?" the man asks.

Mark turns to look at him, but is too dazed to process all that is taking place. "Um, yeah, all good," Mark mumbles, immediately turning his attention away from the intrusion. "On my way to work."

Who does this guy think he is, anyway?

Mark's ears seem to be ringing. Why, he doesn't know. He paws at an ear with one hand while fiddling in the console in search of his phone with the other.

"Hey, buddy!" the man calls again, more forcefully this time. His large brown eyes seem wild with worry. For the life of him, Mark can't figure out what the stranger wants or why he is so insistent about it. "Open the door," the man continues, raising a palm. "I think your gas tank was hit. There are fumes. We've got to get you out of there."

Mark hears the words, but they don't register. Not like they should. He doesn't realize he is injured. Before he can respond to the good Samaritan's pleas, his phone rings. He recognizes the ascending chimes as Reya's ringtone. Filled with heightened motivation to locate the phone, Mark lunges forward. He hoists himself against the dash as he feels along the floorboard for the device. Textbooks are strewn about, their covers rumpled and their pages torn.

"I'm coming, Reya," he breathes.

He doesn't stop to question why she is calling him so soon after they'd both left for work. He isn't aware of how much time has gone by. He isn't aware of the horrific scene that has unfolded just a single car length behind him, either.

As Mark moves, a cold sensation surges through his left shoulder. It's strange. It doesn't feel like pain, exactly, yet it's clear that something is wrong. Is he in shock? He doesn't think so. Not that he'd recognize shock. For all of his misfortunes in life thus far, at least, he hasn't been seriously wounded.

He continues to fish around for the phone, finally laying eyes on the dimly lit display peering at him from the floorboard on the passenger side of the vehicle. He reaches out, but it's no use. Reya's call has ended.

"Oh, no," Mark mumbles incoherently. His head aches. The sensation of spinning continues, despite the fact that the car has come to a stop. Slivers of white light appear around the edges of his vision.

"What's going on?" Mark asks out loud. He tries to swivel his head further to find out for himself, but a searing pain stops him. "Ouch," he groans. "That's gonna need patched up."

For better or worse, the man outside isn't taking no for an answer. He'd disappeared for a time, but is back. Mark sees a gleam of light and thinks the man has a crowbar in hand now. The guy grits his teeth as he does something on the outside of Mark's door. The door doesn't budge.

"What are you doing?" Mark asks through the glass.

That particular window has remained intact. Like a tornado that decimates sections of a home while leaving others untouched, the collision has moved with no rhyme or reason.

"Getting you out, buddy," the man says. "No time to wait. Gas is leaking from your tank. The whole car could explode."

Mark shakes his head as the reality settles over him. "No. That can't be right."

"It is. Now cover your face and help me break the window. Your door's stuck. I don't think it will open."

In a flurry of activity, the glass is broken and the man gains access to the interior of the car. He assesses Mark's injury with the ease of a pro, then rips a piece of cloth from Mark's sleeve and ties it tightly around his upper arm.

As the good Samaritan works, Mark leans out the broken window and stares down at the man's shoes absentmindedly. They are steel-toed work boots. At first, he'd thought the man might be an off-duty medical professional, but the boots don't line up with that theory. They're worn and dirty, like they've been at a construction site.

"What are you? Some kind of boy scout?" Mark asks.

The man laughs, and Mark can see his face clearly for the first time. "Sure. Something like that, if you say so."

A gold tooth catches the light and shimmers in the

man's mouth. The brilliance seems to make his brown skin glow.

"Thank you," Mark says, staring up at the man.

"You're welcome," he replies. "Now, let's get moving. This isn't your day to die. Not yet."

Mark nods, but the ringing of his phone pulls his attention away yet again. It's Reya's ringtone.

"I have to answer," he tells the man emphatically. It's the most lucid he's been since the collision happened, and he means to get that phone. Reya will want to know what has happened. "It's my girlfriend. If I don't, she'll worry."

The man's gaze shoots to the phone on the floorboard, then to something outside of the vehicle. "You can't. There's no time," he says firmly.

"I have to," Mark insists, lunging for the phone.

"Pay attention!" the man shouts. It's the first time he's raised his voice. He'd appeared extremely chill up until now, but he is becoming aggravated. He isn't calling Mark "buddy" anymore. In fact, he doesn't sound very friendly at all. "You have to get out of this car. Right now, I say! Right now!"

Mark lowers his brow, considering the situation. "Why are you helping me?" he asks.

The man grimaces, but he doesn't answer. Instead, he purses his lips and again looks at what Mark now assumes is the leaking fuel outside. The guy seems to be thinking about how to convince Mark of the seriousness of the situation.

"Fine," Mark says without further prompting. He's beginning to smell the fumes himself. "I'm getting out."

The man's strong features soften as he nods. He motions for Mark to follow him through the broken window. Mark complies, wincing when the pain strikes but pushing forward anyway. The stranger's face offers a focal point—something to latch onto. It's an aide Mark hadn't realized he'd needed.

The focus brings to mind Reya's pregnancy and the Lamaze method of childbirth she'd been telling Mark about a few nights prior. Controlled breathing techniques are a staple of the popular method, and laboring women are encouraged to pick something to look at as they breathe through their pain—a clock on the wall, for instance. Maybe Mark isn't any different than a woman giving birth when it comes right down to it. He stares into the man's dark eyes as he carries on, letting those eyes guide him.

Within a few short minutes, Mark manages to get himself out the window. He lands on the soft ground below with a thud. Fortunately, he comes down on his right side, sparing the injured shoulder. The smell of gasoline is pungent now. It fills his lungs and makes him gag. It also provides a much-needed sense of urgency.

"Damn, that smells potent," Mark remarks to the man as he stands and appraises the scene from his new vantage point. "Good call. You were right—one hundred percent. We've gotta go. And fast."

Only the man isn't there any longer. Mark turns, his eyes scanning the area. Nothing. It is as if the guy has vanished into thin air.

"Where'd you go?" Mark asks, his voice carried by the wind.

He stumbles away from his crunched car. He's headed on foot toward the landscaped median, although he is still disoriented.

It's hard for Mark to make sense of the direction he

had been traveling before the wreck. He knows the high school isn't far away. Less than a mile, if his bearings serve him right. The creek is close by, too. He can hear its rushing water. If memory serves, he was driving west, toward the school. Which means he had come from the other way—east.

Without his car or his phone, he'll need to walk the rest of the way to the high school to check in at the office and call Reya. Both she and Principal Heinman are probably good and mad by now. He'll walk the rest of the distance. No problem. But Mark wishes to first thank the good Samaritan who helped him out of the car.

"Hey, where are you?" he calls, cupping a hand around his mouth to amplify the sound. There is no answer. The man has vanished into thin air. "Weird," Mark mumbles. "You've got to be around here somewhere."

A crowd is gathering nearby. Some people stare and point at Mark and his busted-up clunker, their fingers wagging as fast as their tongues. Others are preoccupied, focused on the certain something in the distance that Mark doesn't yet see.

People who live in Thirsty Creek are, apparently, concerned about the welfare of their neighbors. Northerners can say what they want about Southern culture, but small-town Tennessee is genial. That or they are simply curious and gawking.

Mark turns to face the crowd. "What are you all looking at?" he asks. No one replies directly. They just kept looking on, their faces tight with concern. "Never seen a fender bender before?" he continues.

Before anyone has the opportunity to give a proper answer, a whooshing sound fills the space between them as Mark's car goes up in flames. As the kind stranger feared, something has ignited the gasoline that was leaking from the vehicle's tank.

"Wow," Mark says. "That was a close one."

It's the first moment that it truly dawns on him what danger he was in. If he'd been in the car when it caught fire, he probably wouldn't have made it out alive. The stranger saved him.

Mark shoves a hand through his hair as he shifts his weight from one foot to the other. He suddenly wishes he had a cigarette to smoke. He can practically taste the nicotine. His body longs desperately for a puff. Reya made him cut back in anticipation of the baby coming, so he doesn't have a pack on him. The last few in his possession were in the glove compartment of his car. They're smoked now, alright, but not by Mark.

"Damn!" he shouts. "I can't catch a break."

Mark shrinks, immediately regretting the sentiment. Remembering the positive thinking he is supposed to be doing, he takes a minute and tries to calm himself down. Deep breaths of the cool morning air soothe his nerves a little. He attempts to pivot to a more productive thought, like the gurus instructed.

He's grateful to have survived the accident. Honest to God, he is. And he is grateful to the man who made such an effort to help him get out. But he is also sick and tired of being kicked in the teeth by life. He was minding his own business when the pickup hit him, after all. He hadn't done anything wrong.

It isn't fair. Nothing is fair.

"Suckage!" Mark shouts as he raises a fist in the air. He emphasizes the vowels for dramatic effect.

His shouts are addressed to no one in particular.

Even though other people are nearby, they seem separate somehow. Mark feels alone from where he stands.

In the distance, the distinctive sound of police sirens fills the air. They quickly grow louder and more insistent. A fire truck blares its horn as well, adding urgency to the emergency response.

Mark stumbles a few steps, still in shock. His responses aren't as fast as usual, but instinctively, he turns his body toward the sounds.

It's then that he finally realizes what the others are looking at. Something is there, on the other side of the median. He cranes his neck to one side. On the ground is the tailgate of the pickup truck that hit him. It's mangled, detached from the main part of the vehicle.

The hairs on the back of Mark's neck stand on end in response to what, at some level, he already knows: he isn't the only one who was hit. Another, more treacherous accident scene had unfolded behind him.

"Oh, no," he mumbles, picking up his pace and moving toward the wreck. "Oh, God, no. These poor people."

Though his instincts are on high alert now, the full impact of what happened doesn't become apparent until Mark rounds the front of the median and lays eyes on the tangle of metal and broken glass. His own shoulder injury is of little consequence compared what he is seeing. He rushes forward, ready to help.

First responders are close, judging by the volume of their sirens, but they haven't arrived yet. There is an eerie quality to the air, as if a portal has opened and those willing can step through, if they so choose. Maybe someone already has.

As he arrives at the damaged vehicles, it's initially hard to figure out if anyone is still inside.

The entire front half of the pickup has collapsed in on itself making it look like some sort of trailer without a passenger cab. Maybe the front part has been sheared off. Maybe it has spun out and away from this accident site, much like Mark's little car had. A quick examination of the accordion-like metal in front of the truck bed tells a different story, though. It's as if a giant hammer has pummeled the pickup from the front, forcing all of its mass to heave itself into a tiny space.

That can't be good, Mark thinks. *No one could have survived that.*

It's obvious that if anyone is still in that truck, they aren't alive. There's no way. He doesn't want to investigate any further for fear of what horrors he might see. He isn't entirely sure he can handle it.

In an instant, the contents of Mark's stomach find their way upward. He bends over violently, heaving and retching all over the blacktop. His car continues to burn in the distance like some makeshift tribute, memorializing the accident victims.

When he is finished, he wipes his mouth and keeps moving, walking around what's left of the pickup.

The sirens are so close now. It sounds like they are right on top of him. He's relieved, but in too much shock to properly process any of it. He is compelled to keep looking through the rubble. If he can find a way to be of use, he will.

He'd learned basic first aid when he began teaching at the high school. He'd never had a chance to put those skills to use, but he thinks he could probably remember enough to do some good in a situation like this. That is, if there is anyone he can get to. Anyone not completely entangled in metal.

Mark walks around the pickup truck, apprehensive but determined. There, to his horror, he finds an even more sickening sight.

It's a little silver car, about the size of his own. The body of the vehicle is a compact mass that strikes him as looking like a safe in a bank. Or an ATM machine, maybe. It's a tight, dense package, yet the top—what should be the roof— has been ripped off. He scans the area just past the collision and locates the missing piece of metal.

Have mercy, he thinks.

The roof of the car isn't the only errant object in sight. A few feet away from it is a human torso, headless and with a single limb attached at the shoulder.

At this point, Mark loses the remaining liquid in his stomach. He heaves even more violently than the first time, his entire body fraught with revulsion. He doesn't bother to look for the other body parts. He doesn't want to see them. He doesn't want to see anything like this ever again.

2

UNCANNY

As he spins on his heels and attempts to collect himself, Mark feels a small yet firm hand on his back.

"Sir, are you okay? Are you hurt?" Mark turns to see a short, blonde policewoman in uniform. A male colleague is fishing something out of the trunk of their patrol car nearby. "Look at my face, sir," she continues as she guides Mark toward her, making sure he's turned away from the headless torso.

Mark tries to point, but winces with pain. "I … Over there …" he stammers, trailing off. "A man was thrown … A pickup truck hit his car … "

The policewoman looks at him intently. She's cool and calm. Apparently, she's been trained to keep a level head in this kind of situation. Mark is doing his best to stay cool, too, but he is visibly shaken. He's never seen a mangled corpse. Surely, that's what it is at this point. A corpse. There's so much blood. More than he'd realized a human body could hold.

The woman's partner rushes from their patrol car

with a large white sheet. Presumably, he is going to cover the remains.

Thank God, Mark thinks. *Cover him up good.*

"Paramedics are on the way," the woman says softly. "Focus on my face, okay? Don't look at anything else. We'll get you checked out as soon as they arrive."

Mark nods, allowing himself to breathe. He doesn't want to be examined by paramedics if it will keep him from getting to work and calling Reya, but he doesn't tell the cop that. "My car caught fire," he mumbles, coincidentally seeing the firetruck pull up to the scene. Men and women in firefighting gear hop out and tighten their helmets.

"Were you involved in the collision?" the policewoman asks, raising her brows. She doesn't seem skeptical exactly, but she's unsure. She's feeling him out. Deciding if he can be believed. She's eyeing his birthmarks as well. Everybody does when they first meet him.

Mark nods again. "That … that torn-up guy … It was almost me. A few seconds later and it *would* have been me. I would have been … dismembered. God!"

"Sir, what's your name?" she asks gently. "Let's start there."

Mark shakes his head and shoves another hand through his hair. It needs to be cut. It's been bugging him —curling over his ears—but he hasn't gotten around to stopping at the barbershop. He closes his eyes. "I'm Mark," he says. "Mark Edward Simbas." He doesn't know why he included his middle name. That wasn't necessary.

"Good, Mark," she replies. "I'm Officer Rollins.

Dawn Rollins. You can call me Dawn, if you want. Pleased to meet you."

He nods, but his mind is elsewhere. He won't be able to remember this woman's name five minutes from now, and he knows it. She knows it, too. She's a distraction from the enormity of what's going on. That's a good thing in certain ways. A bad thing in others. "Okay," he says simply.

"Why don't we sit down?" Dawn asks when she notices that Mark is unsteady on his feet.

"No!" Mark shouts. "I don't have time. I need to get to work. And I need to call Reya."

She places a hand on his arm to steady him. She's pretty good at this part of her job, actually. She isn't patronizing. "Where do you work, Mark?"

As Dawn talks, she carefully guides him to the hood of her patrol car, then motions for him to sit. At least she doesn't make him sit inside. Mark doesn't think he'd be comfortable with that. He's no goody two shoes but he hasn't seen the inside of a patrol car, either.

"The high school," he replies.

"Thirsty Creek High School? Are you a teacher?"

"Yeah," he says.

He's becoming resigned to this back and forth with Dawn, the police officer. The small talk to pass the time as the headless guy's guts are located and covered. It's all surreal, anyway, so whatever she wants, he supposes. He might feel different five minutes from now. Or one minute from now. They both know that, too.

"What subject do you teach?" she asks. She sounds at least partially interested in his answer.

Marks whips his head up to look at her, anger suddenly surging through him. "Is that really important right now? I told you, I need to call my girlfriend." He thumbs through one of his pants pockets, looking for a smoke. Then he remembers: the glove compartment. He grimaces. He's fiending, and bad.

"Reya?" she asks.

Mark begins to feel like he's being handled. He doesn't like it. He isn't guilty of anything here. So, why does it seem as if he's in trouble? "Yeah, Reya. She was calling, but I couldn't get to the phone. It's toast now." He gestures toward the burning car with disgust. "Along with the last of my cigarettes. She'll be worried."

"Would you like me to call her for you?" Dawn asks.

Mark's face lights up. Reya is a lifeline right now. And Dawn is back in his good graces. "Could you?"

"Yeah, no worries," she says as she pulls a mobile phone out of her pocket. She then reaches up to smooth the sides of her hair. It's pinned into a tight bun at the nape of her neck, but maybe it isn't tight enough. "We'll call her first, then you can tell us everything you remember about what happened."

That reminds Mark of the kind stranger who urged him out of the car before it caught fire. He wants to find him as soon as he can. Even before calling Reya. It seems more urgent, all of a sudden. "There was a guy," he says, standing and looking around. Mark knows he needs to find the guy fast, before the kind stranger leaves the scene and is gone forever. That would be a real shame. "He was with me at my car. He told me I had to get out. Said the car was about to go up in flames. I didn't believe him at first—or maybe I just wasn't paying enough attention—but he turned out to be right."

Dawn returns the phone to her pocket and instead

pulls out a small pad and a smooth black pen to take notes. "Okay," she replies. "What did he look like?"

Mark fidgets, uneasy. "I didn't get a real good look at him," he explains. "I should have. There was a lot going on all at once."

"How about you close your eyes and try to remember?" Dawn asks gently. Mark thinks she's awfully patient for a cop. But he's not complaining. "Tell me what you see," she prompts.

Mark sits back down and does as she asks. It's easy to listen to Dawn's voice and follow her directions. It reminds him of his mother and his sisters. "Brown skin. Smooth features. He was skinny, but strong."

"How old was he?" Dawn asks.

"I don't know. Maybe late twenties. Like me. He was about my age."

"Good," she replies, nodding. "Can you remember what he was wearing?"

"Oh, yeah, I actually can," he replies. "He was wearing a hoodie, with the hood up. The string was cinched and everything."

"What color was the hoodie?"

Mark squints, trying to remember. Keeping his eyes closed isn't doing the job. Not completely. "I don't think I noticed that. Green, maybe? I guess I'd know it if I saw it. I've been looking for him."

"Okay, no worries," she says. "Anything else about his clothes? What kind of shoes was he wearing?"

"Oh! I do remember his shoes!" Mark shouts. He sounds excited, like he's come up with the correct answer on a game show and he's about to win a thousand bucks. "He was wearing boots. I think they were steel-toed. They were filthy. Covered in dried mud. At first, I assumed the guy might be some kind of off-duty medical person. Maybe a doctor or a nurse. But when I saw those shoes, they looked more like they belonged to someone who works construction. No hospital would let an employee traipse all that mud around." He looks at Dawn for approval. "They wouldn't. Would they?"

She shrugs a little, still in control. Her cool exterior remains. She scribbles in the notepad as she eyes him. "You're probably right. That's good, Mark. You're doing a good job."

"Thanks, I guess," he mutters.

"Now," she continues, "you mentioned that the man urged you out of the car."

"That's right. I think he saved my life. I mean, I guess I narrowly escaped death twice. First in the collision and then when my car caught fire. Wow." The enormity of it sends a chill down Mark's spine. Or maybe it's the shoulder wound setting in. Either way.

Dawn nods. "You're lucky," she says.

"You can say that again."

"Did the man tell you anything else? Besides that you needed to get out of the car?"

Mark squints again, doing his best to remember. "No, that's it. I think." He opens his eyes all the way as a man in a business suit approaches. The guy looks out of place in this setting. Mark thinks he must have seen the accident. Probably one of the onlookers gawking from a distance. The guy has a smarmy smile on his too-perfect face. "What does this clown want?" Marks asks out loud. Dawn shoots Mark a look as if to implore him to behave.

"Excuse me, officer," the man begins. He's holding a phone in one hand and a black sunglasses case in the other. Mark wonders why he doesn't stack them and keep one hand free. "Are you filing a report on the accident?"

"Yes, sir," Dawn replies. "Do you have information to share? Did you *see* anything?"

He nods, a serious expression on his face. "I didn't see the accident actually happen, but I arrived before that car caught on fire over there." He points, which Marks thinks is unnecessary. They can all see the burning vehicle. It tends to draw attention. It isn't every day that you encounter a giant flaming object on your morning commute.

"Okay," Dawn replies, flipping to a new page in her little notebook. "What's your name, sir?"

"Theodore."

Mark scoffs. *How pompous*, he thinks. *Theodore*. Irritation rises hot against his neck. Dawn shoots him another look of warning. Why doesn't he like this guy? They've never met before, as far as Mark knows.

"And your last name, Theodore?" Dawn asks.

"Kromsky, with a K," he says. Dawn takes note.

"Hey, mister," Mark interrupts. "Since you saw my car catch fire, did you also see the guy who helped me out just before it did? I've been looking for him. I want to say thanks."

"What guy?" Theodore asks. "There wasn't another guy. Just you, in the driver's seat."

Dawn whips her head in Mark's direction, then back to Theodore. She's intrigued. "You didn't see the other guy? Mark provided me with a solid description of him."

Mark isn't lying. He saw a guy. He is sure of it.

Theodore shakes his head. "No one else was there."

"How long were you on the scene before the car caught fire?" she asks. "Roughly."

"Five minutes, maybe. I'd been watching for a while. I'm the one who called 9-1-1. Well, maybe more than one person called 9-1-1, which sounds logical now that I'm saying it. But that's why I didn't get out of my own car right away. The dispatcher I connected with told me to stay on the line until officers arrived. I gave him a play-by-play of everything I was seeing. All of that should be on record, right? The police department has a recording?"

Dawn nods slowly.

"Are you calling me a liar?" Mark asks. He's growing angry and confused. His positive thinking doesn't seem to be working for him this morning. "Because I know what I saw. The guy got me out of the car just in time. If it hadn't been for him—"

Dawn moves like she's going to put a reassuring hand on Mark's arm, but stops short. They don't know each other. Not really. She turns her attention back to Theodore instead. Sensing her desire to comfort Mark, Theodore backs off and takes it slow.

"I didn't mean anything by it. I'm sorry," Theodore says. "We're all a little shaken up."

Dawn agrees. "That's true. We are." She eyes Mark as she says it. They're being nice to him, but they don't believe him. He's used to that treatment. It doesn't surprise him. What he doesn't get is why they wouldn't believe him about such a simple thing. A guy was there, and he helped Mark out of the car.

"Hey, what happened to you?" Theodore asks Mark as he looks him up and down, a scowl on his entitled face.

"What?" Mark asks. "Can't handle a little blood? It's no big deal. The injury isn't as bad as it might look."

"I'm not talking about your shoulder. I mean the marks all over you. Were you burned?" Theodore steps closer, seeming to want a better look.

A rush of embarrassment covers Mark's face. Self-consciously, he reaches for the sleeve that is ripped and hanging wide open. He had been so distracted that he hadn't realized his arm was exposed. He knows from experience how his birthmarks tend to shock and disgust people. It's a pain that's never far from his mind. Like a modern-day leper, the marks on his skin make for a miserable existence. They mean he has to hide, always careful to keep himself covered.

"Sorry," Mark says, hanging his head. "I wasn't burned. I … Well, I don't …" he trails off, unsure how to explain.

Dawn blinks a few times, then steps in, sensing Mark's distress. "Hey, you have nothing to be sorry for. And you don't owe anyone an explanation about your body."

Theodore steps away, getting the message. "I didn't mean any offense. I've just never seen birthmarks like that. I thought you had scars from a bad burn."

"We get it," Dawns says firmly. "Enough."

Theodore nods.

In the background, new sirens approach and a pair of ambulances park near to where they're standing. Paramedics rush from the vehicles and swarm the scene only to slow down when they see Dawn's partner positioned near the covered body. Her partner—Mark heard Dawn refer to him as Jim—shakes his head, and they know. No survivors. Except for Mark. He's a survivor. But he isn't thinking of himself as in need of medical attention, despite the blood still oozing from his shoulder wound. The shock seems to be wearing off, though, because it hurts like the dickens.

"Zhang! Over here," Dawn says, waving. She recognizes at least one of the medics. "Come check my friend Mark out, will you?"

Friend, Mark thinks. She's being nice, but the truth is, he'd like Dawn to be his real friend. He could use more of those, and he appreciated the way she stood up for him. His colleagues don't yet fall into the friend category, and he's never been very social. That leaves only Reya. A man should have more friends than just his girlfriend.

A tall, thin Asian man bounds eagerly toward Dawn and Mark while the others tend to the mangled body. His name tag reads Zhang, just like Dawn said. The fact that she knows this guy makes it a little better, but Mark isn't interested in wasting any time.

"Mark, hi there," the man says. "I'm Michael Zhang. Let's get you checked out, okay?"

Dawn smiles, pleased with the progress. Theodore hangs back uselessly. Mark wonders why he's still here, but tolerates the inconvenience, for now.

"I'm fine," Mark says. "Really. Nothing a little soap and water can't take care of. Maybe a slathering of antibiotic ointment. I'll take care of it after work."

He doesn't mention his lack of health insurance, but it's on his mind. He hasn't been at his new job long enough for benefits to kick in. And he can't be covered by Reya's policy since they aren't married yet. The last thing they need is a big medical bill, which will certainly come if he takes a ride in an ambulance and is treated at the hospital.

Michael purses his lips sympathetically, then sets his bag down on the ground. "I hear you," he confirms. "Sometimes, though, our bodies protect us from severe pain and we don't realize how bad an injury really is until hours later. Adrenaline, you know? How about you open your sleeve and I look from here? I won't touch you. Is it your shoulder?" He can tell that much from the way Mark is leaning over, favoring the hurt arm.

Dawn nods, approving of her colleague's approach. Michael seems just as nice as Dawn, which is a surprise for Mark. He hasn't had occasion to meet police officers or EMTs before, but he didn't think they'd be quite so compassionate. It makes sense, he supposes. It's just that it's nice to experience their kindness for himself.

"Fine, look if you must," Mark agrees. "Then I really need to find the guy who helped me out of the car. After that, I want to call my girlfriend, Reya, and get on to work." He opens his sleeve, revealing the injury and more of his birthmarks.

Michael doesn't react. He's seen far worse. He simply squints, assessing the damage. "Okay, we're off to a good start, Mark," he says. "I can see the gash. We'll need to wrap that up to stop the bleeding and make sure it doesn't get infected. Would that be alright with you?"

Mark scowls. He thinks about the bills and how mad Reya will be. Their baby shouldn't have to enter the world under the burden of debt. Financial stresses make parents fight. Mark knows that fact well enough from his own childhood, and he doesn't want a repeat performance with himself in his father's old role.

"I'm sorry," he says softly. "I don't want a big bill. I'm sure you understand. My girlfriend is pregnant and we're having a little baby soon. I recently started a new job. Benefits aren't available for another forty-five days."

Michael leans back. He knows this story all too well. He regularly sees patients in need of medical attention who are more afraid of the crippling debt they might accrue than they are of whatever ailment has befallen them. He hates it. He wishes he lived in a place where people could get the help they need. "Look, Mark, I get it," he says. "I see it literally every day in this line of work. But I need you to think about your family. I'd venture a guess that they want you to stick around and be with them. Your health is priority number one. Trust me, that gash needs more than a little antibiotic ointment."

Mark shrugs. He knows Michael is right. "How bad is it?"

"Can I step closer to take a better look?" Michael asks.

Mark nods. He glances at Dawn, who offers a reassuring smile. "What a morning," Mark muses. "It started like any other day. And look at me! I'm a mess."

Dawn sighs. "Like Michael said, we've seen far worse. You made it out largely unscathed. You're going to be okay. Try to focus on the positives."

At that, Mark remembers his guru and his efforts to remain positive. He wonders, in fact, if all of his positive thinking might have kept him from being the other guy. The guy who was just a few seconds behind him in the line of traffic. The guy who didn't survive to see another day.

"Hey?" Mark asks Dawn, grabbing her sleeve as she steps near to help Michael tend to his arm. "Do you believe in the power of positive thinking?" She lowers her brow skeptically. "I mean," he continues, "do you think our thoughts have a bearing on what happens in physical reality?"

Dawn and Michael exchange a knowing glance. "I don't know. Maybe," she replies. It seems like there's more she wants to say. An elaboration for a friend.

Michael cuts away a section of Mark's shirt to gain access to the wound. "Hold still," he says. "I'm going to touch your arm now. It might hurt. Are you ready?"

Mark nods as an excruciating pain bores into his limb like a rototiller. The adrenaline must be wearing off for real now. It hurts worse than anything Mark has ever felt. He can't help it; he roars along with the pain, his eyes closed and his teeth tightly clenched.

"There it is," Dawn mumbles.

"Mark, focus on my voice, okay?" Michael says. "I'm going to reach into my bag and get out some medicine to dull the pain. Then I'm going to wrap your arm up. We have to get you to the hospital. No way around it. I think you may have cut a nerve, and there's extensive tissue damage."

Mark shakes his head. "No. I don't want to go."

"I'm really sorry," Michael says, rummaging around in his bag. "If there was any other way, I promise I'd tell you and we'd do that. But there isn't. If you want to avoid dangerous infection and keep that arm, you're going to need surgery."

"Surgery?" Mark asks loudly. "Oh, no." He shifts his weight, attempting to stand but he's too weak. The energy seems to be draining from him by the minute. He plops down in a sad pile on the grass.

"Look, there are ways to get these medical bills paid. Programs and nonprofits that can assist. I'll help you figure that part out when you've recovered. Right now, take the win and take care of yourself. Please. You could have been that guy," Dawn says as she gestures to the corpse being shuttled on a gurney to a waiting ambulance.

From Mark's vantage point on the ground, it looks like they've gathered the pieces of the poor man and reassembled them to make some semblance of a whole. He's covered with a while sheet, but shreds of his clothing can be seen sticking out around the edges. It's then that Mark sees the pieces of the victim up close, and something catches his eye. Mark's body stiffens. A scrap of sweatshirt material hangs below the white sheet. It's green, and a string dangles on top. It's the kind of string that cinches a hoodie.

"Oh, no," Mark says out loud as it all begins to make sense. A steel-toed boot covered in mud emerges from beneath the sheet, too. In that instant, Mark is sure. "That's the guy," he says, pointing. "The one who helped me out of the car. That's him!"

"How could that possibly be?" Theodore asks, stepping forward as if he's determined to be more involved. "This guy died in the collision. There's no way he could have talked to you. Unless he was a ghost. Which—"

"Okay," Dawn says as she takes hold of Theodore's shoulders and leads him away toward the waiting patrol car. Her partner is available now that the body has been retrieved. "My colleague, Jim, will finish taking your statement. Come with me." Theodore follows begrudgingly, leaving Mark and Michael alone.

Mark can't make sense of what he's seeing. He's lost so much blood, and he's feeling faint. "It's him. I know it doesn't add up, but I swear it's him," he explains to Michael as if he wants someone to validate his experience. To bear witness to his horror. Maybe later, Michael and Dawn will offer reassurance. For now, Michael must focus on the injury and get Mark to a hospital, before it's too late.

3

AWAKE

When Mark opens his eyes again, it's evening. Pinks and purples fill the sky out his window on what appears to be a high floor of the local hospital. His throat is raw, and his whole body feels unusually heavy. Machines beep softly, their tiny lights illuminating the room as the sun goes down.

"Someone should close those shades," Mark mumbles.

In and out of it as the anesthesia wears off, he dreams about the history class he was supposed to teach that morning. For what seems like a dozen or more times, Mark has dreamed that he's late to class and unprepared for the lesson he'd planned to teach. When he finally gets to his classroom—without the books that are now burnt to a crisp along with the rest of his car—and tries to talk about the Pleistocene Epoch from memory, he fumbles awkwardly, unsure of what to say or do to make things right. The cool kids and the jocks mock him, cracking jokes and cracking each other up. The smart kids look on in utter disappointment and disgust. Those in between just look sad. It's like being back in high school all over again. Only this time, Mark has to worry about being fired from his job and becoming unable to support his newborn. The dream seems to loop on repeat with no way out.

He's been dozing as the sun sets but jerks awake when one of the machines makes a loud noise. To Mark's surprise, a figure moves in the shadows along the bottom edge of the window. It's hard to make out clearly but he thinks he recognizes the form. "Reya?" he asks hopefully, rising in the bed. "Is that you?" He hopes she's there, waiting for him to wake up, hoping he's alright.

There's no answer. Mark narrows his eyes, and he suddenly becomes aware of a splitting headache. It seizes him, and all of his muscles tense. This, in turn, makes his heart beat faster and his blood pressure rise. The change on the monitors is enough to draw the attention of the on-duty nurses stationed at the desk in the middle of the unit. In a flurry, two of them come running into the room like something is on fire. "Too late for that," Mark mumbles to himself. It hurts when he laughs.

"Mr. Simbas, how are you feeling?" a young woman asks, her eyes fixed on all the monitors Mark is connected to. He can't tell in the dim light, but he thinks this woman looks a lot like Dawn. It sends a surge of longing through him. He misses her. He wants someone familiar who can provide some measure of comfort.

"My head hurts," Mark replies. "Should it?" He remembers the shoulder injury, which is completely numb. He can't imagine what's going on with his head. "And my throat is sore."

The woman smiles as her colleague, a tall, graying man, scribbles furiously on a clipboard. "You had surgery to repair your injured shoulder, Mr. Simbas," she says. "The sore throat is from being intubated. And the headache is most likely an effect of the anesthesia." Mark nods slowly. He can read her name tag: Abby Guerrero, RN.

"Thank you, Ms. Guerrero," he replies. Mark finds it odd the way he's getting to know a whole new cast of characters. For a homebody who doesn't go much of anywhere other than work, he's met a lot of new people in one day. If it is still the same day, that is. "How soon can I get out of here?"

She smiles again as she reaches for his wrist to take his pulse. "Call me Abby."

"Okay, Abby," Mark says. "Call me Mark. Is that my girlfriend over there?"

She looks where Mark gestures, toward the foot of the bed. "Who? Greg?" Abby and Greg chuckle like they usually do when a patient is loopy and coming off of anesthesia.

"Very funny," Mark replies. "I mean over by the window. I saw someone there, moving around in the shadows."

Greg steps closer and shines a little light in Mark's eyes—one at first, then the other. "Pupils are equal and reactive," he says as he writes on the chart. Mark can see Greg's nametag now, too. It reads Gregory Carmack, LPN. So, Abby is the senior nurse here.

"Pulse ox is good," Abby adds. "Vitals steady." Greg nods as he writes.

"Before you came in," Mark says, "I thought I saw someone over there. When I was first waking up."

Abby follows his gaze. At least, she's entertaining his

delusion. "Where?" she asks. "Over here?" She walks to the window, the light outside growing dim.

"Yeah," Mark says too loudly. The pain in his head lets him know he should talk more softly. "Below the window. Is there a bench there or something?"

Abby does a dutiful job of searching the room but doesn't find anything. Mark watches, wondering if his eyes are playing tricks on him. "I don't see anything over here," Abby reports. "It's just the three of us in the room."

"Are you thirsty?" Greg asks him. "I can get you some ice chips. You aren't cleared for anything else yet. Ice will help, though. Soon you'll be able to have clear liquids—broth, Sprite, that sort of thing."

Mark doesn't like the way Greg is moving on, ignoring the fact that something was in the shadows. "Sure, I'll take some ice," Mark says curtly. "But, Abby, would you check again, please? I know someone was there."

Abby nods and smiles, apparently happy to humor her patient. She's a good nurse, the same way Dawn is a good cop. They both care about people. "Okay. No worries."

As she says it, Mark sees movement in the shadows again. Something is twisting and stretching, just out of sight. He suddenly remembers the mangled corpse on the stretcher and a chill runs up his spine. "There!" he shouts, pointing then gripping his head with his good arm. "Ouch. Damn, that hurts."

"Here?" Abby asks as she points.

"Yes," Mark says. He isn't so sure it's Reya anymore, though. The figure doesn't even seem human, and that thought is unnerving. "Do you see it? It's right there, moving around like it's restless. I'm not sure it's my girlfriend. Maybe it's a kid who snuck in here. Is anyone missing a kid? The more I look at it, I don't think it's big enough to be an adult. I guess it could be some kind of animal. A dog, maybe?"

Greg leaves to fetch ice, unbothered by Mark's distress. Abby purses her lips. "I don't really … Well, let's turn on the overhead lights. Okay?" she asks kindly.

Mark nods. He covers his eyes in preparation for the assault to his senses. When Abby flips the light switch, it's clear that there's no one else in the room. The area where he saw the movement is completely empty. No child, no animal, and definitely no Reya. "Huh," Mark says. "My eyes must be playing tricks on me."

"No worries," Abby says. "It happens. Anesthesia does crazy things to our minds. But you're good. You're in recovery. It will all get better from here."

Mark has a nagging feeling that won't be the case for him, but he returns the kind nurse's smile anyway. "I hope that's true."

"It is. Trust us," Abby says.

Greg returns with the ice chips and helps Mark get one into his mouth. The feeling is glorious. "You weren't kidding," Mark says gratefully. "I didn't even realize I was thirsty. The ice does help."

Greg breaks a smile for the first time. He seems more serious than Abby. Maybe it's best that way. Maybe they have a good cop, bad cop thing going on. Such a dynamic might come in handy with uncooperative patients. "That's what I'm here for," Greg says as Mark shifts his weight in the bed. "Now, we need some information in order to contact your next of kin."

The statement alarms Mark. They know his full

name. They had said Mr. Simbas when they'd first come in, right? "Wait, does that mean no one contacted Reya?"

Abby takes over when it's time to soothe him. "Not yet, but we'll call her right away."

"How could that be?" Marks asks.

"You didn't have any ID on you when you were brought in," Greg explains. The police officer who questioned you had your name and your girlfriend's first name, Reya, but nothing else. No address."

"Oh, yeah," Mark replies. "My wallet and employee ID badge were in the console of my car when it went up in flames. But I told Dawn—Officer Rollins—that I work at Thirsty Creek High. They should have pieced things together by now." He tries to sit up in bed but the pain stops him.

"I'm not sure what has happened," Greg says. "We can get you in touch with anyone you want, though. There's a phone right here beside your bed."

He gestures to an aging beige behemoth that reminds Mark of the phone his parents kept on a wooden stand in the hallway when he was a kid. They'd had a chair nearby and everything, even after they'd eventually upgraded to a cordless handset. The Simbas family didn't exactly keep up with the times. Never early adopters of technology, they made do with what worked well enough.

"Does that thing work?" Marks asks.

"Yep," Greg replies. "Do you know any phone numbers?"

Mark nods. He does know Reya's number, by heart. It seems so strange that she hadn't heard about what had happened to him today. It was one of the worst days of his life, and he wished for her to be there to lean on. Not to mention, she was probably furious by now. If not, she would be out of her mind with worry. "I do. Reya. I need to call her cell. She'll wonder what's going on. I'm usually home by this time of night."

Greg picks up the receiver. "What's her number?"

Mark rattles it off, then waits when Greg hands him the ringing handpiece. Relieved, Mark closes his eyes. He can hardly wait to hear her voice, especially after the shit he's been through. To his surprise, Reya doesn't pick up. It goes to her voicemail.

Hey, you've reached Reya Hughes. Sorry I can't come to the phone right now. Leave a message.

Mark grips the receiver tightly and presses it toward his mouth. "Reya, it's me," he breathes. "I'm sorry I haven't called. I've had a hell of a day, to be honest. It's almost … Well, it's almost hard to believe. But I'll tell you all about it when—"

A long tone interrupts his train of thought and ends the recording.

"Did it cut you off?" Greg asks. Abby is reviewing Mark's chart, not paying full attention to the discussion that's taking place.

"Yeah, it did," Mark replies. He's frustrated. Getting in touch with Reya is beginning to feel like his recurring dream that loops again and again without resolution.

"Hey," Greg begins, "I hope this isn't too personal of a question, but I've never seen anyone with birthmarks like yours. The surgical team was fascinated. Have they always been there?"

Mark scowls. The last thing he wants to talk about right now is his birthmarks. "They got darker as I grew up. Why do you care?"

"Interesting," Greg says. "So very interesting." He reaches for the flap of Mark's gown to uncover his good arm. Mark stops him by burrowing the arm under the covers.

"I don't want to talk about it," Mark snaps. "Would you dial that number again, please?"

Abby shoots Greg a look. He clears his throat and gets back down to business, clicking the button to reset the phone and then pressing the redial button. "Sorry. Here goes."

This time, the phone doesn't even ring. It goes to voicemail right away.

Hey, you've reached Reya Hughes. Sorry I can't come to the phone right now. Leave a message.

"Reya!" Mark exclaims. "You've got to listen to this. I hope you do. I hope you are. Look, something has happened. I'm okay, but I'm—"

The rude tone sounds again, ending the message and severing Mark's connection.

"Bummer," Greg mumbles.

Mark takes a quick breath, then knows what he must do. "Something is wrong. I have to get to her," he says as he begins to unhook the lines and equipment he's attached to. "I need to get out of here."

"Whoa," Greg says. "Slow down, buddy. You just had major surgery. You aren't going anywhere."

"Wanna bet?" Mark asks as he continues to twist and yank the cords. "I've got to find Reya. I didn't want to come to this hospital in the first place. I didn't give my consent."

"Because you passed out," Greg says. He's baffled as to why Mark is putting up such a fight. "If the first responders on the scene hadn't brought you here, it's likely you'd be dead. You should be thanking them. Not complaining about consent."

"I don't care," Mark replies. "I have to go. I'll sign myself out—AMA, right? Against medical advice. Isn't that what it's called? I've seen it on TV. I can fill out a form and walk out of here free and clear. You can't stop me."

Greg puts a firm hand on Mark's forearm. "Just because you can doesn't mean you should. Stop and think for a minute, man."

"He's right," Abby says as she steps closer to the bed. "You could die if you leave before you're ready. I doubt Reya would want that to happen. She'd want you to stay here and get the care you need."

Mark shakes his head. "None of that matters if she's in trouble. I can feel it in my bones. Something isn't right. I have to get to her." He's woozy, but he manages to stand. "Where are my clothes? And help me take out this IV, would you?"

Abby and Greg glance at each other. "Not a good idea, Mark," she says. "Please, stay. We'll help you find Reya while we monitor your recovery."

"I'm telling you, no!" Mark shouts. "Help me take it out, or I'll do it myself."

Greg picks up the call device and pings the nurse's station. "Physician on duty, please report to room 306 as soon as possible. My surgical patient in recovery wants to leave the hospital AMA." He puts the device back down on the tray table as if he didn't just betray Mark completely.

"Why did you do that?" Mark asks.

"Because you need to speak to a doctor before you make what could be the worst mistake of your life," Greg says loudly.

"You obviously don't know much about my life if you think this is the worst mistake of it. Believe me, I've done plenty worse," Mark says as he shrugs Greg off. "Now get out of my way."

Mark rips the medical tape that covers the IV needle at the top of his hand. When the tape is off, a few drops of fresh blood trickle out as the needle twirls around untethered. It only hurts a little. The splitting pain in his head surges with every move he makes, on the other hand, but he pushes through.

"Mark, please." Abby tries to reason with Mark.

"Do you have any pain medicine I can take with me?" Mark asks, ignoring her plea. "Surely, you can send me home with something since I just had surgery. What was in my IV?"

Greg puts his hands in the air as if to say he's giving up. Time for Abby's good-cop routine.

"You've been given morphine in your IV to help control the pain. Your arm is probably numb right now—"

"It is," Mark confirms.

"The morphine we've given you will wear off in a few hours, and you'll be in a world of hurt. It's best to stay here and let us control the pain for you," she says softly. "We're here to help, Mark. We want to see you healed and whole. It's why we do this grueling, thankless work in the first place."

Mark softens a bit upon hearing that. It's not enough to stop him. He's still standing, and he has the IV needle out. "So, what can you prescribe for me to take? Oxycodone?"

"Your doctor could. Yes," Abby concedes. "There are serious side effects. I don't recommend—"

"Fine, let me talk to him," Mark barks. He's beginning to perspire from the exertion. His body is far too weak to be mounting a resistance to the healthcare team that saved him. "It's nothing personal," he adds. "I know you're good people trying to help me. I have to find my girlfriend. And whatever was moving around under the window creeps me out, anyway. I want to get away from here."

"I looked and—" Abby says.

"I know. Nothing there. You said."

"I could look again," she replies. "In fact, I could have someone from maintenance come in here and do a thorough inspection. We want to alleviate your concerns so that you can stay in the hospital until you're ready to be discharged. How about that? And I promise, we will find a way to get in touch with Reya. She'll probably get your voicemails and call the hospital."

"If everything was normal, she would have picked up. She never lets my calls go to voicemail," Mark explains. "She's pregnant. I think something is wrong." His knees go weak and he teeters, nearly falling back down on the bed.

There's silence for a moment as they all think about

what to do. Greg breaks it. "This is ridiculous," he says. "I'm not paid enough to deal with this kind of idiocy."

Mark looks hurt, yet he's too weak to offer much response.

"Easy," Abby says. Her eyes grow wide and Mark can tell that Greg is doing something behind him.

"What?" Mark asks. "What's he doing? What do you see?"

Abby shakes her head. Mark turns around slowly, just in time to catch a glimpse of Greg holding a huge syringe. "I could end this foolishness right now," Greg says. "I *should* end it."

"That isn't your call," Abby says sternly, her good-cop persona out the window.

"You sure about that?" Greg asks.

"I mean it," she replies. "Put the syringe down. That's not how we do things. It wouldn't be fair to our patient and his very real concerns. It certainly isn't worth risking your job over. Keep a level head, Mr. Carmack."

"I'm thinking it's better to ask forgiveness than permission in this instance," Greg reasons. "Keeping this guy here will probably save his life. How is that a bad thing?"

Mark's head spins and he stumbles, landing him in a seated position on the bed. He reaches his good arm to one side rail to steady himself. "Why are you talking about me like I'm not here?" he asks. "I have a right to leave. It's my choice. I don't want to stay. Will you respect my wishes, please? Is that too much to ask?"

Greg isn't anywhere near convinced. He raises the syringe above Mark's neck, poised to inject the sedative that will knock him out. Before he has a chance, a dark-skinned man in a white lab coat walks through the door.

"About time," Abby says, shooting Greg a dirty look. Greg, in turn, slowly lowers the syringe to his side. "Hello, Dr. Tipton."

The doctor is middle-aged with a respectable amount of silver strands throughout his closely-cropped hair. He looks wise, yet still in his prime. Still nimble. Still relevant. "Hello, there," he replies. "I was paged. What seems to be the trouble here?" He walks toward Mark and reaches out his hand for a shake.

"I suppose I'm the trouble," Mark says, meeting the doc's hand. "Mark Simbas, sir."

"Dr. Malcolm Tipton. Good to see you up and at 'em, Mark," the doctor says. "You look a lot different than you did on my operating table a few hours ago."

Mark is startled by this revelation. "You operated on me? On my shoulder?"

"I did," Dr. Tipton replies. "You had lost a lot of blood. We weren't sure we'd be able to save your arm, but we did. If you take good care of yourself and work hard in physical therapy, I expect you to make a full recovery."

Mark's shoulders slump. He knows that should be good news—that it *is* good news—but he wants to leave the hospital. He needs to leave the hospital. "Thank you, sir," he says to Dr. Tipton. "I appreciate what you've done."

The doc nods. "Then what's this about you wanting to check out of the hospital? I intend to keep you overnight. You can go home mid-day tomorrow, assuming everything progresses as planned."

"I'm sorry. I can't wait that long," Mark says. "I don't mean to sound ungrateful. It's just that I haven't been able to reach my girlfriend since I saw her before work this morning. She's pregnant. She doesn't know what happened to me. At this point, I suspect something is wrong. We don't have extended family that we're close to. It's just us, and I have to find her and make sure she's okay."

Dr. Tipton takes off his wire-rimmed glasses and slides them into a pocket on his lab coat. "I see," he says. "Was the police officer who interviewed you earlier able to make contact with your girlfriend? Or the EMTs?"

"I don't think so," Mark says. "I need to go to her on my own. If something happened to her or the baby, I'd never forgive myself."

Abby jumps in. "We've offered to help him get in contact with her," she explains. "He was able to leave her a couple of voicemail messages. We are happy to help him do more."

"We're also prepared to sedate the patient to ensure that his vitals are under control," Greg adds. "Standard recovery room procedure."

Abby raises a brow and Mark agrees. He definitely doesn't want to be sedated. Dr. Tipton purses his lips as he considers the situation. "Did you take the monitors off yourself?" he asks.

"Yes, sir," Mark says. "I'm prepared to leave the hospital against medical advice. I understand the risks. If you good folks will show me where my clothes are and send me with some prescription pain medicine to get me through the next few days, I'll be good to go."

Dr. Tipton sighs. "You're within your rights to refuse our treatment plan and go out on your own. I don't recommend it. In fact, I think it's a very bad idea. You could suffer any number of complications which could threaten your life. Do you realize that? I didn't simply stick a few stitches into your arm. You had serious damage that required intensive reconstruction. You were on the operating table for nearly six hours. With that comes intubation, catheterization, and general anesthesia, all of which carry their own risk of complications."

"I understand," Mark replies, although the medical professionals in the room aren't sure he actually does. "I'm prepared to leave. Once I find Reya, maybe I'll come back … if I have any complications, that is."

Dr. Tipton sits silently for what feels like a long time. Mark's head continues to pain him and he's weak and weary, yet he's determined to follow through. "Bring me the form," the doctor says to Greg with a wave of his hand. "He's within his rights. We have to let him go."

Greg shakes his head. "I think this is a bad move." Abby shoots him another look. "But, okay. I'll go get the form. Be right back."

Dr. Tipton nods reassuringly as Greg leaves the room. He turns to Abby. "Please get this gentleman his clothing and personal effects. While you do, I'm going to review some discharge instructions."

"Thank you," Mark says. He's more grateful than he can adequately express.

"Don't thank me yet," Dr. Tipton says. "Wait and see if you survive the next forty-eight hours first."

Mark swallows hard. That statement makes it real. But still, he's determined. "I intend to do just that," he says. "I'll come back to thank you."

"I certainly hope it happens that way," the doctor says, then he proceeds to inform Mark about what to watch out for. He emphasizes the most serious, life-threatening emergency warning signs that mean Mark will need to return to a hospital right away.

Mark agrees to follow the doctor's instructions. He does his best to listen dutifully and catalog the information in case he needs to recall it later. Deep down, he knows that he's too out of it to commit the information to memory. He also knows his odds aren't good.

Maybe I have a death wish, he thinks. The thought surprises him. He's never put words to the feeling. Not even in his own mind. But it's there, close to the surface.

"Any questions?" Dr. Tipton asks.

Mark shakes his head, which induces more pain. "Only how I get that prescription for pain pills."

Dr. Tipton chuckles, then stops himself. He's treating Mark's situation with the seriousness it deserves. That doesn't mean he doesn't find it every bit as absurd—and funny—as Nurse Greg. It isn't often that they see patients so unreasonable. It happens … just not very often. "We'll order an initial supply of OxyContin from the pharmacy downstairs. You can stop and pick it up on your way out."

Greg returns with the discharge form just as Abby retrieves Mark's belongings from somewhere across the room.

"Um," Abby begins, "to be clear, he doesn't have a wallet or ID. Or a shirt."

Mark hadn't thought that far. His shirt sleeve was torn in the accident. They probably had to cut it off during surgery. His wallet went up in flames with his cash, debit and credit cards, and driver's license inside. "Will that be a problem?" he asks. The obstacles are almost enough to cause him to change his mind and stay put. He's getting weaker by the minute and desperately wants to lie back down.

"OxyContin is a controlled substance," Greg says.

"That, it is," Dr. Tipton adds. "Do you have any way to verify your identity, Mr. Simbas? We can treat you with pain meds here in the hospital, but sending you home with them is another matter due to the street value of those drugs. It's important that we keep track. You understand."

The thought of going home without pain meds makes Mark's blood pressure rise. He doesn't need the monitor to tell him it's happening. He can feel it. "What then? I have to take over-the-counter painkillers after a major surgery? You're the ones who said how serious it all is."

"We said you should stay here in the hospital," Greg blurts. The irritation is obvious in his voice. He sounds like he's close to saying *screw it all* and walking out. Maybe Mark would do the same in Greg's position.

"And a shirt?" Mark asks.

Abby shrugs. "I can help you tie a gown tightly in the back. You can tuck it into your pants. I'd say you could purchase something in the hospital gift shop, but—"

"No way to pay," Mark replies, finishing her sentence. "Dammit. This sucks."

Dr. Tipton vehemently agrees. He nods, his eyes wide. "I can imagine," he says. "I'm sorry you're faced with all of this. Accidents are never fun. The good news, though, is how well you did in surgery. If you take it easy and take care of yourself, you have an excellent prognosis. I think it's wise to focus on that. Everything else will be worked out in time."

Something about the tone of Dr. Tipton's voice sends

Mark over the edge. "I can't wait any longer. I have to go," he says as he stands again. Hurriedly, he signs the discharge form and tosses it onto the bed. He puts his pants and shoes on, then tucks the back of his gown into his waistband like Abby suggested. He doesn't ask for her help tying it closed. When he's dressed, he thanks them and bursts out of the hospital room as fast as his wobbly legs will carry him.

4

GET AWAY

Once downstairs, Mark speed walks past the information desk without acknowledging the concerned looks on the faces of the two ladies staffing it. He waves as he exits through the front door, smiling as he finally feels the cool night air on his face.

What now? he wonders. He isn't certain how far away his house is. From what he remembers about the location of the hospital, it's less than five miles. Not far, yet a huge distance for someone in his current physical condition. He's not completely sure he knows the most direct route, either.

Strangely, the long, thin purple birthmarks on the sides of Mark's neck begin to itch and throb. There are eight of them there. Four on each side. They've never done this before. It feels like something is crawling under his skin, and that something lines up exactly with the marks. The affected area and boundaries are the same. Surely, that isn't an effect of the anesthesia. Is it? Mark doubts that researchers could find enough people with big birthmarks like his to study. *I must be losing my mind*, he thinks.

As he looks left, he notices an Uber idling. It doesn't appear to have a passenger. Mark walks to the driver's side window and motions for the man inside to roll down the window.

"Yeah?" a dark-haired man says skeptically.

"I need a ride," Mark says.

"In an ambulance?" the driver asks, only half joking. "If so, I think you're heading in the wrong direction."

Mark isn't amused. "I need a ride home. To my house. It's about five miles from here, on the other side of town." The man doesn't respond. He just looks Mark over with his face balled up. "Are you available?" Mark continues. "Can you give me a ride?"

"I am available."

"Good," Mark replies, relieved. "The only thing is, my wallet burned up when my car caught on fire this morning. I can get you cash to pay the fare when we get there."

"Did your house key burn up, too?" the man asks.

Mark hadn't even thought that far. This day keeps the hits coming. "Shit," he mumbles.

"Um hmm," the cabbie murmurs. "Anyone home to let you in?"

Mark looks hopeful, then his face falls. "My girlfriend should be there but she didn't answer when I called her a little while ago. So, I don't know."

The guy scoffs. "Yeah. Sounds about right."

"Look, I know how this seems," Mark continues. "I was involved in a bad car accident this morning—not my fault—then my car caught fire and I had to have surgery—"

The man raises a hand to stop him. "Save it. I'm sorry for what you're going through. I'm not your guy. I have mouths to feed." Abruptly, he rolls up the window and pulls forward in the circular loading lane.

Stunned, Mark stares for a minute before collecting his wits and trying again. He walks the fifteen feet or so to where the cab is now parked. He bangs on the driver's window with his good hand. "Hey, haven't you ever been down on your luck? Help me out, man, please."

An older couple walks out of the hospital and cringes when they see Mark's aggression. They steer clear, swinging to the far side of the crosswalk in front of them.

"Get out of here," the cabbie says through the closed window. "Or I'll call the police. You'll drive my customers away. Like I said, I have mouths to feed."

Suddenly woozy, Mark stumbles backward. When he does, the cab driver speeds away, apparently deciding to look for passengers elsewhere. If Mark were in his right mind, he wouldn't blame him. At the moment, rage fills every cell in Mark's body because it feels like that cab driver was his last hope. He raises his good arm and punches the air while letting out a few choice expletives, all within earshot of a young family exiting the building.

A gangly African-American man in a gray uniform follows the family, then makes a beeline for Mark. "Sir, you can't be here like this," he says. "I'll have to ask you to return to your medical team inside or else you'll need to move along."

Frustrated, Mark nods. "Yeah, okay," he says.

He turns around slowly and heads for the road behind the hospital complex even though he has no real idea if he can make it home that way. He doesn't know if there are sidewalks along the path or crosswalks at the traffic lights. All he knows is that he must get to Reya. He doesn't have a logical plan. He thinks his house is west of the hospital, so he decides to follow the setting sun. It takes him a full couple of minutes to realize that it's dark, and there's no sun to follow. Not tonight, anyway. Not on this part of the Earth. Mark plods across the parking lot, focusing on the simple process of placing one foot in front of the other.

He barely makes it two blocks before he trips on a crack in the sidewalk and lands face first in a row of bushes. He narrowly misses falling into the street, where traffic is whizzing by. Luckily, he manages to keep his injured arm from taking the brunt of the impact. At this point, though, everything hurts. The pain in his head has intensified. It feels like someone is taking a jackhammer to his skull.

As he writhes on the ground in pain, Mark breaks out into a cold sweat that soaks him so thoroughly it looks like he's been swimming. Even his scalp is drenched. This leads him to get chilled and to shiver uncontrollably. It's September and it isn't very cold outside. The low for the evening won't dip below sixty. That doesn't matter right now. The slight chill in the air seems to get all the way into Mark's bones. It soon feels like he'll never warm up. Not good for a man who just had surgery.

Mark waits. He isn't sure what he's waiting for. A part of him hopes that some kind stranger will happen by and help him in his hour of need. Maybe Dawn will be out on patrol. Nevermind the fact that she was working this morning and isn't likely to be on duty now. Maybe Michael will be passing by in his ambulance.

Although he, too, should be off duty by now. Mark could really use a ride home right now, and some strong painkillers. For a moment, he considers trying to buy OxyContin from someone on the street. Anything to make his head stop pounding and to prevent the wall of pain sure to descend on him when whatever they gave him to deal with his arm wears off.

"Fuck!" Mark yells. It's the best summary statement he can come up with. No sooner does the word leave his mouth than he hears one short whoop of a siren. Blue lights flash in his peripheral vision. He hears a car door close and turns to see who has arrived. "Dawn, is that you?" he asks.

The beam from a powerful flashlight meets his eyes and drowns out the blue. "Sir, are you injured?" a deep male voice asks.

"Yes!" Mark replies, sitting up. "I was in an accident this morning. I've been to the hospital. I'm trying to get home now."

The officer steps closer. He isn't a tall man, and his light hair and pale skin make him look almost like a boy. As if he hasn't grown all the way up yet. "Did I hear you ask for Dawn?"

"Yeah," Mark replies. "I thought maybe you were Officer Rollins. She helped me out this morning. After the accident. I'd sure love to see a friendly face right now. As you can probably tell, I'm having a shit day."

The man turns off the flashlight and returns it to a designated spot on his belt. "You're the guy whose car burned up. The one with all the unusual birthmarks. Right?"

Self-consciously, Mark pulls the gown down as far as possible over his arms. He hates it when people mention his birthmarks. He's never understood the fascination with them. As far as he's concerned, the marks could be ignored completely. "That's me. How did you know?"

"I'm Officer Rollins' partner. Jim Perkins. I was there this morning. We didn't have a chance to get properly introduced, though." He reaches down and extends a hand to Mark. "Pleased to meet you."

"Same here," Mark says. Mustering his remaining strength, he stands. Traffic is slowing down to go around the stopped patrol car. People in vehicles stare as they move slowly past. They probably think Mark is in some kind of trouble. Or that he's drunk. Or crazy. Maybe he's all of those things. He doesn't ask why Jim is still on duty. He's curious but decides it wouldn't be prudent to inquire.

"Say, could I offer you a ride somewhere? Are you trying to get home?" Jim asks.

"Yes! Please," Mark replies. "I've been trying to get to my girlfriend ever since the accident this morning. It's been one delay after another, and I haven't been able to reach her. I am sure she is worried sick about me. Now I've begun to worry about her. She should have tracked me down by now. And she should have answered her phone when I called. A lot of what's happened today doesn't make any sense."

Jim gestures towards the car. "Come on, then. We'll put an end to this no-good day. Let's get you to her."

A wave of nausea moves through Mark along with a wave of relief. He pushes past the discomfort and moves toward the cruiser. "Thank you," he says. "You have no idea how glad I am to see you. I was trying to walk. It's about five miles, and I'm not sure I was heading the right direction."

"No problem at all," Jim replies. "I'm afraid you'll have to sit in the backseat, though. It's nothing personal. Department policy."

Marks agrees and climbs in. He's in no position to be picky. They make small talk as they ride. Jim doesn't ask about Mark's hospital gown or why he didn't call a cab or a rideshare service instead of stumbling around in the dark. Mark doesn't mention the dismembered corpse from the morning and how Jim had to retrieve the pieces. Neither has the energy for heavy discussion. They keep it short and light.

"This is me," Mark says as Jim pulls his car against the curb in front of Mark and Reya's house. "Home sweet home."

"Cute house," Jim says as if it's obligatory that he make some positive compliment. Mark doesn't care. He's just happy to be home. "Do you need help getting in? You looked like you were on your sea legs earlier."

"No, thank you," Mark replies as Jim opens the door to let him out of the backseat. "I'm good. Happy to be home. I appreciate the ride."

They say their goodbyes and Mark stumbles to the front door. He doesn't have a key, as the cabbie at the hospital astutely pointed out. He tries knocking but can already tell Reya isn't home. The outdoor lights are off and the shades are still open. She doesn't answer the door. "Reya?" he asks, just in case. There's no answer.

A quick glance at the curb tells Mark that Jim has driven away. *Thank God*, Mark thinks. He would have wanted to help more. Mark isn't sure what the man could have done. With nervous energy coursing through him, Mark spots the trash bin that he promised Reya he'd take out tonight. At least he can do something right.

Something that Reya will appreciate, if she returns home safely to find out. He grabs it with his good arm and heads for the curb, near where Jim's patrol car was parked. He peers into the darkness as he walks, thinking about what an unusual sight he must be. If any of the neighbors see him, they'll have questions. Mark doesn't want to answer any questions right now. He simply wants to place the trash bin on the curb and get on with whatever else this hellish night might hold. Namely, he wants to find Reya, once and for all. A dose of painkillers wouldn't hurt anything, either.

As he wheels the trash bin flush against the curb and drops the back down against the section of grass between the road and the sidewalk, Mark suddenly hears a low, guttural growl. The sound makes his entire body stiffen with terror. It's a primal response. One that he can't control or override. He's petrified. He turns slowly and faces the sidewalk as it heads north up the street.

There, crouched in front of him, is a living, breathing saber-toothed tiger. He saw one just like it in his dream a few hours before, only that one was two-dimensional on the pages of a textbook he was staring at while trying to get his shit together as the class mocked him. *Smilodon*, he thinks, remembering the technical name for the creature. Latent energy pulses from the big cat's muscles as it waits, ready to pounce. It's staring at Mark with an evil, predatory look in its eyes. It opens its mouth to growl again and huge, razor-sharp teeth glisten in the soft glow of the moonlight. Saliva drips from the teeth and falls onto the sidewalk below. The cat means to attack, that much is clear.

The birthmarks on Mark's neck come alive again and seem to want to crawl right off his body. He's so frightened, he loses control of his bladder. Warm urine soaks the front of his pants. There's no time for shame. Only fear.

Before he can take another breath, the saber-toothed tiger lunges for Mark in a flurry of muscle and teeth, knocking him to the ground with the force of a moving freight train. He hits the sidewalk hard, certain he won't make it out of this alive. The killer cat places its long, sharp claws on Mark's neck, right over top of the marks. He covers his face with his good arm as he waits for the cat to end him. He lets a long, agonized moan escape his lips. His suffering has reached levels he never imagined possible. Maybe it would have been better to be the dismembered guy from the accident this morning. At least that guy didn't suffer. He was gone in an instant.

When Mark believes the saber-toothed tiger has him and there's nothing else left, Reya's face flashes in his mind's eye. *I love you, Reya, and I love our baby. I'm so sorry*, he thinks, defeated. Then he closes his eyes tightly and accepts his fate. There's nothing else left to do. This is the way it goes for countless animals on this planet. He's but one in billions who has lost out to a bigger, stronger predator. It doesn't feel good to be on the receiving end, but it's nature's way.

It's all over now.

A long moment passes. Mark stays still, his eyes closed and his body tense. Until he notices that it's quiet. No growling. No gnashing teeth. No ripping flesh. *Am I dead?* he wonders.

He gathers his courage, then removes his arm from his face and opens his eyes. To his utter surprise, he's alone on the sidewalk. There's nothing there. The big cat is gone. Mark thinks he's still alive. The pain tells him that he is, anyway. He props himself up, nervously peering into the darkness around him, sure that—if he is alive—the creature is nearby and ready to take another run at him. Only he doesn't see anything at all. Not even a neighbor outdoors. He shakes his head, too upset to think through the possibilities clearly. He'll try to make some sense of this later. He stands, feebly, just as the porch light flips on and someone opens the front door. It creaks, breaking the eerie silence.

"Mark?" a soft voice calls. "Is that you?"

Mark's eyes widen. It's the best sound he has ever heard in his entire life. "Reya? You're here?"

She chuckles. "Of course, I'm here. We live here. Where else would I be at this time of night?"

He stumbles up the driveway as tears stream down his face. He's overwhelmed with gratitude and relief after having been chewed up and spit out by whatever powers that be have had him in their grips. As he nears the house, Reya's face falls. Concern takes over and she covers her mouth with both hands.

"I'm home. I'm okay," Mark says. "Are you okay? The lights were off. And you didn't answer the door or your phone."

She lowers her hands slowly as he comes into her view. "I was in the back bedroom reading a book. My phone was on silent. I didn't mean to get so carried away. I guess I lost track of time. I had a long day at work. Wait … What happened to you? Is that a bandage on your arm? Are you wearing a hospital gown? You look terrible! Oh, Mark … Did you … *wet* your pants? What in the world?" Her voice escalates with each new revelation.

Mark stops a few feet away from her, unsure if he

should approach like normal. He glances over his shoulder to be sure the tiger isn't around. "I've had the absolute worst day of my life," Mark says somberly. "And as you know, that's really saying something."

Reya reaches out and takes his hand. "Can I hug you? I mean, will it hurt?"

Marks laughs out loud. The absurdity of their situation strikes him as funny for some reason. Maybe it's because he's exhausted beyond all belief. Maybe he's still loopy from anesthesia. Either way, he never expected to find himself here. "Hug me, anyway," he says as he embraces his love. He breathes her familiar scent in as he holds her as tightly as he can with one good arm. "I was worried about you," he says. "I thought something was wrong since I hadn't heard from you. I left you voicemails."

Reya pulls back. "I didn't miss any calls from you."

"You did, but they didn't come from my number. My phone got destroyed this morning when my car went up in flames."

Reya's mouth drops so far open it looks like it could hit the concrete of the porch below. "Your car did what?"

Mark takes a long, slow breath. There's so much to explain. "So, you really didn't hear? My boss didn't call you?"

Reya narrows her eyes, confused. "Your boss knew? Mark, what the hell is going on? Did you hit your head? Should you be in the hospital right now?"

"Ha!" Mark exclaims. "Yes. Yes, I should." Remembering the big cat, he glances over his shoulder nervously. The last thing he wants is for Reya to get hurt.

She takes a step back and looks hard at him. She's silent for a moment, taking it all in. "Mark Simbas," she begins, "are you being followed? Is someone after you?"

Using his good hand, Mark reaches for her cheek. He cradles it in his palm as he stares deep into his love's eyes. He then lowers his hand to her pregnant belly. He rests his fingers on what feels like their little one's rump, where it's tucked just below Reya's ribs.

"What are you doing?" she asks. "How can you be so calm at a time like this?"

"I'm far from calm," he replies. "I'm exhausted. Overdone. Downright miserable. But beyond all of that, I'm simply relieved to be here with you and the baby. At home. Can we go inside?" He double-checks over his shoulder again, to be certain they aren't in any danger from the predator he had a brush with.

Reya nods. "Of course. Let's go in."

Reya goes first and closes the shades. Mark follows. He locks the deadbolt tightly once the door is closed. He closes his eyes and breathes a sigh of relief to be in his own home, presumably safe. The pain he's been feeling seems to ease, if only a slight bit. "Is there still Tylenol in the bathroom?" he asks. "Because I could sure use it."

Reya says there is, then she goes to get him some with a glass of water while he gets as comfortable as possible on the sofa. "Here you go," she says as she hands him two little round pills.

"Two? That's all?" he asks. "I just had major surgery. I'd think—"

"You what?" she asks in disbelief.

"Two will be fine for now," he replies. "Sit down." He takes the pills and the water from her as she eases down beside him.

For the next hour, Mark tells Reya what happened to him since they left for work that morning. Piece by piece, he explains the accident, the stint at the hospital, and his dumb luck in finding a ride home. Reya gasps time after time as she learns what Mark's been through. The irritation she felt for him that morning has disappeared, replaced with genuine concern and sympathy.

What Mark doesn't tell her is that he saw a saber-toothed tiger on the sidewalk out front. Or that the birthmarks on his neck seemed to come alive before it happened. They're still throbbing, the pulse perceptible under his skin. He also doesn't tell her about the man who helped him out of his vehicle and then vanished into thin air, only to later be seen in pieces on a stretcher. Or about the figure he's certain was moving in the shadows under the window at the hospital. Those tidbits might make him sound certifiably insane. Maybe he is. If so, he wants to sort the details out on his own. Reya has enough to worry about without adding her boyfriend's hallucinations to the list.

Reya stays mostly quiet while she listens. When Mark is finished and has leaned his weary head against the back of the sofa, she finally speaks. Her words are measured. Her voice is soft and loving. "Mark, honey, I think I need to take you back to the hospital. Your condition seems serious. I don't want to lose you."

Mark jerks his head upon hearing this. "I don't want to lose you, either. Why do you think I came home? I had to be sure you and the baby were okay."

"Good. Then we're on the same page," she replies. "I'll pack a bag and then drive you back. I can stay overnight with you."

"What? No way. You won't be comfortable in a

hospital chair or cot or whatever they give you. You'll wake up stiff and sore, if you can sleep at all," he says. "I'm fine. I can stay home with you. That way, I can make it to work on time in the morning. I don't think my boss knows why I wasn't there today. I might already be in trouble."

Reya sighs. The pain of their financial situation doesn't need to be spoken about. They both know it. They feel it every single day. The pressure is only going to get worse when the baby comes and Reya has to take time off. The need for health insurance is especially pressing.

"Mark," Reya begins, "I know you want what's best for us. None of the rest will matter if you aren't alive and healthy. We can figure out the money …"

Mark shakes his head. "I'm sorry. I really am. But I'm sure I racked up a huge bill with the ambulance ride and surgery today. It might take us the rest of our lives to pay off that much. No joke. Medical bills ruin people, Reya. I don't want to add a dime more than is necessary. And I do *not* want to lose my job. Again."

"We can work it out. When the baby is older, I can pick up a second job. We'll take turns staying home with the little one," she tries.

"We'll never see each other," Mark replies.

"Okay. Then I'll ask my parents for money," Reya says. "They'd be happy to help. They've offered again and again—"

"Absolutely not," Mark says, sitting up straighter. "I don't intend to fail my family. *I* will provide for you and our baby. I won't take handouts from *those people*."

She bristles. "That's a little harsh, don't you think?"

Mark raises a brow. He bites his tongue because he

knows whatever he says next won't be kind. He's so tired and overdone that his filter probably isn't what it would normally be. He generally makes a habit of not mentioning Reya's parents. It's easier that way. "You're right. I'm sorry. I'm not in my right mind at the moment."

"You think?"

Mark chuckles, then leans back and settles more deeply into the soft cushions. "My head is killing me, I'm beyond exhausted, and this arm is beginning to hurt, too. I'm going to take a little rest. I'll be better—*friendlier*—when I wake up. I promise."

Reya watches as Mark closes his eyes and immediately dozes off. "Should you be sleeping? What are you feeling? Mark?"

He's asleep before Reya finishes her line of questioning, which leaves her to decide whether or not to intervene. She thinks about the money, and about Mark's job. She rubs her protruding belly absentmindedly as she considers the risks versus the rewards. Mark begins to snore. It seems like he's okay. Against her better judgment, Reya lets him sleep. After all, she really needs him to keep his job. If he can go to work in the morning, he should. They need the money.

5

DAYDREAMS

Mark sleeps fitfully on the sofa once Reya retires to their bedroom. He isn't sure, but he thinks he develops a fever at some point during the night. He becomes restless, flopping around as he tries to find a comfortable position. The Tylenol helps for a short time but does little to keep the pain at bay once the anesthesia and the heavy-duty pain meds given to him in recovery wear off. The pain becomes excruciating, yet he's too weak to get up and take another dose. When his fever finally breaks near dawn, he wakes up shivering, covered in sweat.

In his daze, it crosses Mark's mind that fever is one of the emergency symptoms Dr. Tipton warned him to watch out for. He pushes the thought out as fast as it enters. He's focused on making it to work before the first bell rings. He knows it's foolish to be so careless with his own health, but he's still young enough to feel invincible, most of the time.

The accident shook him up. So far, though, it hasn't changed him for good. He's still willing to burn the candle at both ends. Still willing to sacrifice himself. His intentions are good, though the execution is lacking. Maybe that will all change when he becomes a father.

"Up and at 'em," Mark mumbles to himself when he sees light begin to fill the gaps around the window shades. He's barely slept. If he had to guess, he might have gotten three cumulative hours of shut-eye. Not nearly enough.

It's quiet in the bedroom and Mark doesn't want to wake Reya, so he moves as quietly as he can. He winces as he tries to stand. The pain in his arm cuts deep. It's sharp, and it takes the wind right out of him. He falls back onto the sofa, attempt number one an utter failure. He closes his eyes and steels himself, then tries again. This time, he leans on his good arm and uses it to push forward. That works much better. He manages to get onto his feet.

Woozy at first, Mark teeters from side to side before stumbling to the kitchen and using the countertop on the island to steady him. He takes the Tylenol bottle out of the cabinet and dispenses a handful. He fills a glass and tosses the pills back. He doesn't bother to count them. He's in so much pain that he'd take anything that would make it stop.

"What are you doing?" Reya asks. She's leaning against the door frame with her arms crossed over her chest.

Mark hates the way she makes him feel like a child sometimes. Like she's keeping score. Keeping close tabs on him. He isn't in the mood for it. "Taking some pain medicine," he says without looking her in the eye. "Is that alright with you?"

"Don't be snippy, Mark," she replies. "I'm only looking out for you."

He sighs. "I know. Forget it."

She shakes her head. "You don't look so good. How did you sleep?"

"Fine," he says. He doesn't mention the fever. If he did, she'd want him to go back to the hospital instead of to work. She eyes him skeptically. "The weekend is only three days away, I think. I can catch up on rest then. Today is Wednesday, right?"

She nods. "So, you plan to go into work?"

"I don't have much choice. You know that," he mumbles as he rubs the top of his head. It still hurts, too. "It will have to be fine. It *will* be fine."

Reya is quiet for a moment, then finally, she shrugs her shoulders. "I can't watch. I'll get ready first and leave for my job. You do whatever you wish. Just be home for dinner tonight, okay?" Mark nods. "And get yourself a new phone," she adds. "Text me when you do, so I have your new number."

"That might be tricky without an ID," Mark muses. "And I don't have time to go get a new one of those today. I suspect I'll be tied up figuring out how to pay for the textbooks that got destroyed when I don't have a debit or credit card. The bank probably won't give me new ones without an ID, either. It's a mess."

"I can help you on my lunch," Reya says. Her job as a billing manager for a dental office doesn't allow her to get away often.

"Yeah, we both have bosses breathing down our necks," Mark says. "It's a frustrating life for two smart people who graduated from college to be this poor and to have such little control over our own time. It's maddening, in fact. It sucks."

"You always wanted to be a history teacher," Reya says softly.

"I know," he replies. "And I know you were passionate about your vocal performance degree. It's a shame there aren't more jobs in that field."

"Yeah," she says. "At least, I had a scholarship. I didn't go into debt over it." She's referring to Mark's student loan debt from college. It's something of a sore subject between them.

"You don't have to remind me," he grumbles. "I'm well aware of my shortcomings." It's easy to feel sorry for themselves but they both know it isn't productive. That's why Mark has spent so much time focusing on positive thinking. It's the thread of hope he clings to. That maybe, somehow, some way, things will get better. "Get ready for work," he says. "I'll handle my issues. No need to worry about me. I'm telling you, I'm fine. Just go."

She nods, even though she knows what he's saying is complete and utter bullshit. She should worry about him. But she has to keep her own job and her own schedule. If he's well enough to stand here and argue with her in the kitchen, she figures he's well enough to go to work and teach history to high schoolers. He ought to be able to sit down at his desk while he lectures if he isn't strong enough to deliver the lectures while standing.

"Are you sure you're good?" she asks. "Like I said last night, your health has to come first. None of the rest matters if we don't have you here with little Joey and me."

"Joey?" Mark asks, grinning from ear to ear.

"Short for Joseph," Reya adds. She cradles her

pregnant belly, a playful look on her face.

"You think it's a boy?" Mark asks.

Reya beams. "I know it is."

Mark's eyes grow wide. "What? How? Why didn't you tell me?"

"Because I haven't had a chance," she explains. "I found out by accident at my sonogram appointment yesterday."

"I thought that was just to check the baby's size and to make sure there is enough amniotic fluid sloshing around in there. I didn't know you were going to find out the gender. If I had, I might have been somewhere different when the accident happened," he explains. "It could have changed the course of things."

Reya walks to Mark and cups his cheek in her hand. "I get that. And I didn't mean to leave you out. I promise. The ultrasound tech let it slip. She seemed to think I already knew."

Mark smiles. He isn't mad at Reya. His thoughts center more on the remnants of dirt, blood, and sweat on his face. He knows she'd probably prefer he shower before she touches him much more. He steps backward. "I'm pretty grimy—"

She nods before he can finish his sentence. "We'll get cleaned up now. Little Joseph and I, that is." She turns and heads for the shower, a cheerful spring in her step.

"Why Joseph?" Mark calls behind her. Only, the bathroom door is closed mand she doesn't hear him. "I guess time will tell," he mumbles to himself. "Joey isn't a bad name for a little guy, I suppose. Huh. I kind of like it."

While Mark waits for the Tylenol to kick in and contemplates the prospect of becoming a father to a son,

Reya gets ready for work. She kisses him quickly on the lips as she breezes out the front door. "See you tonight. Call if you need me to do anything about your phone on my lunch break. I'll tell the other ladies in the office to put you right through."

He agrees, smiling and attempting to look as normal as possible. When the front door is closed and Reya pulls out of the driveway, Mark flings himself against the wall near the window. His level of pain continues to be nearly unmanageable. He put on a good show for Reya, but this won't do. He adds finding heavier-duty pain medication to the day's mental to-do list. He's wincing, trying his best to bear the pain when there's a knock at the door. He's still beside it, and the knock practically rattles his teeth, it's so loud.

"What did you forget?" he asks as he flings the door open, expecting to see his girlfriend. He pastes on the smile he knows she'll want to see. Only it isn't Reya. "Dawn? I mean, Officer Rawlins?" he asks when he sees her familiar face.

"Good morning, Mark," she says as she cocks her head to one side. Her hair is slicked back again, pulled tight into what must be her go-to ponytail. "My shift just started a little while ago. I went to the hospital to visit and they said you'd checked out last night. I, um, well … I thought I'd check in on you. How are you feeling?" She leans one hand on the door frame as she talks. Her posture is confident. Powerful.

"I've been better," Mark replies. He shoves his good hand through his hair. "I'm guessing Jim told you how he found me last night?"

Dawn smiles. "He did. Nothing to be ashamed of."

"Easy for you to say," Mark replies.

"I'm serious," she continues. "You had a rough day. It happens to the best of us. All told, you're one lucky man." She glances over his shoulder and into the house as she says it. "Your girlfriend home? Reya, right?"

Mark looks over his shoulder, following Dawn's gaze. It makes him nervous the way she's peering into his house. He knows he's probably paranoid, but he isn't sure why she's here. He doesn't like the uncertainty. "That's right," he confirms. "Reya. Tell me something, if you will."

"Okay."

"You knew my address and Reya's name. Why didn't you come here yesterday when I was in surgery to tell her what had happened?"

"I did." Dawn's words were sure. Her voice was calm. Her demeanor professional. Yet the statement didn't make sense. Reya was surprised to see Mark when he arrived home last night.

"No, you didn't," Mark says. "She didn't know."

"Yes, I did," Dawn insists. "After completing the report from the accident scene, I came straight here. Your girlfriend wasn't home, but I tracked her down at her job— The Creek Dental. There, we went out back and I explained everything. Didn't she tell you? She must have."

Mark shakes his head. "No. When I finally got home last night, Reya said she had lost track of time reading a novel and that her phone was on silent. She didn't know what had happened to me."

He can't imagine Dawn lying. She's an officer of the law, for God's sake, and she seems like a good person. But he can't imagine Reya lying, either. Why would she do that to him? Why would she play dumb? Why wouldn't she have rushed to the hospital the minute she heard he'd been in an accident. Something isn't right.

Dawn looks down at her feet as if she's considering the weight of the situation. When she looks up, she asks, "Can I come in?"

Mark hesitates. He still has a lot to do before work and he's running out of time. On the other hand, though, Reya left him here without transportation, which is strange, in hindsight. He may need to ask Dawn to give him a ride. "Come in," he says. "But I can't talk for long. I have to get to my job on time."

Dawn nods, then follows him inside. She takes a seat in a recliner chair and waits for Mark to get settled on the sofa. She can tell he's in a lot of pain. She has questions that she'd like to have answered. But she's used to being patient. There's plenty of time. "You changing into something else?"

"Yeah, I'd better," Mark says.

They eye each other, an awkward silence between them. Neither wants to make small talk but they don't want to jump right into the heavy stuff, either.

"You lived here long?" Dawn asks.

"Three years next month," Mark replies. "Why do you ask? Am I in some kind of trouble?"

Dawn shakes her head. "No, of course not. I'm just trying to make conversation. I wanted to check on you, but I don't want to intrude."

"I see," Marks says.

"Am I?" she asks. Her bright eyes flash, a mix of emotion in them.

"Are you what?"

"Intruding."

"Shit, no," Mark says. "While you're here, I do have

another question for you." He saves the ride ask for later. There's more that's on his mind.

"Anything. Go ahead," she says.

"Okay," he replies. "Did you contact my boss at the high school yesterday? To tell them why I didn't show up? I mean, I told you I was a teacher there, so I kind of figured—"

"I'm sorry," she says. "I didn't reach out to them. I thought your girlfriend would. She didn't contact them?"

"I don't think so."

Dawn pauses, thinking. "Is that why you checked yourself out of the hospital? To go to work?"

"Well, that and I was worried that something had happened to Reya. She didn't answer her mobile phone when I called. Not to mention, there was this strange shadow creature …" He stops himself before saying more.

"What kind of shadow creature?" Dawn asks. Something about the tone of her voice makes Mark think she might be open to hearing about his more unusual experiences. He'd sure love to tell someone about them, to get the weirdness off his back and out of his system. He hates keeping secrets.

"Do you really want to know?" he asks. His face is hopeful.

"Sure," she says. "If you want to tell me." After a pause, she adds, "I won't think you're crazy, if that's what you're worried about. You wouldn't believe some of the things I've seen. My grandma says I have a gift. I don't know about that. But I promise, I won't think you're crazy."

He's leery, and he doesn't want to cause a rift between himself and Reya. Maybe she had a good reason for lying to him. He feels like he ought to give his girlfriend the benefit of the doubt. Also, he isn't sure he should be confiding in Dawn instead of Reya. Desperate for someone to understand him, he decides to go ahead.

"I should back up," he begins, "and tell you what happened at the scene of the accident. Did you pick up on the fact that the torn-up guy looked like the one who urged me to get out of my car before it caught fire?"

She nods. "I thought so, yes. Theodore swears he didn't see anyone with you. I found that odd. I was curious and wanted to ask you more questions."

"Then I lost consciousness and had to be taken to the hospital," he adds.

"Right. Tell me more about it now. Did the man actually do anything physical that you could see when he was near your car?" she asks.

"I didn't realize it as it was happening, but as I look back, I don't think he did," Mark replies. "Maybe he was a figment of my imagination."

Dawn sighs. "Yeah. He didn't open your door?"

Mark shakes his head. "It was stuck. I thought, anyway."

"Did he break your window?" she asks.

"I thought that, too," he says. "But no. He didn't." Mark reaches his good hand up and cradles his bandaged shoulder as he remembers the injury. "Could I have imagined him there?"

"Maybe," she replies. "I've heard of stranger things happening. It seems like anything goes when life and death is on the line. Almost like the veil between this world and the next is thin."

"Kind of like a portal opens up and the rules are different?" Mark asks.

"That's one way to describe it," she replies. "Do you think the accident opened something that followed you?"

A chill runs up and down Mark's spine when she says it. That's exactly what he's been thinking about. He just hasn't found the right words to describe it. He scoots forward on the sofa and rests his good elbow on his knee. "Maybe so. The thing I saw in the shadows of my hospital room didn't seem human."

"Wow," Dawn mutters. A chill hits her spine, too. There's an eerie quality to the air all of a sudden. She can't help but feel like something otherworldly has made its presence known. "If not human, then what was it?"

"I thought of a child at first, but it didn't move like any child I've seen. It sort of rolled and twisted over on itself. I thought about a dog, maybe," he explains, "but that didn't make any sense. How would a dog get into the hospital?"

She nods. "Unlikely."

"That leaves more sinister and creepy answers," Mark says. "I was still groggy from anesthesia, and at first, I thought that might explain what I was seeing."

"Except that you weren't under anesthesia at the scene of the accident," she says, finishing his thought.

"Yes, you're right," he replies.

"You weren't under the influence of alcohol or drugs, were you? Because I didn't put that in the—"

"Of course not," Mark says. "I'm a high school teacher, for Christ's sake. I'm not a substance abuser.'

Dawn laughs, caught off guard by his candor. "Understood." She looks at him, waiting for him to continue if he has anything else to share. She's good at letting people talk. It's an asset in her profession. In her friendships, too.

Mark pauses, deciding whether to tell her about the saber-toothed tiger and the corresponding birthmarks. That vision is perhaps the strangest of all. He wonders who in their right mind would take his word about such an incident without thinking he was actually crazy. "Hmm," he mutters nervously.

"What's on your mind?" she asks as she leans forward in her own seat to meet his intensity. "Seems like there's something else."

"It's out there," he replies. "Even more so than what I've already said. I don't want you referring me to the loony bin." He laughs, his anxiety about the subject on full display.

"Try me," she says.

He purses his lips and shakes his head. "I don't know if I should."

They stare at each other, neither willing to give up their stance. It's so quiet in the house that the ticking clock on the kitchen wall suddenly sounds loud enough to wake a person from a deep slumber. Funny they didn't notice it before. It almost seems like some metaphor about time running out is being thrust upon them. "Go on," Dawn prompts.

Mark shakes his head again. "I've got to get to work. I should get cleaned up so I'm halfway presentable."

Dawn glances at the clock. "Tell me quickly, then. Give me the CliffsNotes version. You never know. You might end up needing a friend."

Mark raises a brow. This logic speaks for itself. "A friend who is aware of what's been going on could be a big help," he confirms. "Fine. You talked me into it."

She leans farther forward, as if she's about to hear a juicy piece of gossip. Maybe she is. "That was easier than I expected. You're a softie at heart, huh? Now *what* happened?" she asks eagerly. "Was it the thing in the shadows? Did you see more?"

"To the best of my knowledge, it was something … different. And it's going to sound so insane when I explain. Please, promise me you won't tell anyone else. I haven't even told Reya," he says.

"Yeah, no problem," she confirms. "My lips are sealed."

Mark likes the way Dawn is becoming a friend instead of merely a police officer. At least, he thinks that's what's occurring. Perhaps he's being presumptuous. Only time will tell. "Good. Thank you," he says. "So, at the hospital, the birthmarks on my neck seemed to come alive." He gestures to them, making sure she can see which marks he's talking about.

"All of the long ones right there?" she asks, pointing.

"Yes."

"They seem to be similar in length," she adds. "You … *felt* them?"

"It was strange," Mark explains, "like they were suddenly activated or something. I could feel the edges of them. It wasn't my entire neck or even a portion of my neck. It was precisely where the birthmarks are. I could feel the edges."

"Interesting," Dawn says. She continues to wait for him to keep going.

"I didn't think that much of it until I got home," he continues. "Granted, I was in bad shape and had to focus on putting one foot in front of the other. I thought maybe it was some weird side effect of anesthesia."

She winces with sympathy. "Jim told me as much. I'm sorry you've had such a rotten twenty-four hours."

Mark smiles. "I appreciate that. Really, I do. You've been very kind to me."

Dawn smiles back, then after a beat, slaps him on the knee like a friend would. "Now quit stalling and tell me the rest of the story. What happened when you got home?"

"Okay, okay! I didn't think Reya was home, so I took the trash bin down to the curb. I had promised her yesterday morning that I wouldn't forget," he explains. "I walked down there and had just placed the container on the sidewalk when I heard the loudest, most horrible growling from some*thing* nearby."

"Get out!" Dawn shouts, becoming more animated than Mark has seen her. "Was it a mountain lion? They've been spotted in these parts before. It's been a while. They aren't usually bold enough to wander into neighborhoods like yours."

"This was, well, much larger," he says.

"Yeah?"

"Larger and ... older."

She looks confused. "What do you mean, older? Like an old, slow mountain lion? Was it wounded?"

Mark balls up his face, bracing for her reaction. He closes one eye. "Prehistoric."

Dawn lowers her brow as she tries to decipher what he's talking about. "I don't get it," she says. "You're gonna have to spell it out for me. Prehistoric what?"

"*It* was prehistoric," he continues. "The awful growling got louder, and when I turned to look in the direction the sound was coming from, I saw an enormous saber-toothed tiger. I recognized it immediately because I'm teaching about that era in my class this week. I had an illustration of the same creature in one of the textbooks that got burned up in my car."

Her eyes widen, then narrow as she processes the revelation. "It was real? In the flesh? Err … fur?"

"It looked that way, yes."

"What did you do?"

"I thought about tucking my head between my legs and kissing my ass goodbye," he jokes. Dawn chuckles, but waits to hear more. "I was terrified. I just sort of stood, dumbly. There wasn't time to do anything else. It lunged at me, knocking me to the ground."

"Oh, my God!" she exclaims. "Are you alright? Did it hurt you?"

"The creature went for my neck, and its claws lined up with my birthmarks … *precisely*," he says. "I closed my eyes thinking that was it. I truly thought I was done for. But when I finally got the guts to open them, the thing was nowhere to be seen."

"Oh, no!! That's—"

"A hallucination," he says, finishing her sentence. "I know. It's the kind of thing people get heavily medicated for. Or labeled as mentally ill. It's not the kind of thing I should report, which is why I was hesitant to tell you. You won't flip on me and have me sent to some overeager shrink, will you?" He fiddles with the seam on the sofa cushion as he talks. He isn't sure he can trust Dawn to keep this to herself. He hopes he can.

She leans further forward. "Mark, no, I won't. I'll be concerned about you and will probably check in on you another time or two, if that's okay. It's probable that you did hallucinate the tiger. But the connection with your birthmarks is fascinating."

"I thought so, too," he says.

"That grandmother I mentioned earlier?" Dawn asks, her voice low and serious. "She always had the gift, as she called it. She used to say that birthmarks are placeholders, showing where fatal wounds happened in past lives. She had a strawberry-colored birthmark that ran from mid-calf on one foot all the way to her toes. She claimed she'd lost a foot when she was a young girl in the mountains of Germany who stumbled into a bear trap."

Mark is astonished by this theory, and it shows on his face. "Seriously?" he asks. "She believes that? She *remembers* that?"

Dawn nods. "I'm not saying I believe *her*. I'm not sure how I feel about the concept of past lives. It sounds so woo-woo, you know what I mean?"

"Yeah," he replies. "You can say that again."

"Her theory about the birthmarks is interesting, though," Dawn says. She shrugs her shoulders, ready to move on. She hardly knows Mark. She doesn't want to freak him out. "I don't know. Something to think about, maybe."

He smiles politely and leans back, a stabbing pain catching in his arm when he moves it. "Ouch." He doesn't mention the fact that the birthmarks on his neck are still humming, as if they're ready to be activated again at any time.

"You really are hurting, aren't you?" she asks. "I sort of keep forgetting that. You look and sound pretty good, all things considered."

Mark winces again. It all seems to hit him harder now that he's actively thinking about it. "Yeah, this sucks. They couldn't send me home with any prescription painkillers since I didn't have an ID."

"Gone in the fire?"

"Yep, along with my wallet, debit and credit cards, cash, and my work ID badge and textbooks. My boss may kill me when he finds out," he says. "I had better get moving. I can't be late."

"Okay, but how are you getting to work? Is Reya coming back to get you?" Dawn asks.

Mark sighs. "I don't think so. "I'm pretty sure she forgot about me not having a car here today. She offered to help me get a new ID on her lunch break, so there's that."

"Need a ride?" Dawn asks. "So far, it's been a slow morning. There's nowhere in particular I have to be." She turns a dial on a radio that's affixed to her belt. It has, apparently, been off because it comes to life with low tones and official conversation. Nothing sounds urgent.

"Actually, that would be great," Mark says. "Can you wait a few minutes while I get cleaned up?"

"Sure."

He pauses, feeling embarrassed about Reya's odd behavior. "She's a good woman. I guess she's stressed out by my … situation. Or maybe it's pregnancy brain."

"You don't have to explain to me," Dawn replies. "I didn't ask."

"You didn't have to."

They leave it at that without delving any further. It's the first time Mark has felt embarrassed about Reya. Usually, she's the one feeling uncomfortable about something he's said or done. Without another word, Mark turns and heads for the shower while Dawn settles back in her chair to wait.

6

THE SCHOOLYARD

I t's another bright, sunny morning as Mark rides in the back of Dawn's patrol car on the way to Thirsty Creek High School. He feels self-conscious about being in the backseat, but he understands that it's department policy. He knows he hasn't done anything wrong to land himself in the criminal category. Not yet. Hopefully, not ever, but that much remains to be seen.

"Comfy back there?" Dawn asks with a smirk as she glances at Mark in the rearview mirror.

"It'll do," Mark replies. "I appreciate the ride."

"All kidding aside, I'm sorry about the accommodations," she says. "I think it's dumb how strict the captain is about this kind of thing. We ought to be able to exercise our own judgment. You're obviously not a threat to anyone."

"Gee, thanks," Mark says. "I'm sure that's what every man wants to hear from a pretty woman. That he's not a threat to anyone at all. How very unmanly."

Dawn blushes but doesn't mention the compliment. They both stare straight ahead as they approach the intersection where the accident took place the morning before. She slows the car as if she owes it to those involved to show the area a certain amount of respect. "There it is," she says quietly.

"Huh," Mark says. "Almost exactly twenty-four hours later. It looks different."

"It's all cleaned up now," she replies. "Our department has the process down to a science. It's what we do."

"Yeah, but that's not all I'm seeing," he explains. "I came away from this place a different person. The experience changed me in ways I suspect I don't yet understand. I can … *feel* it."

She nods. "There's a heaviness here. Maybe it was there before your accident."

"Or maybe it's a lingering result of my accident," Mark says.

"Maybe."

They proceed through the intersection and remain silent the rest of the way to the high school. Mark's focus shifts to the day ahead as Dawn parks her patrol car around the quiet side of the building. She doesn't want to make a scene, which Mark is grateful for. His mysterious return with a giant bandage on one arm after being absent yesterday will be scene enough. He wonders who filled in and taught his classes.

He figures the students will pick on him for it. They're a short-sighted bunch. Most of them don't yet realize the effect their pettiness has on other people. They'll probably learn the hard way—alienating friends, relatives, and maybe even significant others and spouses before they straighten out and develop a healthy sense of compassion. They aren't all that way. But enough of them are to make Mark squirm as he waits for Dawn to walk around and open his door from the outside. The inside latch is locked so criminals can't let themselves out. It makes sense, but it's still embarrassing to be the guy in the back.

"Come on," she says once the door is open. She senses his reluctance. "You can do this. March right in there with your head held high and make them show you some respect. You deserve it."

Kids are already slowing down to look as a group of them walks through a breezeway in the distance. They're craning their necks to see if they recognize the poor sap being escorted this way. Some of them whisper to each other, throwing hands up to cover their mouths even though they're out of Mark's earshot by a long margin.

"Thanks," Mark manages to say as he maneuvers around his injured arm and out of the vehicle. The Tylenol has kicked in now and he's feeling some renewed energy. He isn't ready to play flag football at lunch or anything foolish like that. But he might just make it through the lecture to the students in his first-period class. That is, if he makes it through the inevitable discussion with Principal Heinman unscathed. "I'll try," he says to Dawn. She closes the car door behind him and he knows there's no use turning back. He has to face his fears.

"Hey," Dawn says, leaning toward him and lowering one eyebrow. "These kids can't be as bad as a saber-toothed tiger, can they?"

He laughs. The tension is broken, and Mark appreciates it. "Maybe not," he says, "but Marty Heinman probably can."

"Your principal?"

"And boss," Mark adds with a nod.

Dawn crosses her arms over her chest, her crisp black uniform and all its adornments shimmering in the morning sun. "Want me to do a background check on him? Dig up some dirt to give you leverage?"

"What?" Mark says cautiously. "No. I wouldn't. I mean, why? Do you know something about him?"

"No."

"Then why would you ask me that?" Mark asks.

Dawn chuckles. "Lighten up, Simbas. I was only joking."

Mark likes her calling him by his last name. It feels like they're buddies. "Were you?" he asks. "Because I haven't refused the offer yet. Depends on what kind of leverage we're talking about."

Dawn winks at him, then gives his good shoulder a shove, pushing him in the direction of the front office. "Have a good day," she says. "Call me if you need anything."

"With what phone again?" he asks, wincing.

"Yeah, well, I'm sure this place has a landline, you crybaby. In fact, I know they do because it's required."

He smiles, assuming she's joking with him about being a crybaby, but the banter is getting too aggressive for his tastes. He decides to get on with what he has to do. The two of them can decide what kind of friends they want to be later. "See ya," he says simply as he walks away. A moment later, he hears Dawn's car door close, then her tires on gravel. The sound grows quieter as she retreats into the distance.

On his own again, he does his best to appear confident. For some reason, Mark notices the pain more when Dawn isn't there. His head aches and his shoulder throbs. He needs a distraction.

Suddenly, a trio of stoner kids step out from where they've been standing under an exposed stairway on the outside of the building. They're upperclassmen, and Mark doesn't have them as students on his rosters. He's seen them around, though. His colleague, Susie Jeffers, who teaches remedial math for those who need it to graduate, has mentioned this crew's antics on numerous occasions in the short time Mark has worked at the school.

"What's up?" the biggest one asks as he slinks around in front of Mark on the sidewalk. This guy is huge. He plays on the school football team and looks like he could go right from Thirsty Creek to the NFL if he wanted to. Apparently, he's their leader. The others wait on his cues. They don't speak a word.

"Aren't druggies generally thinner? Sicklier?" Mark mumbles out loud, immediately regretting it. The big guy crosses his arms as a show of strength. "I'm sorry," Mark says. "I'm not thinking straight this morning. I didn't get a lot of sleep last night." He points to his bandaged arm.

"What'd you do?" the big kid asks.

"To my arm?"

"No, to your shrimp dick, asshole," he says, then waits for a reaction. The other two boys smirk, pleased with the insult. "Yeah, to your arm."

Mark's conflicted. He's the teacher here—not to mention the *adult* here—and he shouldn't let these losers push him around. At the same time, though, he's the one with the physical disadvantage. He doesn't want to get beaten up on top of his other issues. It won't matter how much trouble they get in when he's the one hurting.

"I'm talking to you," the big kid prompts when Mark takes too long to respond.

"It was a car accident," Mark says. "Yesterday."

The kids look at each other excitedly. They're practically salivating. "Did you go to the hospital?" the big guy asks.

The crowd in the distant breezeway is growing thicker now. It's getting late. The warning bell ought to ring any minute. "I did. Had surgery and everything." It takes him a beat, but Mark finally realizes what they're after. He sighs heavily, knowing what's coming next.

The big guy steps closer. He's so close that Mark can smell the cigarettes on his breath. He'd like to have one of those for himself. "They give you anything?"

"For the pain?" one of the other kids asks nervously, stepping forward. He's gangly and is wearing a beanie cap even though the temperature is pleasant outside. The big guy shoots him a look and he quickly steps back, all too aware of his error.

"They actually didn't. My ID … I didn't have my ID, and I checked out of the hospital early, so I couldn't get any prescriptions. Now, if you'll excuse me, I need to get to Principal Heinman's office before the second bell rings."

Mark moves to walk away but the big guy pulls on his shirt, halting forward progress.

"He's lying," the gangly kid blurts. "Surgery means drugs. They wouldn't send him home without drugs."

"How would you know?" the big guy asks, still holding onto Mark's shirt with one tightly clenched fist.

"I know because my mom works at the hospital," the skinny kid says defensively. "She's a nurse."

"Ross, shut up!" the third kid shouts. He seems to be the youngest. He's gangly, too. Perhaps he's a little brother who wants to protect his sibling.

Mark makes mental notes and plans to chat with Susie as soon as possible. Someone should intervene and set these kids straight.

"Move out," the big guy instructs under his breath. He lets go of Mark's shirt and the kids disappear into the stairwell as fast as they first appeared.

Mark stares in the direction they went but doesn't try to go after them. It's remarkable, really, that such an underbelly exists at Thirsty Creek High. The school is well funded and in an area with upper-middle class families who are actively involved in their kids' education. It's not the kind of place you'd expect students to try to shake down a teacher for prescription drugs. "Incredible," he says as he turns back toward the front office.

"What's incredible?" a deep voice asks. This time, it's an adult's voice, belonging to a well-groomed black man who Mark has seen at faculty meetings but hasn't yet met. He smiles politely as they make eye contact.

"Oh, hello," Mark replies. "Just some kids—delinquents, I suspect—hanging out in the stairwell. Are they allowed to do that?"

The man laughs. "Define allowed." Mark stares at him, unsure whether the question was meant to be rhetorical. After a pause, the man extends a hand. "Al Muth. Pleased to meet you. You're Mark Simbas, history. Right?"

"Thanks," Mark replies, shaking Al's hand. "Good to meet you, too. And yeah, that's me. How did you know?"

"You're the new guy. There was an announcement made about you and the lady art teacher from Wyoming during our first day back after summer break."

"Ah," Mark says as they begin to walk together. "I guess I didn't realize that. I knew the art teacher had recently moved to town. I didn't know we'd been announced to the faculty. What do you teach?"

"Chemistry. I'm the guy praying those dipshits from the stairwell don't blow us all up one day in my lab."

Mark laughs. Al seems friendly. Yet something about that fact puts Mark on edge. He's met a string of friendly, helpful people since the accident the morning prior, which seems too good to be true. Granted, his positive-thinking gurus wouldn't want him to be so skeptical. Maybe all these nice people are, in fact, a direct result of his positive thinking. That sounds great but doesn't feel quite right. In fact, Mark gets a weird vibe from Al that he can't explain.

"A penny for your thoughts?" Al asks as he puts a finger on his chin. His posture is formal, as if he was trained to move the way he does.

"Oh, I was just thinking about how nice everyone is around here. The adults, anyway. The kids are another story, but most of the adults I've met lately have been very kind," Mark explains.

Al nods. "I hope that continues. Talk to me in another few weeks. I'll be curious to know if you still feel the same way."

They're nearing the breezeway where students swarm. Mark needs to take a right to get to the front office. "This is me," he says, gesturing. "Which way are you going?"

Al points to the left just as a short, stalky man slams into Mark's back, causing him to lose his balance. The impact hurts. He stumbles a few steps before regaining his footing. The man gives Mark a dirty look without stopping. "Watch where you're going," the guy grumbles.

"See?" Al says as he shakes his head.

"Who is that?" Mark asks. The man is gone before Mark has time to speak to him directly.

"Gill Watson. Geometry and boys' soccer."

"He's a coach?" Mark asks.

Al nods, then does a mini salute, turns on one heel, and walks away. "Hope to see you around," he calls over his shoulder.

Shaken, Mark stands still as he considers just how precarious his injury is. He's never had any vulnerability like it before, and he didn't realize how easy it would be for someone to bump into him and cause a world of hurt. He could sustain permanent damage. How would he throw a baseball with his son—like good dads are supposed to do—if his arm is permanently screwed up? He's getting tired, the Tylenol holding for now but he suspects it won't last much longer. He really needs to find something stronger for the pain.

"Out of the way!" a tiny girl yells as she moves past. She seems awfully little to be in high school, much less have that attitude. Strangely, she looks sort of like Abby, the nurse from the hospital last night. Apparently, though, this girl isn't nearly as friendly as the kind nurse. She's gone before Mark can respond to her rudeness.

"What's wrong with people?" he asks under his breath. He shakes his head hard, in disbelief.

Suddenly, a bell rings and the crowd thins. Kids scatter, disappearing into various doorways, their backpacks bobbing behind them. Mark will be late if he doesn't hoof it. He turns toward Principal Heinman's office and speed walks down the long corridor that leads to the office building. He reaches the door and grips the handle, then heaves himself inside just before the second bell rings. He ought to be in his first period classroom by now. He hopes the principal will consider making it into the office as good enough.

"Can I help you?" the secretary asks curtly. She's new. At least, Mark hasn't met her yet. She's older with badly dyed red hair, and she seems to be wound pretty tightly. Her features are not friendly despite the forced smile on her face. An engraved silver placard on her desk reads Misty Sullivan.

"Yes, certainly, ma'am," Mark replies. "Ms. Sullivan. Have we met? I think I'd remember you." Reya says you catch more flies with honey, so he figures he'll try being polite and complimentary. Only, he doesn't come off that way.

"What do you think this is? Hello Cupid?" Misty asks, her wrinkled skin rippling with every word. The lines around her mouth reveal decades of heavy smoking, which the gravelly voice confirms. "We *haven't* met, but who cares? Do you have official business here?"

His face falls. He clears his throat and adjusts to her hostile tone. "I work here."

"You do?"

"I'm a teacher. History," he says.

"Then why are you standing in front of me instead of in your classroom? You do have a first period class, right? And where's your ID badge? You aren't supposed to be on campus without it."

She's full of questions. "I was in an accident," Mark says, gesturing to his bandaged arm. How could she have missed it? "I'm here to speak with Principal Heinman about my absence yesterday. Is he available?"

She narrows her eyes. "What kind of accident?"

"A car accident. A truck ran a red light and hit me—"

Raising one hand, she stops Mark before he can say more. "The one near downtown? Yesterday morning? Was that you?"

Mark nods. "That's right. I passed out and couldn't call—"

She raises her hand again. "Hold on," she says through gritted teeth as she picks up the phone on her desk and pushes a few buttons. After a moment, she slams the receiver down. Apparently, no one picked up. She looks at Mark and points. "Sit there. You might have to wait a while. Was he expecting you?"

"No, I guess not," Mark replies. His face feels hot and the pains in his arm and head threaten to return with a vengeance. He's genuinely afraid of being in trouble and losing his job. Reya would be livid if that should come to pass. Livid.

"Then get comfortable," Misty says with a grunt. Her irritation is obvious.

Mark nods, then takes a seat at the end of a row of chairs against the front window. The main door quickly opens and closes a few times as student aides shuttle deliveries of various kinds. It doesn't take long for things to settle, everyone eased into the rhythm of the new day.

As Mark sits obediently, he thinks about the disdain

in Misty's voice—a woman he doesn't even know—and how it's the same tone that Reya strikes more often than he'd like. What is it about him that makes people grouchy? He doesn't mean to offend anyone. He definitely doesn't want people pissed off by virtue of his very existence. That's no way to live.

The down time gives him a chance to mentally review the events since the accident, which he does with a careful seriousness. He thinks about the nice folks who have come to his aid. There have been a lot of those. He also thinks about the hostile and inhospitable people. Too many of them, truth be told. As he ponders his situation, he isn't completely sure which category to count Reya in. He decides that he doesn't have to decide yet. He only needs to observe. And keep from losing his job. *That* is priority number one.

"Mind if I turn it up?" Misty asks out of the blue.

"What?" Mark asks. He's been lost in his own thoughts. He has no idea what she's talking about.

"The radio," she says, tilting her head toward an old-school radio alarm clock situated on one side of her desk. "It's one of my favorites. Aerosmith."

No one is in the office lobby besides the two of them and a female student aid who is highlighting something on papers at a desk in the corner. "Sure," Mark says. "I like Aerosmith. Which song is it?"

Misty's eyes grow wide as if she can't fathom anyone not knowing. "Listen," she says.

He does, and he soon recognizes the distinctive intro. When the first few words about looking in the mirror are sung, he knows for sure. "Dream On," he says with a smile.

"That's right," Misty confirms. She doesn't look so

angry anymore. In fact, the two of them might be bonding. "I thought you might know it. These kids don't. They wouldn't know good music if it knocked them upside the head."

Mark laughs. He guesses she's right. "Yeah," he says. The girl with the highlighter looks up briefly but doesn't seem to care what he and Misty are saying about her generation. She goes back to what she was doing without a reaction. "My dad liked this song," Mark muses. "He played it a lot when I was a kid." As he listens, he remembers being back in his dad's garage again. The sights and smells return right on cue, as if they never left.

"Are those memories happy?" Misty asks. She reaches up and tightens a messy bun full of white hair that's piled on top of her head.

He shrugs. "Mostly."

"My memories of this song are the happy variety," she offers. "I'm older than you. I can't say that I listened with my dad. Yeah. I remember making out to this song with my high school boyfriend. That clown became my first ex-husband." She grins now, her thin lips spread wide across her face. "It was fun while it lasted."

Highlighter girl doesn't react to this either. She really is uninterested in the old folks. For some reason, that irks Mark. He isn't that old, after all. Does he look older than he actually is? "Excuse me, miss," he says to her. He points when she looks up. "That's right. You."

"Yes, sir?"

"Do you know this song?" he asks. Then he says, "Misty, turn it up louder, would you?"

Misty obliges gleefully. She cranks the volume, apparently unconcerned about Principal Heinman on the other side of his door. "Oh, it takes me right back to the seventies," she coos. She closes her eyes as the band prompts listeners to sing with them. "That may sound like a long time ago, but I remember it like it was yesterday."

"I don't think I know this song," the girl says bashfully. "Sorry."

In a surprising move—at least, surprising to Mark—Misty stands, her ample thighs sending the rolling chair she's evacuated hurtling backward against a wall. She raises her hands in front of her face and wraps her fingers into loose fists as she moves her elbows to the beat. Her eyes remain closed as she moves and sways with the music. Mark suspects she's actually envisioning the ex-husband's face in her mind's eye. He smiles at the sight. He can't help himself. Her delight is contagious. Mark is in dire need of moments of joy. Life's simple pleasures are incredibly valuable to him at this juncture.

"Dance with me," Misty says without opening her eyes. Her voice doesn't sound so gravelly now. Her expression is enticing. How can he say no?

"I don't know if I should," he says, but it's obvious he wants to dance. His toes are already tapping to the beat.

Misty shuffles and scoots her way around the edge of her desk and into the open floor area in the middle of the room. Aerosmith continues to croon about dreaming on and singing for the year, the laughter, and the tear. Their distinctive voices are a balm to her aging heart. Mark wonders what kind of life this woman has lived since the days of the ex-husband she mentioned. He gets the impression that her best days are behind her. He hopes the same isn't true for him.

"You'll wish you did," Misty says to him. "Life's short, Mark Simbas. You'll know that for sure when you get to my age. Don't miss a chance to let your hair down." With that, she reaches up and literally does let her hair down. White curls shake loose of the bun and fall freely as she keeps up with the front edge of beat.

Mark shrugs. "You know what? Why not?" He stands, his bandaged arm dragging yet unable to hold him back. The pain returns, worse than before. He doesn't let it get him down. He raises his good arm to match Misty's signature move. His elbow keeps the rhythm as his knees bend and his body sways. He bobs his head to the beat. "Dream on!" he sings enthusiastically. "Dream on."

The girl excuses herself, then slinks past them and disappears out the front door. Mark and Misty laugh like old friends, an unspoken understanding between them. "Oh, well," Misty says. "Her loss."

"She's too young to appreciate the goodness that is Aerosmith," Mark adds. "I figure our elders said the same about us. I remember my grandpa talking about Nat King Cole and Buddy Holly. I wasn't terribly interested."

"She'll understand one day," Misty says without slowing her body down. "One day, she'll be a wrinkly, white-haired woman who lets herself get lost in an old song while a teenager looks on. To everything there is a season."

"You can say that again," Mark replies. "I'm having a baby soon. Well, my girlfriend is, anyway. I'm not actually the one having a baby." He stops dancing and laughs nervously. "I hope he doesn't think I'm too much of a dork."

Misty stops dancing, too. A serious expression covers

her face. "So, this meeting with Heinman … I guess it's pretty important, huh?"

Mark nods. "I definitely need to keep my job, if that's what you're asking."

Something about the thought of losing his income and benefits sends a chill up his spine. He's been relaxed—having fun, even—but the reality of his predicament hits him hard. He suddenly feels careless out here dancing like he doesn't have a care in the world. What if Principal Heinman thinks he doesn't respect him or the need to remain professional at his place of work. Beads of perspiration form on Mark's brow as his muscles tense.

Misty purses her lips as she thinks. She narrows her eyes, then reaches over her desk to turn the music down. Only when she does, the knob turns the other way and the music blares even louder. "Once Bitten Twice Shy" comes on and fills the room just as a random kid enters from outside. Wind catches the door behind him and slams it so hard that the loud bang of metal against metal can be heard over the music.

"Oh!" Mark exclaims as his body fails him in all sorts of ways. He crumples, landing back in his chair. He then doubles over and puts his head between his knees, feeling like he might be sick. Pain radiates all the way down his injured arm. It has suddenly come to life with a searing sensation that feels like tearing from the inside out. Right on cue, his head pounds. Even his legs and feet ache. He isn't even sure why. Maybe the walk out of the hospital yesterday?

"You okay?" Misty asks. "The door—it's just wind. Happens all the time. You look like you've seen a ghost all of a sudden. What's got you so freaked out?"

Little does Misty know … Mark actually has seen a ghost recently. The guy in the hooded sweatshirt and muddy boots flashes into his mind. That was so creepy. And a ghost isn't the only thing Mark has seen in the past twenty-four hours. The shadowy figure in the hospital and the saber-toothed tiger are both equally frightening. Perhaps he hasn't yet had time to fully process all that he's seen and experienced. Perhaps he can't simply move on as if nothing out of the ordinary has happened. Perhaps he shouldn't even be here at the high school right now. Mark suddenly wants to rush back to the hospital and climb into bed so Dr. Tipton and the nurses can take proper care of him.

He is too shaken up to answer Misty. He lets out a guttural grunt that sounds sort of like "yeah." It's the best he can do right now. Something about hearing the same song that was playing on the radio yesterday morning when the crash happened puts him on edge. Then the bang of the office door that sounded so much like the impact when the truck hit his little car simply did him in. "I'm sorry," he says, finding his voice.

Misty turns the music down but not all the way off. "Sorry for what?" she asks.

He shakes his head. It's answer enough. Bright red blood forms a visible circle on the outside of Mark's arm bandage and begins to leak. Self-consciously, he covers it with his good hand. It's no use. He needs a clean dressing on the wound. He vaguely remembers Abby saying that this could happen. He wishes he'd paid more attention to their instructions. "I've got to go," he continues. "I changed my mind. I shouldn't have come here in the first place. The doctor told me I should stay in the hospital—"

"He did what now?" she asks.

The boy who has entered the office turns around and exits. He's smart, and he doesn't want any part of this. The door slams behind him as the Great White song continues in the background. Meanwhile, Mark's level of distress escalates. His heart pounds in his chest. It feels like an elephant is sitting square on top of him. He can't get a full breath.

"Please tell Principal Heinman why I'm not on duty. Tell him I'll be back as soon as I can, but that I was in an accident and am not well," Mark pleads. "Tell him I need my job." Blood drips from his bandage onto the floor, punctuating his point.

Misty nods. "Go," she says. "I'll make him understand. Don't you worry about it. You hear? Take care of yourself."

Mark nods his gratitude, then rushes out the door. He clasps his arm as he goes, following the same path he walked when he entered. He's in such a bad state of mind that he hardly remembers his lack of a car or a phone. He can barely see straight. With what little awareness he has, he suspects he might be having a heart attack. Or a panic attack. Either way, he needs some privacy and some air. He needs to clear his head. He needs to find a way to make the searing, incessant pain stop.

As he stumbles along the sidewalk around the side of the building, he hears a male voice from the stairwell. "Hey," it says. "Want a little something for the pain?" It takes Mark a couple of beats to process what's happening. As he does, the big kid from earlier emerges from the shadows and waves him over. "Follow me."

Mark doesn't ask questions. Earlier, he was confused

about who the potential buyer and who the potential seller was. Now, he knows exactly what's going on. These kids don't just want to buy the meds they hoped he'd been prescribed at the hospital. They're far too savvy for only that. They know he's desperate and they have what he needs. He no longer cares that they aren't in class. He doesn't ponder the ethics of what he's doing. He needs relief, and he needs it now.

The big guy seems to be alone this time. When they reach the stairway, he pulls a plastic baggie from underneath the bottom stair.

"I don't have any money on me," Mark says. "It all burned up in my car after the accident yesterday morning. No ATM card, no—"

"I know where to find you," the kid says gruffly. He hands the baggie to Mark.

The weight of the cool, smooth pills inside feels delicious in Mark's palm. "Thank you," Mark says, unsure what else to say. The power dynamic between them has shifted irreparably. Mark could be in huge trouble if anyone ever found out about this. At the moment, he doesn't care. Not one bit.

He sits down on the concrete and grabs hungrily for the pills, stuffing several of them into his mouth and forcing his dry throat to swallow. Blood pools around him as it leaks from his bandaged arm. He leans back against the brick wall, feeling the rough edges tug at his shirt. He doesn't have to wait for long. Relief comes quickly. It washes over him like a warm blanket, lulling him into a deep, deep sleep.

PART II

PLUMMET

7

LIKE A DRUM

Two Weeks Later

"Mark, how's it going?" Al calls out as he rolls up to the Thirsty Creek High School football stadium in his pristine white Lexus sedan.

Mark's standing at the gate, showing his shiny replacement ID badge to gain entrance to the game when he hears the greeting. It's early and it isn't crowded yet, but the smell of freshly popped popcorn and warm hot dogs already permeates the evening air.

"Hey there, stranger!" Mark replies. "Long time, no see." He chuckles at himself, knowing that the two of them saw each other at school less than two hours ago.

"Hardy-har-har," Al says with a smirk. He crinkles his face into an exaggerated expression to make Mark laugh.

"Park that fancy car and come on in. I'll wait on you," Mark continues. It isn't the first time he has laid eyes on his new friend's car over the past two weeks. It isn't the first time he's wondered how Al can afford a Lexus on a teacher's salary, either. He doesn't think it polite to inquire. That doesn't stop him from teasing about it.

Al nods and gives a mock salute. "Be right there," he says. The lot is mostly empty. He arrived early enough to get the third spot from the front. Al parks the Lexus, locks it with the keyfob, and walks casually to join Mark at the stadium gates. All indications point to a fun night ahead. The local weatherman mentioned the possibility of strong storms later but there's no sign of them yet.

"You eat?" Mark asks. "Because I think one of those hot dogs is calling my name."

"Not yet," Al says. "I was hoping they'd have pizza tonight. I'm not entirely sure I trust what's in those dogs."

"The trick is to not think about it," Mark says with a laugh. "You'd never catch me reading the ingredients." His arm is in a sling now with a wrap instead of the big bandage he wore right after surgery. It's still sore, though. He doesn't want the pain to get out of hand during the game. He knows he might get jostled in the crowd. Best to take a pain pill now. "Excuse me a moment," he says. "I need to make a quick trip to the restroom, then we'll get whatever kind of mystery meat you desire from the concession stand."

"Okay," Al says. "Be quick. I'd prefer to get our food and sit down before this place is swarmed."

"Will do," Mark replies.

When he reaches the privacy of a restroom stall, he shoves an eager hand into his pants pocket. The feeling of the soft packet of pills against his palm has become a comfort. As long as he can pop a few pills several times a day, he can make it through. He's grateful for their presence. He leans against the locked door and closes his eyes for a moment. It's been a long day at work, and he hasn't taken a pill since lunchtime. If asked, he wouldn't say he's become dependent on the pills, yet his body craves them. More and more all the time.

The restroom is empty now, but Mark knows it might not stay that way for long. He doesn't want to be seen taking the pills if he can help it. He'll need a swig of water from the sink to wash them down. He doesn't want to be seen drinking from the faucet instead of the water fountain out front, either, but stopping at the fountain is too risky. Anyone could show up and see what he's doing. That wouldn't be good.

Moving quickly, he takes three pills out of the packet. He pops them into his mouth, keeping them balanced between his front teeth until he gets the water. He returns the packet to his pants pocket, noting that only three more pills remain. He'll need to find Butch—as he's nicknamed the big kid who sells the drugs—before the game is over tonight. Otherwise, Mark won't have enough supply to last through the weekend.

He hears the door to the restroom open. It's a group of boys. He can tell immediately that it's at least three kids. Maybe four. They're talking and laughing together. Mark knows he'll need to vacate the stall he's in soon, or else it will draw unwanted attention. He shifts the pills further back in his mouth, balancing them between his molars. It will have to do. "Hello there, boys," he says as he exits the stall. His voice sounds strange with the pills in there but they don't seem to notice.

"Um, hello, Mr. Simbas," one says.

They know him. He was hoping they wouldn't. He doesn't recognize them. No matter. "Enjoy the game," he says as he washes his hands at the sink, opting to drink from the water fountain out front, after all.

He walks nonchalantly out of the restroom, even though his mouth is watering. The pills taste bitter as they begin to dissolve. Not to mention, knowing that he's so close to the feeling of relief makes him want it even more. He's restless, keen to wash the pills down and feel them work their magic. He's at the water fountain, bent over the nozzle when he hears a vaguely familiar voice.

"Mark, is that you?"

Mark freezes, a guilty man caught in the act. He doesn't know who's recognized him, but he won't let them keep him from his relief. Not this time. He pitches himself forward, guzzling water and swallowing the pills. When he's finished and they're down, he straightens up and turns to see the man standing behind him. It takes him a minute. He doesn't immediately place the smiling face. "I'm sorry," he says. "I know that I know you. I'm not remembering, though."

"I wouldn't expect you to," the man says. "You were having one hell of a day when we met."

That does it. Mark remembers. "Right," he says. "You're the medic who patched me up after my accident. "Michael ... Zhan?"

"Close," Michael replies. "Michael Zhang. Good memory."

"Michael Zhang it is. You look different without your uniform," Mark says. "Plus, you don't have your ambulance parked nearby. Or do you?"

"No, sir," Michael says. "I'm off duty tonight. I'm here to see my girlfriend's kids play ball."

"Nice. Do they attend Thirsty Creek High?" Mark asks.

Michael nods. "They do. One is a freshman. Drew is his name. I doubt he'll do more than warm the bench this season. The other one is a junior, though, and he's pretty good. Ross Guerrero. Have you heard of him?"

Mark's brows shoot up as he pieces the bits of information together and makes the connections. "I'm not sure I do," he lies. He remembers the youngest kid in the trio of druggies calling one of the older boys Ross. He also remembers them mentioning a mom who worked at the hospital, and he's pretty sure nurse Abby's last name read Guerrero on her badge. "I don't have them in class, if that's what you mean."

"They're good kids," Michael says. "Their dad died a few years back. It's a sad story. Cancer took him within months of being diagnosed. Their mom's a nurse who works long hours. She does the best she can for them. I try to be supportive and fill in when I can."

Mark swallows hard. The group of boys is on their way out of the restroom now. They excuse themselves as they step past where Mark and Michael are standing. Sometimes, it feels like the kids could dominate Mark. Like they could physically overtake him. He tries not to let on. "You say your girlfriend is a nurse?" he continues, refocusing on the conversation.

"Indeed, she is," Michael replies.

"Where does she work?"

"At the hospital," Michael says. "The same one we took you to. You might have actually seen her there. She works in recovery."

Mark nods. There's no point in denying it. He figures he might as well face the facts. "Is her name Abby?"

Michael smiles big, like his most favorite name in the world has just been spoken. Maybe it has. "That's right. Abby Guerrero. Did she take care of you after your surgery?"

Mark smiles back. "She did. She was very nice. I can tell you're proud of her. You should be. She seemed great."

"She sure is," Michael replies. "I'm her biggest fan."

In his peripheral vision, Mark sees Al hanging back and watching. He seems to want to join in but is giving Mark and Michael space. "Hey," Mark says to Michael, "I'd love to introduce you to a friend. He's waiting for me to get some concession food with him. Want to walk with us?"

"Sure," Michael says enthusiastically. "Maybe Ross and Drew won't think I'm such a loser if they see that I've made friends. You might score me some points with the teenagers."

Mark laughs. "Tough crowd, huh? I know how that goes. I sometimes wonder why I ever wanted to become a high school teacher in the first place. Kids this age can be brutal."

Michael laughs along, too, as they walk. "Glad I'm not the only one who thinks so. Like I said, Abby's boys are good kids. But that doesn't mean I don't feel inadequate around them. I do. More than I care to admit."

Mark catches Al's attention and waves him over. "Al, I'd like you to meet someone!" Mark calls as his friend makes his way across the main walkway between the gate and the restrooms. It's beginning to get crowded. Kids dart around excitedly, greeting friends and forming groups. Everyone seems to be arriving at once.

"Hi, there," Al says confidently. He isn't a shy man. Quite the opposite. "Al Muth. I'm a colleague of Mark's. I teach Chemistry."

Michael reaches out his hand to shake. "Michael Zhang. Pleased to meet you. I'm an EMT. I helped patch this guy up a few weeks ago. I'm off duty tonight."

"He's here to watch his girlfriend's kids," Mark adds, shooting Al a knowing look. "They play football. Ross and Drew Guerrero. Do you know them?"

Al hesitates, unsure what Mark is getting at. "The names sound familiar," he says. "I'm not sure I've had either of them in class. Maybe I've just seen their names on the team roster."

"Hmm," Mark replies. "That might be where I've seen their names as well. I knew they sounded familiar."

Michael smiles without adding anything more about Abby's boys. Maybe he doesn't want to sound preoccupied with them. They aren't even his own kids, after all. Taking the cue, Mark turns the conversation to food. "Hungry?" he asks.

"Famished," Al says. "Will you join us, Michael? I can't promise fine dining at the concession stand, but it's usually edible."

With a laugh and another broad smile, Michael accepts the invitation. Chatting as they go, the three of them buy and then scarf down a variety of lukewarm and overpriced menu items. It isn't that bad. It's all part of Friday night lights at a high school football stadium. They're making memories that they will, no doubt, look back upon fondly. When their bellies are full, they make their way to the bleachers to wait for the game to start.

Mark is hesitant to get too excited, yet he can't help feeling good to hang out with friends. He tells them as much. "You guys," he begins, "this is really nice. The three of us hanging out like this."

"We could do it more often," Michael offers. I work mostly days and am always up for a cold beer ... or a mediocre hot dog."

Al agrees. "Works for me. I'm single, so no one is waiting for me at night. I'm down to hang with you two cats."

"Cats?" Marks asks with a laugh. The saber-toothed cat comes immediately to mind.

Al shrugs. "It's an expression. Something my dad used to say."

Michael nods, seeming to understand.

Out of nowhere, Mark feels a hot, burning sensation on his back that radiates all the way through to his chest. It's a thick, round, and full feeling, as if a rod or a pole is lodged all the way through him. He winces at the sensation. It isn't pain, exactly, but his flesh feels like it has come alive. It takes him a minute to remember, but the sensation is a lot like what he felt on his neck before he saw the prehistoric beast in his front yard.

An announcer's voice booms through the loudspeaker. It's time for the game to start.

"There they are!" Michael says, pointing out Abby's boys as they make their way onto the field.

"Alright, alright," Al says, oblivious to Mark's distress.

Beads of perspiration begin to form on Mark's brow. He narrows his eyes as he thinks about what might be happening to him. Could it be the Oxy? He has been taking more and more each day—probably more than he should. He could ask Michael, but he doesn't want to let on that he's becoming dependent on the drugs to get through the days. He also doesn't want to be asked where he got it. Now that he knows about the connection to Abby and the hospital, he wants to avoid opening that can of worms if at all possible.

Wait, Mark thinks. He pats his chest and closes his eyes, remembering that he has two round, purple birthmarks in the exact spot that feels funny now. One is on his back, and the other is on his chest. If he's right, the birthmarks line up exactly with the sensation he's feeling, just like the birthmarks on his neck corresponded to the places where the saber-toothed tiger placed his massive claws when he pounced.

"I have to go to the restroom," Mark says as he leaps up suddenly. "Sorry."

"Weren't you just in there?" Al asks.

"Dinner not agreeing with you?" Michael jokes.

"I'm fine," Mark says, even though he doesn't feel fine at all. The space in his body between the two round birthmarks is absolutely crawling. Before he can exit his place on the bleachers, the announcer asks the crowd to stand for the singing of the national anthem.

"You'd better wait a few minutes," Michael says. "You know, out of respect."

Mark forces himself to focus on the scene around them. Members of the Thirsty Creek High School JROTC Color Guard are marching to the middle of the football field. Two of the cadets have flagpoles leaned against their shoulders. One bears the American flag and another one the Tennessee state flag. The young men look ultra-serious about their duty to bear the colors. Folks in the stadium seem to meet their mood. A hush falls over the crowd and it gets so quiet you could hear a pin drop.

"Are you a veteran?" Mark whispers as he tries not to squirm.

"I am," Michael replies. "U.S. Navy."

Al leans over and gives Michael a hearty slap on the back. "Thank you for your service."

Michael smiles, appreciative of the words of support. He nods his thanks. "How'd you know to ask?" he inquires of Mark.

"Just a hunch. You have a certain look about you." Mark barely gets the words out before he has to close his eyes to collect himself. The sensation in his chest is intensifying. He fears that soon, he will be completely overwhelmed by it and won't be able to carry on an intelligible conversation. He wants to get to the bathroom, out of sight. He knows Michael is right, though. It would be disrespectful to leave his seat and walk in front of everyone before the national anthem is finished.

The announcer comes back, talking quickly as he says the names of the color guard members and then asks the crowd to stand for the singing of the anthem. Mark's grip on the space and time around him is slipping. Michael and Al stand on either side of him. He knows he should stand, too, but his legs don't feel like they'll work. He's dizzy, and it seems like the entire stadium is spinning.

"Are you okay?" Michael asks.

Al has noticed as well. "Buddy, you don't look so good," he adds.

Mark opens his eyes and forces a smile through gritted teeth as a tall, thin girl with long black hair takes her place on a podium and begins the familiar intro to

"The Star Spangled Banner." They have her miked up. Her smooth alto wafts through the air. She's confident, and she ought to be. Her voice is strong and sure. Mark wishes he had even a fraction of her self assuredness. "I'm fine," he says, not sure whether he's trying to convince his friends, or himself. "I might need to splash some cold water on my face."

Michael looks at him skeptically. He keeps one hand firmly over his heart, but he uses the other to feel his friend's clammy forehead. When the anthem is finished, he says, "you're sweating. A lot. Something's wrong. Are you in pain?"

Mark attempts to shake his head. His movement is subtle. Strained.

A look of concern spreads across Al's face. He looks past Mark and addresses Michael instead. "You're the EMT. What do you think?"

They stand silently while the songstress hits the high note on the word free and holds it out for dramatic effect. When she takes a big breath and concludes the song with the next line, the crowd erupts into cheers. The cacophony of sound pushes Mark further into his own mind. He recoils, dropping to his knees on the bleacher in front of him. He nearly topples over due to his injured arm in the sling being tucked against his torso. He braces with his good arm just in time to avoid crashing into an older couple who is standing in front of him, oblivious to what's happening. They're focused on the show that's taking place on the field.

"Watch out!" Michael shouts as he grabs Mark by the back of his shirt to steady him.

"Umm hmm," Mark grunts. His head truly is

spinning now. The pain in his chest intensifies even further, and it radiates throughout his limbs. It's all he can do to keep from dissolving into a puddle on the ground.

"Should we call for help?" Al asks Michael. "They always have an ambulance on standby. Not that you don't know what you're doing, I mean. The equipment is all there … in the rig. That's what I'm saying. Should we get someone?"

"I hear you," Michael replies. "Let's give it a minute. You're exactly right, though. We might need medical help from the crew on duty."

"No!" Mark manages to shout. He's in distress, yet he doesn't want to be taken to the hospital. Even in his impaired state, he knows they'll do bloodwork and find out about all the Oxy he's been taking. He'd surely lose his job—and Reya—if that should come to pass. "No hospital," he mumbles.

The marching band takes its place on a section of the stadium near to Mark and his friends. The drum major raises his arms as the ball game begins. With a boom, the band is playing loudly, stomping their feet on the metal bleachers in a one-two rhythm.

"I'll help you sit down," Michael says in an encouraging tone. He takes Mark's forearm and guides him to the seat below. "There. Rest for a minute, okay?"

Mark allows himself to be led. Inside his mind, though, a world of wonder suddenly begins to unfold.

As the crowd roars with excitement and the band members blow their horns, reality begins to fade. The rhythmic foot stomping seems to push Mark along on an inward journey that he can hardly perceive, led alone believe. In a flash, the football stadium is gone from sight. It's replaced by an ancient scene, and Mark finds himself smack dab in the middle of it.

He's on a boat. A huge, lumbering vessel made of rich brown wood that's being rowed by what looks like a thousand oars. It's a battleship of some sort. An ancient one. The rotting stink of dead fish and body odor from a hundred men permeates the air. The odors are putrid, yet the smell of fear and the look of terror on the men's faces is even worse.

Mark looks down to find himself in an entirely different body. One dressed in some kind of tunic that stops mid-thigh. The soft cloth sits underneath rigid armor that fans into sections when he moves his legs. He has a metal helmet on his head. In one hand, he holds a round metal shield. In the other, he grips a long, thin spear. He shakes his head as if the movement will shake loose the vision, but it doesn't. For better or worse, Mark is immersed. He's there, experiencing the scene fully.

The space between his round birthmarks throbs now. Searing pain seems to dance from the front to the back of his body within the space. *What is this place?* he thinks. *Why am I seeing this? Why am I here?* The rowing of the giant boat keeps pace with the foot stomping in the Thirsty Creek High School stadium. He feels the smooth sway of the boat on the waves as it approaches a foreign shore.

Although he can't explain why, the answers to his questions spring to his mind. It's as if he already knows what's going to occur. With that knowing, Mark makes his way to one side of the vessel and looks out at the sea spray and birds flying overhead. Precisely as he intuits, the ship he's on has nearly made landfall on a beach where countless opposing warriors await their arrival. Those men intend to kill Mark and his comrades, and the intense burning under the round birthmarks tell him they were successful.

In another flash, time seems to skip ahead and Mark is on that beach, fighting for his life. He intuitively knows that he's part of the Peloponnesian War. Specifically, the Battle of Pylos. It's fresh in his mind because he taught it to his World History high school students just the other day. The Athenians battle with the Spartans in this ancient war. The scene unfolding in front of him is even more brutal than the history books depict. Blood oozes and severed body parts thud to the ground as intense, angry men stab, slash, and muscle their way through the lines. It's raw. And it's ugly. It's far uglier than the dismembered man in the car crash that shook him so thoroughly. The battle scene that surrounds Mark makes the accident scene pale in comparison.

As he watches, there's a dual sense of urgency and helplessness. He has the urge to use his weapon to fight the men around him. At the same time, though, he feels like he's watching a replay—something that has already happened, and that can't be changed. He braces himself for what he senses is coming. It doesn't take long.

A hulking man who seems larger than life surges toward Mark, his spear leveled at Mark's chest. In the distance, a second man follows closely behind. His spear is ready, too. He means to be a backup to his friend. Mark has a split second to decide how to handle the attack. If he meets their assault and fights back, he'll surely go down within minutes. He'd be lucky to hold these two off for one minute, in fact. If he turns and runs, there might be a chance. He might get lucky and manage to escape without being killed. It would be a cowardly move to turn and run, but every fiber of his being wants to do it. He wants to flee. To get as far away from here as possible.

Overcome by sheer terror, Mark feels a warm wetness running down his leg. He looks down to see urine forming a puddle as it reaches the ground. His lizard brain is overwhelmed and has decided he must turn tail and run. He does just that.

He drops his spear and his shield in the hopes of making a better escape without their weight slowing him down. He runs, his legs and feet wet with the evidence of his cowardice. He pumps his arms, moving as fast as he can. He doesn't have to look behind him to know that the big man and his countryman are giving chase. Mark can feel the weight of the large man's momentum, heavy in the air. Then, as he closes the gap, he can hear his footsteps booming like thunder behind him. Finally, as Mark's round birthmarks and the space in between glow white-hot like fire in his chest, the big man plants his spear. It enters Mark's back at the exact place of the first birthmark and exits his chest at the precise place of the second.

Mark writhes in pain as he collapses onto the ground, full of thoughts about his birthmarks, the man in the green hoodie and dirty boots, the creature in the shadows at the hospital, the saber-toothed tiger, and the crawling sensation beneath his skin leading up to the vivid vision of the cat.

Is this the same? he ponders. *I felt the birthmarks come alive again.*

He remembers what Dawn said about her

grandmother and the belief that birthmarks are connected to mortal wounds in past lives.

Do I believe in past lives? Am I high on Oxy and tripping right now? Or worse, am I losing my mind?

And then, there is nothing. Everything goes dark. Mark's mind gives him a few blessed moments of rest.

8

RULES OF REALITY

Mark opens his eyes to see clouds in the evening sky above, silhouetted by familiar faces. They're huddled around, looking down at him with earnest concern.

It takes him a beat to get oriented and realize he's on his back, staring upward. He can feel the hard, unforgiving metal of the bleacher below. It's uncomfortable but it lets him know that he's still at the high school. Still in the stadium. *Still alive.* Thank God he's not in an ambulance—or at the hospital. At least there's that.

He can feel his pulse racing. His chest still burns where the spear went in. Instinctively, he grabs at the spot.

"Are you having chest pain?" Michael asks. His voice is remarkably calm. Years of experience as an emergency medic has taught him how to stay low-key during situations like this.

Mark looks hard at Michael, squinting his eyes to

make them focus. "It's strange," Mark says. "It felt like I was really there. It still does."

"Where?" Dawn asks, her face coming into view as she leans around Michael. Mark is surprised to see her.

"What are you doing here?" he asks with a smile. The two of them have become friends, and he's happy to have her join Al and Michael. The four of them make for a nice group. Mark likes that he has friends in Thirsty Creek now.

"I was nearby and I noticed a commotion, so I stopped by. It wasn't until I recognized Michael that I decided to come see what was going on for myself," she explains.

"Working tonight?" Mark asks.

"No, I'm off duty," Dawn replies. "I was heading to the pizza joint around the corner to grab something to go."

Michael lowers his brow. "Enough, already," he says. "Can we dispense with the friendly reunion? At least, long enough for me to check you out?"

Mark chuckles. He's discombobulated after the ordeal he's just been through, but he's beginning to get back to normal. "Okay. Easy there, tiger," he says, immediately questioning his choice of words. He doesn't really want to focus on the saber-toothed tiger, yet the beast seems to be taking up residence in his thoughts. He remains on his back, too weak to sit up or stand yet.

Michael squats beside him. "Are you having chest pains? I noticed that you touched your chest as soon as you came to."

"Was I unconscious?" Mark asks.

"Yes, you were," Michael replies. "Chest pains?"

Mark is avoiding the question. He shrugs. "Sort of,"

he says. "It's complicated. Oh, no," he mumbles under his breath as he detects wetness streaming down his leg. The spillage of urine wasn't limited to the guy in his vision. He slowly closes the gap between his legs, hoping no one will notice.

"What?" Michael asks.

"Nothing."

"You look like you got the wind knocked out of you," Dawn says. "What happened?"

Al takes the opportunity to jump in. "Yeah, what happened? Should we call for more help?"

Michael smiles a flash of white teeth to thank Al for using the qualifier. "I've got you," he says to Mark. "But I really need to know if you're having chest pain. It's important. Okay?"

Several people sitting nearby had gathered around Mark after he collapsed. They've been watching intently —some to offer help and others out of sheer curiosity. They begin to turn their attention back to the game. Mark is pleased that the game continues on and that no one besides those in the immediate vicinity are aware of the incident. He'd like to keep it that way.

He props himself up on his good elbow, his head swimming as he moves. "Whew," he mutters.

"Woozy?" Dawn asks. She puts a hand on Mark's forearm, and he's reminded of her calm, steady presence the day of the accident. It's a comfort to him now.

He nods. "I am. And hey, I'm not trying to be difficult," he says. "It's good of you all to be here, lending a poor sap like me a hand."

"Stop it," Dawn says. "I won't stand for that self-deprecating bullshit. Answer Michael's questions so we can take care of you. We know you'd do the same if it were one of us sprawled out on the bleacher like a casualty of war."

Mark snickers. "If you only knew." He and Dawn share a look, and she instantly knows that he's seen something else. Something that most people wouldn't believe if he told them. People are funny like that.

Dawn is the only person he's told about the other bizarre visions. He'd like to keep it that way. At the same time, though, he trusts his new friends. He supposes that Michael and Al would hold anything he wanted to share with them in confidence. It might be nice to let them in on his secret. One of his secrets, anyway.

"You want me to call Reya?" Dawn asks.

"No!" Mark says emphatically. "Definitely not."

"Fine," Dawn replies, her eyes wide as if to scold her friend for snapping at her.

"Sorry," Mark says.

Dawn lowers her gaze and lets her face relax. "It's okay," she says. "I just thought—"

Mark raises a hand to stop her there. Meanwhile, Michael is getting impatient. "Last time," he insists, "or I call the guys from the rig parked near the end zone. Chest pains?'

Mark takes a breath. He knows he has to answer, and he doesn't want to lie. "Yes," he admits. "But on the right side, not the left. The left is where my heart is, right?"

"That's correct," Michael says. "Although that doesn't mean pain on the right side is something to ignore. Tell me about the pain."

Mark stares up at him, trying to figure out how to begin. He's still dizzy. He's going to need more time to regain his strength and his bearings. "I'm not sure how—"

"Try," Michael says.

Mark shrugs. "I guess it kind of feels like a burning sensation."

"Does the pain—the burning—radiate to your back?"

Mark takes another breath, then nods. He knows enough about heart attacks to know that this sounds bad. He must find a way to convince Michael that he doesn't need to go to the hospital.

"Do you feel anything strange under your breastbone?" Michael asks as he touches Mark's chest. "Pressure? Squeezing? Tightness?"

"Not really," he replies. "Well, maybe tightness, but I'm pretty sure that's just stress. It feels like my entire body is tense."

Michael narrows his eyes and thinks.

"Did you check his pulse?" Dawn asks. She's stalling for Mark. Giving him a chance to collect himself and make a case for this all being nothing more than an isolated episode. She wants a chance to hear what he saw. Her eyes are alight with curiosity.

"I did check," Michael replies. "Let's check again." He takes Mark's wrist in one hand and presses firmly until he feels the rhythmic thump. After a moment, he declares his findings. "It's a little fast. Nothing too concerning, in and of itself."

"See?" Mark says. "Nothing to worry about. I'm feeling better already. Maybe I got overheated or something. I don't know."

"Overheated?" Al says skeptically. He raises a finger to his chin, the same way he did the day they met. Mark now knows that it's one of his signature poses. It makes Al seem more formal than he really is. "It's been cool the past few days," he continues. "It can't be much above sixty degrees right now."

Instead of responding verbally, Mark pushes himself into an upright position, swinging his legs around the front of the bleacher and sitting on his own.

"That's good," Dawn says with a smile. "Looking good, my friend. Rally for us so we know you really are okay."

She doesn't know the intensity of what Mark's just seen. And she doesn't know about the Oxy. She wants to support him, though.

The crowd suddenly goes wild in response to something happening in the game. Michael turns to look, then jumps up and down. "It's Ross!" he shouts. "He's headed for a touchdown!"

Dawn looks confused. She, apparently, doesn't know about Abby's kids and Michael's interest in them. Ross scores, and cheers fill the air. Michael is so excited that he high fives Al, then hugs both Dawn and a random old lady in the row behind him.

"It's his girlfriend's son," Al says to Dawn, happy to fill in the blank.

"Ah, I see," she replies. Then adds, "I don't think we've met yet. I'm Dawn Rollins. Thirsty Creek P.D."

"Oh, sorry," Michael says, turning his attention back to the group. "I should have introduced the two of you."

"Not a problem," Al says. "I'm Al Muth. I teach chemistry. There. Introductions are done. Now, let's figure out what to do with our friend here."

"Yes, let's," Michael agrees. He sits beside Mark, then feels his forehead. It's still clammy.

"I told you," Mark says. "I'm fine. I'll bet it's just stress, what with the new baby coming soon and all.

Nothing a few beers after the game won't solve. Anybody want to go with me to the pub?"

It's the first time Mark has mentioned the baby in a long while. He's been so preoccupied with his own drama that he's scarcely had time to think about the baby as anything other than a reason for Reya to be mad at him. He perpetually feels inadequate to be a father, or a partner. Oxy helps, but he can't tell anyone that.

They look at him skeptically. Michael crosses his arms over his chest, appraising his friend. "Look," Michael says, "if I were to go down the list of when chest pains warrant an emergency room visit, you'd have most —if not all—of the warning signs. Confusion, sweating, dizziness—"

"I never said I was dizzy," Mark inserts.

"Ya look dizzy," Al says, his nose crinkling and pushing his glasses upward. "Dizzy as hell."

"Forget about dizziness," Michael says. "You have pain that sounds like it radiates to your back and tightness in your chest. Are you having any trouble breathing?"

Mark inhales slowly and deeply, filling his lungs with as much air as he possibly can. His primary goal right now is to throw Michael off the scent and avoid a hospital visit. As such, he pushes the ancient war scene from his mind, compartmentalizing it and shoving it into an imaginary box where it can wait until a better time to come traipsing out. "I'm breathing okay," he says, finally. "You just saw. I can take a big breath."

Suddenly, Mark remembers the little packet of pills in his pants pocket. Someone could have taken it when he was unconscious. He grabs at his pocket, pawing like a desperate animal. It's there. The feel of it makes his fingers tingle as his body remembers the relief the Oxy provides. He leaps up, determined to get somewhere private for a few minutes.

"Whoa," Michael says, putting a hand on Mark's shoulder. "Where do you think you're going?"

Mark needs the steadying. He's shaky on his feet. "To the restroom," he replies. "I'm okay. I'll go slowly."

Michael shakes his head. "If you must, I'll go with you."

"I think that's a good idea," Al adds.

Mark remembers that he won't have enough Oxy to get through the weekend if he doesn't find Butch and buy some more. The last thing he wants to do is run out of pills. Especially after the ancient war scene lit up his chest like fire. He needs them to cope. To get through. "Nonsense," Mark says. "Michael, you need to stay here to watch those boys play football. Ross might get another touchdown. Abby wouldn't want you to miss it."

"This takes priority," Michael replies. "Abby and the boys will understand." It's then that Michael spots the wet spot on the front of Mark's pants. His eyes follow the darkness down Mark's leg. Mark bites his lip as he waits to find out how Michael will handle the situation.

"See?" Mark mouths.

The others are gazing out at the field. They don't seem aware of the silent communication taking place.

"You know what?" Michael says, winking at Mark. "You do seem to be recovering quickly. Maybe you did just get overheated. Go ahead to the bathroom. I need to get something out of my car, then I'll meet you back here."

Mark's entire body relaxes. "Will do."

"Wait. What?" Al asks. He turns to Michael. "Should he be going by himself? I mean, really?"

Michael crosses his arms over his chest again. "I think he's okay," he says. He sounds at least halfway sure.

"Let him go," Dawn says. "It isn't like we'll be far away. We'll check on him if he doesn't have his ass back here soon."

Mark nods. "Okay, then. Thank you all for your concern. I'll be back as soon as I can. After the game, I hope you'll join me at the pub. How does that sound?"

"I'm game," Dawn says. "Sounds better than takeout."

Al shrugs. "I suppose I can hang out a while."

Mark looks at Michael. "Sure," he says. "Ross can drive his little brother home. They probably want to stop by the ice cream place with their friends anyway. Which pub?"

"Thirsty Soul," Mark says. "It's not far from here. Near the old library downtown. They renovated an old factory on Main Street. Opened a few weeks ago."

"Then it's settled," Dawn says. "Need a ride?"

They all know he does. Mark hasn't been able to replace his car yet, what with the hospital bill from the day of the accident and the upcoming new baby expenses.

"That would be great," Mark says. "Thanks."

"You got it," she replies.

Marks glances at the scoreboard in the end zone. It's almost half time. The marching band will take the field soon, then things will move quickly as the second half of the game is played. He didn't realize so much time had passed, but he's glad it has. Now, to take care of what he must and get out of here. He doesn't really care about the game, anyway.

"The band will play soon," Al says. "You going to be back in time?"

"I don't know," Mark replies. "It's loud in here. I might step outside the stadium for some quiet. If I'm not back soon, don't worry. I'll catch up with Dawn for a ride, and I'll see you all at the pub."

They agree and part ways. Finally. Mark thought he might go out of his mind trying to evade their inquiries. He simultaneously hates them for getting in his business and appreciates the hell out of them for caring enough to do so. Having friends is harder than he expected it would be. No matter. He's alone now and can tend to pressing concerns.

First things first-—Mark urgently needs a pair of dry pants. It's humiliating enough to live with the damn birthmarks. He doesn't wish for wet pants to make him look like any more of a loser. As he makes his way across the walkway in front of the crowd, he feels a familiar hand on his shoulder. Michael had started off in a different direction. He must have taken a short cut to catch up with Mark without the others seeing. "Hey," he says.

"Yeah?" Mark asks.

Michael leans close to Mark's ear so no one else hears. "I have some sweats in the gym bag in my trunk. They're about your size. Can I lend them to you?"

Mark doesn't hesitate. "Please," he says simply.

With a nod, Michael heads to the parking lot. Presumably, he'll meet Mark in the bathroom. Mark makes his way there, eager to close the door behind him and relish the solace a stall will provide.

Alone with his thoughts as he walks, the vision of the battle scene knocks at the door of his conscious mind once again. Mark can feel it pressing, insistently. It wants to be acknowledged. In a flash, he sees the boat again and all the terrified men rowing in sync. He hears the yelling of the warriors as they ready themselves for battle. Some are more frightened than others, but they do their best to psych themselves up.

"Watch where you're going!" someone shouts as Mark feels a bump against his chest.

He's crashing into the figure, unsure whether it's a male or a female, young or old. When he turns to look at the person as they walk away, he sees metal armor on their body and a round shield in their hand. Panic surges through him. *Oh, no*, he thinks. *God, please. No! They can't be here.* He remembers the scene from the beach. Turning to run. Dying a coward.

As quickly as he perceived the ancient armor, he looks again and sees a member of the color guard with a round prop in her hand. Relief washes over him. He's overwhelmed with gratitude that it's just a high school student and not a warrior here to kill him—again. "Sorry!" he calls out. She nods, then keeps walking.

Mark's emotions shift again as he considers what's occurring.

Am I crazy? he wonders. *Like seriously, certifiably, off my rocker? Did I get a bad batch of Oxy that's making me hallucinate? Can Oxy even do that to a person?*

A flurry of questions swirls in his mind. It's all he can do to keep from screaming in frustration. He tells himself to focus. If one of his students came to him for advice on how to navigate a difficult situation, he'd tell them to tackle the problem by breaking it into smaller parts. Yes. He decides to do that now, too. It makes perfect sense. And it's what the positive-thinking gurus would say as well. He's gotten away from his positive-thinking routines. He desperately wants to get back to it. At this point, he needs to get back to it. He ducks behind a section of bleachers and begins to go over his plan out loud.

"Step number one," he begins. "Get yourself cleaned up. You're a damn mess." He rocks back and forth as he talks because the war scene is pressing again. He decides that maybe if he moves with the rhythm of the rowing, he can somehow keep it all at bay. Like lightning that courses through a person and exits into the ground, perhaps he can let this flow right out of him.

"Step number two," he says. "Restock your supplies. Be prepared. Don't let your reserves get so low. You've got to stay on top of things better. Prior proper planning, and all …"

He hears someone walking near to where he's standing but ignores it. He's too distracted to do anything but continue.

"Step three," he mutters. "Get a car. You're a grown man, for God's sake. Stop acting like a little boy whose mama has to pick him up. You can take control of it. It doesn't matter what Reya says. It doesn't matter what anyone says. You are an adult. Adults need cars."

"I agree," Michael says, his voice coming from somewhere in the distance. He made it to his car and back awfully fast. "Adults do need cars."

Mark shakes his head. In the span of the few seconds it takes, he sees both the underside of the bleachers and the underside of the ancient warship as it makes landfall on the beach. "What?" he asks, struggling to regain his composure. He isn't acting normally, and he knows it.

Michael steps closer. "I said I agree. You should get a car. Need a ride to the dealership? I can take you tomorrow." He has a gym bag in one hand. Mark eyes it, remembering the sweats and the kindness Michael is showing him by keeping this quiet. "I have a clean pair of underwear and socks in there, too," he says. "They're yours, if you want them."

Mark takes the bag gratefully. "I do. Thank you," he says. His face is balled up, an indicator of the battle raging inside his aching head.

"Would you like me to take you to the car dealership tomorrow?" Michael asks. "Or we could go Sunday. Whatever is best for you."

Mark shakes his head again, harder this time. "Oh, well, maybe."

"Maybe?"

"Maybe."

"But you were just making a to-do list. I overheard you. You said adults need cars," Michael explains. "I'm happy to help you out. If money is a problem—"

"No, thanks," Mark says before he has a chance to hear what Michael has to say. He's sensitive about money. If he wasn't, he would have accepted financial help from Reya's rich parents a long time ago.

"Okay," Michael says. He eyes his friend cautiously. After a moment of silence between them, he says, "You can put your dirty clothes in the bag. My Jeep is in the parking lot. It's red. Parked in the third row, over near the softball field. The top's down, so toss the bag in the backseat when you're done. I'll wash your clothes and we'll exchange them later. No one has to know."

"Thank you," Mark says, making eye contact for the first time since the vision overtook him.

Michael smiles when he meets his friend's gaze. "There you are. Nice to have you back."

Mark hasn't meant to be cagey with his friends. There's so much on his mind. He breaks eye contact with Michael and stares at the ground beneath his feet. "I'm really sorry," he says. "Truly sorry. I don't mean any disrespect. You're a good friend. I mean, I'd like us to be friends. Maybe I'm jumping the gun."

Michael's lips curl at the edges. He sees people at their worst. He knows what it's like to go through something that distracts from every other thing in your life. "It's okay, man," he says. "We *are* friends. And I like it that way. You don't need to apologize to me."

"It feels like I do," Mark says. "I seem to end up disappointing everyone I care about. Maybe not right away, but it eventually happens. I don't want to do it to you. Here you are, handing me clean clothes … after you found me talking to myself under the bleachers like a crazy person."

"Are you a crazy person?"

"Maybe," Mark says. Michael probably thinks he's joking. He's not.

Michael shakes his head. "Seriously, though, man. Don't mention it. But you should probably go and get changed before anyone else notices."

Mark agrees. He wants to get this show on the road before Michael remembers the chest pain and starts grilling him again. "On my way," he says.

Before Mark can leave, he hears footsteps on gravel. Someone else is coming toward them. A quick glance at Michael tells him that the lighting has his friend hidden in the shadows. Whoever is approaching will see Mark, and they'll think he's alone.

"Mr. Simbas?" a familiar voice calls.

The sound sends Mark's heart racing. It's Butch. He's here to sell drugs. Mark had better play it cool or all hell is about to break loose, with consequences that will change the course of his life forever. How sad would it be if he crashed and burned before his son even made it into the world? "Um, what?" Mark tries as he scrambles to come up with a plan.

Michael lowers his brow and shoots Mark a questioning glance. He stays still. He doesn't speak.

"Mr. Simbas?" Butch tries again.

In his haze and confusion, Mark had forgotten that he and Butch were scheduled to meet here and now. Apparently, Mark's subconscious had filled in the blanks and prompted him to duck under the bleachers, moments before the appointed time. Suddenly sweating bullets, Mark had better do something. And fast.

"Sorry, kid," he squeaks out. "I'm not feeling so good right now. Would you give me some space? Please." He steps forward, further into the light. He hopes that Butch will see the expression on his face and get the idea.

"I thought you said—" Butch grumbles.

Mark cuts him off. He raises his voice. "I said I'm not feeling well. Give me some space. Would you?"

Hopefully, Michael will think that Mark is simply embarrassed about the wet spot on his pants.

As Butch stands silently, processing, Mark says a silent prayer. *Help me out of this*, he thinks. *For Reya. For our son. I'll do better. I promise. I'll be better.*

To his great relief, Butch seems to get the idea. Maybe the kid is smarter than he looks. Butch grunts, then tucks his hands in his jacket pockets and turns around to walk away.

"We'll talk another time," Mark says. "When I'm feeling better."

Butch turns half way and gives him a nod. *Thank you,* Mark thinks.

Without pausing to allow Michael to ask questions, Mark clutches the gym bag and heads for the men's restroom.

The sweats fit perfectly. Mark places his dirty clothes in the bag and drops it in the backseat of Michael's Jeep, as instructed. Then he waits near the front gate— shoulders hunched and deep in thought—until the game is over and his friends gather at the pub.

So many troubles swirl in Mark's mind that he begins to wonder what's real and what's imagined. Above it all, a singular fear drowns out all the rest. He hears the words of warning, as if someone is issuing a stern directive.

Another close call like that, and your entire life will unravel like a ball of yarn being used as a cat's plaything. Get it together, Simbas. Or else.

9

THE AIR

It begins to sprinkle as Dawn eases her blue Mustang into the parking lot of Thirsty Soul. Mark has been her passenger enough times now to know that she hates getting her car dirty after it's just been washed. And as luck would have it, the car has just been washed.

"Dammit," she says reluctantly, as if maybe the rain will change its mind if her tone remains tentative.

"Didn't you check the weather?" Mark asks.

Dawn slides her hands around the steering wheel slowly and methodically as she turns into a spot. "No, I didn't. I should have. Or I should have kept Gigi in the garage and driven my cruiser."

"I thought you weren't supposed to use your police cruiser on personal time," Mark muses.

"I'm not," she replies. "I'm just saying."

He smiles sympathetically. "Is this a good time to ask why you named your car Gigi? I've always wondered."

"Seriously?" Dawn quips. "For all two and a half

weeks we've known each other? That's the burning question on your mind?"

Mark laughs, but he can't help thinking about his car burning up after the accident on the day he met Dawn. "It's odd how certain words take on new meaning, isn't it?" he asks.

"Yeah, I heard it. I didn't mean anything by it," she replies. "I hate that you don't have another car yet. Not to say that I mind giving you rides when I can. I don't mind at all. I promise. I know you need wheels of your own, though."

"I do," he confirms. He considers telling her about Michael's offer to take him to a car dealership but decides against it. That conversation would likely lead to talk of why Mark was under the bleachers in the first place.

He wants to open up to his friends. And he feels most comfortable confiding in Dawn. Still, he isn't sure how much to share.

"My grandmother is the reason," Dawn says.

Mark narrows his eyes. He's been lost in thought. "What?"

"My car. I named it for my grandmother. We used to call her Gigi, and she gave me money to buy the car before she passed away. That's why I take such good care of it, I guess."

Mark tries to remember everything Dawn said about her grandmother when she visited his house the morning after the accident. He doesn't want to be rude. His mind was foggy then. He can't quite extract all of the details from that discussion. He remembers the thing about the bear trap and Switzerland. Or maybe it was Germany. But did Dawn say her grandmother had passed away? "Is that the same grandmother who believes in past lives?" he tries, broaching the subject cautiously.

"That's the one," she confirms. "Believed in past lives. I suppose I should use past tense when I talk about her. It probably sounds silly, but I feel like she's still around. You ever felt like that?"

Mark shakes his head and leans against the window. "I can't say that I have. I guess I haven't lost anyone I was really close to. My childhood was … complicated. The people I've lost didn't always have my best interest at heart. As bad as it sounds, it's probably best that they're gone. I don't want to draw those connections out any further."

"I'm sorry to hear that," Dawn says. "I know I'm lucky to have known a woman like Gigi. She's the best. Warm, funny, generous. And she had the most infectious laugh I've ever heard. I'd rather have her for the years I did than another grandma who would live to be one hundred and twenty."

Mark smiles. "That's nice." They sit quietly for a moment. He considers his unborn son and wonders if, one day, he will have grandchildren of his own who will think so highly of him. He hopes so. Will they say he was warm? Generous? Funny might be too far of a stretch.

As the precipitation falls more heavily outside and the sun makes its final retreat for the day, the ambience reminds Mark of the battleship he saw, when the sea spray hung thick in the air around him. The vision wants to make its way into Mark's conscious mind again. Like a wild creature desperate to gain entry, it skulks, searching for an opportunity.

In need of a reprieve and feeling comfortable with

Dawn, he leans his head back against the headrest and closes his eyes.

"Take it easy for a bit," she says quietly. "No hurry here. There's time for a catnap, if you need one. I'll keep watch."

The simple gesture touches Mark. He doesn't get much rest these days. Not when Reya's around, anyway. She wants him fixing up the house for the baby and jumping to serve her every time she gets a weird new craving. He doesn't blame her, exactly. He knows she's growing their child in her body. She's still working full-time, too. But stack her demands with Mark's own personal troubles, and it feels like his every waking moment is filled to the brim. He can barely breathe. "That's mighty kind," he says to Dawn without opening his eyes. "I just need a minute."

"No worries," she replies. "I've got you."

The Peloponnesian War vision has drained him. Nearly getting caught buying drugs from a high school student didn't help either. Not to mention, Mark must now figure out how to connect with Butch over the weekend or else go without the Oxy his system desperately needs.

It doesn't take long until the vision seizes him. The ancient scene isn't done with him yet. The round birthmarks come to life once more as the space in his chest between them feels as hot as fire. He grabs at the hot spot, his body tensing as he remembers the big guy with the spear, running for his life, and the cowardly end. Mark's eyes jolt open. In a panic, he rolls down the window and juts his head outside. He breathes in the misty air and lets it settle deep into his lungs. He's overwhelmed by the ancient scene that weighs heavily on him. The line between what's real and what's imagined blurs.

"What are you seeing?" Dawn asks. She seems to know what's happening, although Mark isn't sure how she could.

His body convulses, his eyes blinking rapidly as he struggles to make sense of what's happening. "I … I don't … uhhh …" His words are unintelligible. His chest burns. It hurts so much. He can't find words to describe what he's experiencing.

"Mark, are you having a heart attack?" she asks, as if he would know.

He shakes his head, then pulls back his shirt and points to show Dawn the round birthmark. Once she's seen the purple mark on his chest, he swivels in the passenger seat, taking care not to disturb his arm in the sling. Using his good arm, he moves his shirt and shows her the mark on his back. It lines up perfectly—front to back, all the way through. "See?"

A look of recognition washes over her face. "Like the tiger and your neck?" she asks.

He nods.

"Wow," she mutters. "That's crazy."

Mark can only grunt, his mind shifting from the present reality to the beach where the big man planted the spear. He's drawn to the mist outside, as if some part of him wants to integrate the two scenes. *What does it want with me?* he wonders. *Why won't it let me be?*

Remembering the tiger, a jolt of terror moves through Mark's belly. He's suddenly afraid that the big warrior might appear and come at him again. "No!" he shouts, finding his voice. "Stay away from me!"

"Mark!" Dawn says, grabbing his shoulder and

pulling him back into the vehicle. In his distress, he's climbing out and into the ever-increasing rain and mist. If he isn't careful, he'll topple over the side. "Sit down! It's okay. You're okay."

He shakes his head again, frantic. "Leave me alone!" he shouts into the distance.

"What are you seeing?" Dawn asks. "No one is there, Mark," she tries to explain. "Calm down. No one is there …" Her voice trails off. They're parked against a row of trees in a far section of the parking lot, away from the crowds gathered near the front door.

She wants to help Mark but isn't sure how. She considers trying harder to pull him back inside the car. If she could get him all the way in, she could roll the window up and lock it in place. Dawn is physically fit and strong for a woman, yet she knows Mark could overpower her. Especially if he's out of his mind and doesn't realize what he's doing. More and more, it seems like he is out of his mind.

As fast as Mark lunged to fling himself out of the window, he collapses and melts into a sad heap on the passenger seat of Dawn's car. Tears spring from his eyes. "I'm a coward," he wails.

"Mark, slow down," she says, placing a firm hand on his forearm. "Do you see something?"

He nods, then wraps his good arm around his torso. It's a self-soothing move, but it has little effect. "Yeah. A war."

"Okay," she replies. Her voice is calm and even. Like Michael, her professional experience has shown her how to maintain a level head in even the most stressful situations. "Good. Were you in this war?

He nods again. "I think so. There was spray from the

sea around the boat. The mist outside tonight reminds me of it. Maybe this weather triggered the vision." Talking about it helps center Mark. The ancient scene begins to fade as the current reality takes prominence.

"Were you on a ship? In the Navy?" Dawn asks.

"An early Navy, I guess. The ship was made of wood, and there were hundreds of men rowing long oars that stuck out of the sides. I can't explain why but there is a knowing that came with the vision. I *knew* things. I knew it was the Peloponnesian War. The Battle of Pylos."

Dawn's eyes go wide. She keeps her hand on Mark's arm. "Okay," she says. "That must be unsettling ... to see something so strange."

He nods enthusiastically. "Yeah, especially since I teach history. I've seen illustrations from the war based on artists' renderings. To see it in vivid, living color, well, it's something."

"And your birthmarks ... hurt?"

"They do. Part of the time, they sort of tingle. As the scene becomes clearer the feeling intensifies and turns into a burning pain," he explains. He shoves a hand through his hair. "This sounds crazy. I'm sorry to be freaking out in your car. Maybe I'm hallucinating. Maybe ..." He thinks about the Oxy but doesn't mention it. *Could Oxy make me hallucinate like this?* he wonders once again.

Before Dawn can comment further, a bolt of lightning flares in the sky. Mark startles. Judging by the loud popping sound and the thunder that follows a couple of seconds later, the bolt was close. As if on cue, rain starts to pour down harder. No longer a fine mist, the rain falls in sheets that block out all remaining light.

Mark grips the armrest on the side of his door. His

knuckles turn as white as a sheet under the pressure. He closes his eyes. "It's back. It's happening again," he says. His voice is thin.

"It's just a thunderstorm," Dawn says. "We're safe in the car. The rubber in the tires grounds the vehicle. Even if we're struck by lightning while in here, it won't hurt us." She searches his face for understanding but doesn't find it. He's in no frame of mind to listen to logic or talk about science. She'll need to try a different approach.

"The war …" he mutters, trembling. "I see it again. My eyes are full of it, like it's really happening right now. And my chest … my birthmarks … it burns …"

She grips his arm tighter. "You're here with me, Mark. It's Dawn. Your friend in Thirsty Creek, Tennessee. Look at me."

He glances over at her but doesn't keep his gaze fixed. His eyes wander to the front window and the storm raging outside. He stares out, and it soon becomes clear that he's somewhere else entirely. He's *there*. In the war.

As the scene takes complete hold on him, more lifelike details emerge. He's back on the boat again with his fellow soldiers as they prepare for battle. This time, Mark can see the boat in sharper focus. He looks at the holes where the oars exit the body of the vessel, and he sees that it isn't just sea spray that's swirling around them. It's a full-on storm that's raging out there, complete with terrifying lightning and deafening thunder. More knowing settles over him. He's from Athens, and the Athenian fleet he's part of is being washed ashore in the storm. The fierce Spartan soldiers waiting on the beach are out for blood. The fact that

Mark now knows his fate makes the ship's approach even more horrifying.

He hears Dawn's voice from somewhere in the distance. She's calling his name. He can't seem to connect to her, though. He's too immersed in the ancient vision. Too consumed by what's happening there. The stink returns, filling his nostrils with unpleasantness. These men are filthy. They've been in unsavory living conditions for some time. The stench of dead fish and other rotting sea creatures creates a noxious cocktail that's probably dangerous to breathe for any extended period of time. Now that Mark is more firmly rooted in the scene, he also detects the scent of human waste. It's disgusting. It smells like fear.

Fear is something that Mark hasn't spent much time living with in his modern-day life. More accurately, he thought he'd known fear, but he actually hadn't. Sure, he was scared of the boogeyman as a kid, and he always thought spiders were creepy. Now that he understands what it feels like to face a saber-toothed tiger and an army of Spartan warriors, the boogeyman and spiders of his youth no longer seem like much of a threat.

In the ancient vision, a hardened man with dirt and grease on his face steps in front of Mark's face. He has the air of a leader. Mark can tell this man is afraid but that he will keep moving forward anyway. "Ready?" the man asks.

Hearing his words sends a chill down Mark's spine. He didn't expect the figures in this vision to actually speak. *Can I interact with them?* he wonders. *Are these people real?*

"I asked you a question," the man says. "Are you deaf, hoplite?"

Mark hesitates. He listens, and sounds around him come to life. He hears the roar of rain, the crackle of lightning, and the screams and chants of his fellow men. It's remarkable how real this all seems. Out of the blue—at least, it seems that way to Mark—the man slaps him across the face. Hard. "Ouch," Mark says. "Damn, man. No, I'm not deaf. Why'd you have to do that?"

"Because I need you ready for battle. Get ready!" he commands.

Mark nods, instinctively recoiling his energy from the distasteful exchange. The effect of doing so is that he seems to move to a different place in the timeline of this scene. It's as if he's skipped ahead. The ship has come ashore now. Mark is in the middle of the group of soldiers who are rushing out of the boat and onto the beach. They have their shields and spears raised, at the ready.

The rhythmic rowing he heard earlier that seemed to pull him into the vision is replaced by the sound of running feet on the wood below. He can feel his own feet moving with the crowd. The rumbling, plodding sound is overwhelming. At the same time, though, the sound seems somehow hollow. Maybe it's because Mark knows that most of these men will be dead by the time the battle is over—himself included. They're quite literally dead men walking. He's seen this type of scene in movies and TV shows, but this seems so *real*. The stakes are high. The panic is visceral and justified. It's an eerie feeling.

Mark looks at the man to the left of him, then to the man on his right. Both are steely-eyed. "How are you so brave?" Marks asks.

The man on his left grunts. He's older compared to

most of the soldiers. He wears heavy lines on his face and gray hair at his temples. Mark doesn't think he knows the man personally, but it's clear he is more experienced and war savvy than many of the others. "Bravery isn't the absence of fear," he says in a low tone. "It's being afraid and doing what you have to, anyway."

Mark finds that sentiment interesting in a heady, detached sort of way. What isn't heady or detached is the impending doom that awaits him on the beach. No philosophical ideal will spare his life. He wishes he could be brave like the other men. He knows they're scared, too. He can feel a collective fear in the air. But Mark isn't like them. At least, he isn't brave *enough*. He's already seen his cowardice play out on the battlefield. These men marching beside him would be outraged if they knew he'd soon turn tail and run from his enemy. The thought makes him nauseous, and he feels like he might throw up. He isn't sure whether that feeling is simply a part of this vision or whether he might actually throw up in the present, in Dawn's car.

The present seems thousands of miles—and thousands of years—away.

He looks up and notices a single black crow who is braving the storm. The poor creature is being tossed in the wind and rain like a ragdoll, yet it perseveres, hanging in the sky despite the difficulty in doing so. The seabird coos, and it seems like it's speaking directly to Mark, urging him on. Telling him to have faith in a compassionate universe that saw fit to place him in a new, modern-day body that is healthy and whole, even if it is marked up with wounds from his past.

"What are you doing out here?" he asks the bird. "Go find shelter. Get someplace safe." Mark waves an arm in the air. The bird coos again, but Mark doesn't have time to watch him any longer. His group is on the beach now, and the opposing soldiers are poised to engage.

In what seems like a strange haze, Mark observes the battle from a distance, as if he's floating above his Athenian body, hanging in the stormy sky like the bird. Spears fly, shields clash, and bodies fall to the ground as he watches it happen below him. He knows his time is coming. He remembers seeing it before, and not just earlier in the football stadium. Suddenly, Mark sees the big man in the distance. The man who will end his life. Complete and total terror grips him. He jumps, electricity coursing through his body. His limbs become numb and his breathing heavy. He wants to flee. To run far away from that man and that beach. To follow the bird over the open seas, if he must. To get away, at any cost.

Gripped by the scene from the past, Mark's body reacts in the present. In one swift motion, he flings the car door open and hurls himself out into the storm. He breaks into a sprint, throwing off the sling and quickly picking up speed. Rain soaks his hair and his clothes. It's a cool rain. Temperatures have dropped as darkness sets in. He doesn't notice.

"Mark! It's dangerous out there. Come back!" Dawn calls, to no avail. She gets out of her car and stands, the driver door open and getting wet. Mark barely registers her words. He's running from the Spartan soldier. "Mark! Please! Come back."

He raises his shoulders and picks up his knees to push himself across the parking lot and into the forest beyond. There's no trail into the woods. No path to follow or signs to light the way. Nothing but trees and darkness.

Terror has a firm grip on Mark. He sees the large Spartan soldier behind him each time he turns to look back. He feels his footsteps, massive on the ground. He knows he's gaining on him. He knows the man will soon plant the spear firmly into his back, harpooning him like a whale or a caribou. Reducing him to prey.

He runs as far and as fast as he can, his birthmarks alight with a fiery sensation matched only by the burning in his legs as they strain under the pressure he's exerting. His entire body is engaged in the act of escape. It's primal and it's gritty. Mark wishes he could hide from the ugliness of it all. He wishes he could be good and pure, unmarked by the horrors of his history. Is that why he was drawn to the subject when he set out to become a teacher? Is it why he feels compelled to delve deep into the nooks and crannies of the past to learn what motivated the most memorable stories we've passed down from one generation to the next?

While he runs, his muscles firing at peak intensity as he barrels through the woods behind Thirsty Soul, it becomes clear that Mark isn't only running from the Spartan. He's running from Reya and her gnawing disillusion about what a life with him will be. Running from their son, who will inevitably be disappointed in his dad. He's running from Butch and the cruelly addictive OxyContin the teenager pushes. From Dr. Tipton and Abby and Greg who wanted to give him more help than he had the guts to accept. From his crushing lack of enough money to support his family the way he'd like to. From his parents and his sisters and everything they did to scar and limit him. From Dawn and Michael and Al, who are good people he doesn't want to hurt. From the damned, hideous birthmarks that ostracize him. And—last but not least—from the positive-thinking gurus who promised him things would turn out okay if he simply eliminated negative beliefs. *Those bastards.*

Mark Simbas is running from nothing and everything, all at once.

Just when he thinks he's cornered, all alone without a way out, the crow reappears. The bird's wings are outstretched. It teeters as if on an invisible tightrope strung high across the battlefield. Its feet are pedaling against the wind, working hard to remain upright.

"You?" Mark asks. The bird moves its head to one side. It seems to be gesturing for Mark to follow. Grateful for any sense of direction, Mark nods, happy to oblige. "I'll follow you," he says. "Show me the way."

Pushing from the balls of his feet instinctively, Mark is surprised to find that he can move up and into the air, floating along behind the crow as it makes a sharp turn around the ship and toward another section of beach. Relieved, he looks back to find the Spartan shaking his fist angrily. The Spartan can't float in the air like Mark and the bird can. He can't rise off the ground and take himself to safety. He must stay and fight. "See ya!" Mark says with delight. "I'm outta here."

Not wanting to lose sight of his rescuer, he turns around and follows the bird. Thanks to that blessed creature, he didn't have to relive his terrible death again. He didn't have to face the shame of being stabbed in the back while running away from battle. He didn't have to be reminded what a coward he truly is. That, he'll save for another day. Another journey through his inner world.

After what seems like a long while later when time has stood still, the bird and Mark float to a section of the beach where they find a shallow cave. The cave is dry, and it provides protection from the elements. It also hides them from any people who might be searching.

The bird enters first and seems to indicate that it's okay to take up residence there for a time. Mark follows appreciatively. He sits down against a rock wall at the back, then tucks into a ball with his knees against his chest and falls into a deep sleep.

10

———

INTERVENTION

"Once we set up a search perimeter, I want you to stay in the car," a male voice says from somewhere in the distance. "It may be a long day, and given your condition, you should take it slow."

"Fine," a female voice replies. "I agree. I don't want to put the baby at risk by traipsing through the woods in the heat. It's supposed to be a warm one today."

Reya. That's Reya's voice.

Mark's waking up, bleary eyed, in the cave. He's disoriented. Sun shines in from a low angle. It must be morning.

"You can sit in the passenger seat while you wait," the man adds. "You don't have to sit in the back or anything. There's a case of water bottles in the trunk. If you get hungry, there's a bag of beef jerky in the console. Sorry I don't have anything better to offer you, but it'll do in a pinch."

Is that Jim Perkins? Mark wonders as he works to get

his bearings. The man's voice is familiar. *What's he doing with Reya? Why are they here?*

"Thank you, officer," Reya replies. "That'll be great. I appreciate the kindness. I have some trail mix in my bag, too. These days, I don't leave home without a snack. You know, since I'm eating for two and all."

He says something too quietly for Mark to hear, but Mark doesn't like the sound of it. Jim and Reya seem too chummy. Too comfortable with each other. Even Dawn insists that Mark sit in the backseat of her cruiser with the cage in between them when he rides along. She says it's department policy. What does that mean for the level of closeness between Reya and Jim?

Where am I? Mark thinks. He doesn't remember being here—or getting here.

He squints his eyes against the sun, then looks around to survey his surroundings. The cave is small. Slowly, a memory of another cave on a beach comes into his mind. The memory is foggy, but that cave seemed much bigger than the one he finds himself in now. There's no beach in Thirsty Creek, either. Just the winding creek that the town is named for. He thinks he might hear running water, so maybe he's close to the creek now. That doesn't make much sense to him, though. Last he remembers about his life in Tennessee, he was in Dawn's car, in the parking lot of Thirsty Soul. They were waiting for Michael and Al to arrive. It was storming.

Mark looks down at his clothing. The sling is gone from his arm. His shirt is tattered and ripped, as if he's been through barbed wire. Maybe he has. His shoes are beaten up, too. The brown suede is scuffed and one sole is missing a chunk.

This is insane, he thinks. *What's happened to me?*

Luckily, the sweatpants Michael lent to Mark seem to be in good condition. And they're dry, so no round two of wetting his pants.

A loud, garbled noise, presumably from a police radio, pulls his attention back to Reya and Jim. He wonders what they're doing out there. It doesn't register that they're searching for him. In Mark's mind, nothing is out of the ordinary. At least, he doesn't think other people in his life notice anything out of the ordinary.

The thought crosses his mind that he should crawl out of the little cave and flag them down. Then he considers how rough he looks and thinks better of it. He decides he should probably lay low until he figures out how he got into this situation.

Is my mind playing tricks?

"I'm just glad he didn't pull this stunt on a weekday," Reya says, her voice rising again. "I can't afford to miss any days of work right now. Mark can't either."

Jim chuckles but quickly reins himself in, probably realizing he shouldn't laugh at Reya and Mark's predicament, no matter how he feels for Reya. "Understood," he says. "Hopefully, we'll find him soon and things will go back to normal for you both."

Good thing Jim didn't stick around to see my reaction when the saber-toothed tiger pounced, Mark thinks. *It doesn't sound like he's on my side.*

"There's no such thing as normal anymore," Reya muses. "I think Mark has lost his ever-loving mind. Can you believe he never got a new phone since the accident a few weeks ago? He kept saying he was going to. I even offered to meet him at the phone store on my lunch break. But he keeps avoiding it. Or maybe I should say that he's avoiding me. Yeah, that sounds more accurate."

"I'm sorry," Jim says. "It's true that if he had a phone now, we could triangulate its location and find him pretty easily. That is, if he's somewhere with a cellular signal."

"I wish," she replies. "I guess this is my lot in life. I might as well accept it. Don't you think?"

Is she fishing for sympathy? Mark wonders. *Does she want him to comfort her?*

"Well, no," Jim says. "I don't think that's true. You could always choose something different. You aren't obligated. The two of you aren't even married."

There's a pause. Reya is thinking. Finally, she mutters something about loving Mark and how she wants the two of them to be together, especially since they have a baby on the way. Jim makes a few polite comments, but Mark can tell that he'd probably be interested in Reya, if given the opportunity. And she's right. He has been avoiding her. If pressed, he couldn't even explain why.

Tires crunch on gravel and it sounds like the police car is driving away. Mark is relieved. He doesn't want to worry Reya, but he knows he should figure out what's going on before he heaps more stress onto her shoulders. He tells himself to forget about Jim and focus on his own troubles. He'll ask for Reya's forgiveness when he sees her later. It shouldn't take too long for him to sort things out.

He realizes he's probably being paranoid when it comes to the relationship—or lack thereof—between Reya and Jim. It's most likely nothing to worry about. Reya is a beautiful woman. She's smart and kind, too. What single, red-blooded man *wouldn't* be interested in someone like her, if she was available? That doesn't mean there's any attraction from Reya's half of the equation. She's never given him a reason to doubt her loyalty.

Delusional and paranoid. What a combination, Mark thinks.

A bird chirps from a perch near the entrance to the cave. Something about the sound unhinges what's been locked in his brain. In a flash, everything from the night before comes flooding back. The battleship, the storm at sea, the Spartan, the burning pain in between the round birthmarks on his back and chest, leaving Dawn's car, the run for his life, and the crow.

"Oh, fuck," he says out loud.

Mark sits, pain rushing to his head with the change in position. He isn't even sure what's causing his head to ache at this point. It's been several weeks since the surgery to repair his arm injury.

Maybe it's the Oxy, or more specifically, a withdrawal symptom, he thinks. He hasn't had a pill since before the football game started the night before. Granted, he's beginning to wonder if most of his troubles can be traced back to becoming a drug addict. *There, I said the word. Addict.* Until his accident, he'd never taken anything with the potential to become an addiction.

At least the pain in between the round birthmarks where the spear entered is gone. He rubs his chest above one of the marks to double-check. *Nope. Nothing hurts.* That's a relief. He checks the marks on his neck that came alive before the vision of the tiger. They don't hurt either, which begs the question as to whether Dawn's grandma was onto something about birthmarks being connected to fatal wounds in a past life. Now that he's experienced that possible connection twice, Mark isn't sure what to think.

He doesn't know what he believes, but he decides right then and there to find someone who can help him figure it out. Not necessarily a traditionally trained counselor, but perhaps someone who is open to the more unusual aspects of life and death. He realizes he might have to leave Thirsty Creek and drive into Nashville to find such a person. Once he gets a car, that is.

He reviews the summary statement out loud. "Once I get a car, I'll drive into Nashville to find someone who can make sense of the strange experiences I'm having. So, the first order of business is to get a car. Michael offered, and I will take him up on a ride to a dealership this weekend. Who cares that finances are tight and Reya doesn't want another monthly payment? An adult should have a car. Is she trying to infantilize me?"

Mark stops talking when he hears a loud rustling in the bushes outside. It's too loud to be the bird he heard chirping. This sounds more like a large animal. *A dog, maybe? Or a deer?* Curious, he hoists himself onto one hand and both knees, and slowly—yet awkwardly—crawls out of the cave to investigate.

The sun is shining brightly when he extends his neck into the open air. The familiar yellow sphere is beginning to climb high in the sky. Mark looks around for whatever made the rustling sound but doesn't see anything. Deciding it was probably an animal passing by, he figures he might as well take a walk now that he's out of the cave. He urinates behind a bush first, then pulls the sweats up and turns toward the sound of the running water. He's about to walk in that direction when, to his surprise, a couple of familiar faces appear not far from where he's standing.

"Mark? Is that you?" his friend says.

"Dawn?"

"Oh, thank God," she blurts, gripping one of Michael's arms in celebration as they walk to Mark. "We've been so worried about you. We've been combing these woods all night. Where have you been?"

Mark lowers his brow. "You've been looking for me all night?"

Dawn nods. Michael doesn't speak. He doesn't seem as quick to forgive. Or maybe he's skeptical of Mark's motives. Whatever the case, Dawn is the vocal one. "Yes. I followed you into the woods right after I called Michael," she says. "I didn't want to get into the dense forest until I'd called for help. I knew there might not be a good phone signal in here. Once I made the call and began to pursue you on foot, you were too far gone. You were blazing through the line of trees last night. I'm not sure I've ever seen anyone move so fast."

"Now you have," Mark says, a poor attempt at humor.

"You run into trouble?" Michael asks, gesturing to Mark's tattered clothes. When Mark doesn't reply right away, he adds, "I caught up with her. We searched as much ground as we could."

Mark feels embarrassed around Michael. He knows he has to be careful what he says, or his friend will insist he goes to the hospital. Mark still doesn't want that. Those doctors and nurses won't know how to help him. Not really.

"I guess it looks like I ran into trouble. Yeah," Mark answers sheepishly.

"It looks that way? Or yeah?" Michael asks.

They're silent for a moment, the tension thick between them. Mark doesn't mean to be rude. He simply doesn't know how to explain. He feels terrible to have kept them out all night, looking for him. He remembers the ancient war scene and assumes he must have been running through this forest while envisioning running in ancient times. He remembers next to nothing about what actually happened here, to his physical body. Nothing until he woke up this morning in the cave. "I'm not sure," Mark says.

Ever the mediator and protector, Dawn intervenes. "Michael, we need to let Reya know he's all right. Will you try your phone signal in the clearing we just came through?"

Michael eyes her, knowing exactly what she's doing. He knows that Mark and Dawn share secrets, and he wants in on them. In fact, he plans to insist that he be allowed in on them if they expect him to go against his better judgment when it comes to handling Mark's … oddities. "Sure," he replies. "But I want to hear what happened. Don't ice me out."

Dawn nods, then Michael turns and heads for the clearing. "We'll be right here when you get back," she calls after him.

"We will," Mark adds, feeling useless. "Right here."

Now he's been reduced to an echo.

When Michael is out of earshot, Dawn takes Mark's good arm in hers and guides him to a large, flat rock where they can sit down. "Sit," she says. He gets situated first, then she settles onto a spot beside him.

"You called Reya?" he asks.

"Yeah. Had to. You took off your sling?" she replies.

"Don't remember," Mark replies. "But it's gone. So …"

Dawn taps her foot nervously. It isn't like her to fidget. She genuinely cares about Mark. More now than she did when they first met. Even though their friendship is new, it feels to them both like they've known each other forever. Like their allegiance to each other was predetermined. Perhaps it was already won, in another time and place.

"Do you remember getting out of Gigi?" she tries. "In the storm?"

Marks purses his lips. "Sort of," he says. "I wasn't exactly seeing the present reality, which I realize sounds strange."

She nods. "I get it, Mark. Believe me, I do. I'm not your enemy."

"I didn't say you were."

"When we walked up on you, the look on your face said otherwise," Dawn explains. "You looked like a balloon that just had the air let out of it."

Marks shakes his head. "That's not it. It isn't you. I trust you."

"Then what?"

"When I first woke up a while ago," he explains, "I heard voices and realized it was Jim Perkins with Reya. They were having a good old time as they cruised by in his police car."

"They're looking for you," Dawn says, a hint of frustration in her voice.

"I know. I mean, I didn't at first," he replies. "I guess I wasn't ready to face other people's opinions of what I'm going through. And when I saw Michael's face, it was clear that he wants to see me in a hospital bed."

Dawn sways from side to side as she chooses her words. "I always try to consider a person's background and perspective, you know?"

Mark nods. "You are good at that."

"Thanks. If you think about Michael's perspective, he's an emergency medical professional, right?"

He nods again. "I know."

"His entire career centers around recognizing signs of trouble and saving lives by getting people the help they need. You get that, yeah?"

"I do. But I don't want to go to the hospital again," he continues. "I can't afford it, for starters, and I don't think medical doctors will be able to fix what's wrong with me. Actually, I think someone like your grandmother is who I should be talking to."

Dawn raises her brows, admitting that he's right. Mark smiles, glad for her understanding.

"Okay, yes," she says. "I think you should talk to someone like Gigi. I wish she was still here. If she was, I would have already taken you to see her. Believe me."

"I'm not sure Michael would understand that," Marks says.

"Understand what?" Michael asks as he rounds the corner to reunite with them.

Mark startles. "Damn. You came out of nowhere, and with supersonic hearing to boot."

They all laugh, nerves playing a part. They know that the actions taken next will determine the course of their friendships.

"Umm ..." Dawn starts. She doesn't want to betray Mark's confidence. She also doesn't want to hide warning signs and keep him from professional help he might truly need. It's a balancing act. "We were talking about Mark's night out here in the woods. Discussing how much he remembers."

Mark remains silent.

"What's this about Gigi?" Michael asks. "Dawn, isn't that the name of your car?"

She nods. "It is. And it's named after my grandmother who gave me the money to buy it."

"Okay," he says, taking a seat on the rock nearby. "What's she got to do with Mark? And what won't I understand?"

Mark takes a breath. He's still regaining his bearings. He feels mostly back to normal since waking up in the cave, yet he also feels changed in a fundamental way. He isn't sure he could explain how. He doesn't want to answer the question about Gigi. When he doesn't speak, Dawn jumps in again.

"Did you reach Reya?" she asks Michael.

"No, unfortunately," he replies. "I couldn't get a signal. We'll have to walk further to find a better spot. Maybe this way," he says, pointing.

Dawn smiles. "How about you walk a bit and try again?" she asks. "Mark is still shaken up. I think he should rest here for a while."

Again, Michael knows exactly what Dawn is doing. She wants more time with Mark. To discuss what happened, plus the mysteries of the universe and how life and death work, probably. Michael's annoyed. He sees her determination, though. He knows that Dawn is strong-willed enough to get her way, when she wants to. He doesn't bother arguing with her. "Okay," he agrees. "I'll walk around and try to get a signal so I can call Reya. You two stay here until I get back. Fair?"

They nod their understanding, then Michael

disappears into a thick grove on the way to the creek. At least, it sounds like the way to the creek. Running water can be heard coming from that direction.

Alone once more, Mark and Dawn resume their conversation.

"I thought about who I could find to help me," Mark continues. "I assume I'll need to go into Nashville. I'm not sure anyone in Thirsty Creek is forward-thinking enough to believe … well, whatever this is."

"Don't sell us short," Dawn quips. "We're more than a bunch of backward hillbillies."

"I didn't mean any offense," Mark adds. "This town and the people in it have been pretty good to me. I'm just thinking about logistics." A wave of discomfort moves through him. It's probably his body jonesing for more Oxy, he figures. He had three more pills in his pants pocket but he can't remember what he did with them when he changed into Michael's sweats. He winces and folds over toward his knees.

"What's wrong?" Dawn asks.

He thinks fast. "I think I need a cigarette," he says. It's the first time cigarettes have crossed his mind in weeks—since the day of the accident, now that he looks back on it. He supposes the Oxy took the place of the cigarettes he'd been missing. It makes sense. Oxy is easier to hide. It doesn't stink. It doesn't leave residue on your hands and clothes.

"I don't smoke," Dawn says.

"I know," he replies. "I would have noticed if you did because I used to be a heavy smoker. The day of the accident—the day I met you—my last pack of cigarettes burned up in the glove compartment of my car. Reya had been on me about quitting, so I did. I guess it's good that I haven't thought about having a smoke until just now." He doesn't mention the fact that, apparently, he has an addictive personality and has conveniently replaced one addiction with another. He sits upright as the uncomfortable feeling passes. "Maybe I'm just hungry," he adds. "That concession stand hot dog isn't holding me anymore."

Dawn leans back slightly to get a good look at him. "You know, Mark, you're talking in full sentences, you seem lucid and reasonable, and you look okay, physically. How does a person go from the state you were in when you left my car last night, to sleeping in a cave, to this? Talking to you now, it's as if not much happened, yet the chain of events is quite unusual."

"I honestly have no idea," he replies. "You'd probably think it even more miraculous if you knew what I saw."

She leans closer, bumping his shoulder with her own. "Then tell me. What did you see? Last night in my car, I could tell you were somewhere else. I was talking to you then, pleading for you to stay with me, actually. But you didn't seem to hear anything I said. You were sort of … gone."

He nods. "I felt gone. I was gone, I guess."

"Where?"

"Promise you won't laugh?"

"Of course not," she replies. "When we left off, you were telling me about the Peloponnesian War. You saw yourself on a ship, right?"

"Yeah," he confirms. "When we were at the football game and I passed out—or fainted or whatever—I saw myself fighting in that war. A huge Spartan warrior chased me down and planted a spear into my back."

"Here," she says as she touches the birthmark he showed her. "And it came out the front. Here." She moves her hand around and touches that mark, too.

Mark nods. "That was intense enough, but in your car, things escalated even further. The storm outside made me remember—or see—the storm there. It washed our fleet ashore. We were Athenian. The Spartan army was waiting for us on the beach. It was brutal. Once the battle began, there was blood and gore as far as the eye could see."

"Wow."

"It's a long story. I could describe all sorts of details, if you want to hear them," he says. "It all sounds nutty, I know."

She inhales a deep, compassionate breath. "What made you run all the way here? To this part of the forest? Any further and you would have been in the creek."

Mark looks down at his feet and scoffs. He hadn't considered his proximity to the Thirsty Creek as being dangerous. He's still relatively new to the area and hasn't ever been to this part of town. While it's hard to imagine drowning in a creek, this particular one is certainly large. It's much wider and deeper than most flowing bodies that are called creeks instead of rivers. Had the crow saved him from more than he initially realized? "That's the part you might laugh at," he says to his friend. "I wouldn't blame you. I might laugh, if our roles were reversed."

"Tell me," she insists. Her voice is steady. She intends to be there for him, through thick and thin. None of this is scaring her away. Not in the slightest.

"I was running from the huge Spartan man. I mean

really running, for my life. I'm not sure how the timing of what I was seeing lined up with what these legs did, but I know I was moving as fast as I could. I was terrified. I had to get away. I didn't want to watch my death a second time. Didn't want to watch my cowardice cause my demise in that horrible place."

"Okay. That's intense," she muses, noting how Mark speaks of his visions as if they are memories instead of hallucinations. "And then?"

"And then I saw a bird."

"A bird?" she asks.

"A crow," he explains. "The crow saved me."

"It saved you?" she asks. He nods. "Saved you here? Or there? I'm not sure I understand."

He shrugs. "Here. There. I don't know. Maybe both places. Maybe neither place. Maybe I've lost my mind."

"Stop saying that," she replies. "You don't have to do that with me. Just tell me what you saw. What you think it means."

Marks exhales. He looks up into the sunny sky, half expecting the bird to be somewhere in the trees above them. "Like I said," he continues, "I was running for my life at top speed, desperate to get away from the Spartan warrior. I think there was more to it—like, metaphorical stuff—but anyway, I was running and just when I thought the man was going to spear me again, the crow appeared. It was braving the storm, which I found inspiring. And then, it motioned like it wanted me to follow."

"So, you did?"

"I did," he says with a nod, meeting Dawn's gaze. "It led me to a cave where I'd be safe from the weather. Where I wouldn't be chased."

"Do you remember anything else?" she asks. "Anything else before you woke up this morning?"

He shakes his head. "Nothing. I went to sleep in the cave with the crow and woke up to the sounds of Jim's police car and his conversation with Reya."

They sit silently for a moment, reflecting on the events of late. Mark isn't sure what to do next. He tries to imagine what will happen when Michael reaches Reya. He supposes she'll insist he go to the hospital. Or to a shrink. That will put a huge dent in their tight budget.

"What are you thinking about?" Dawn asks. "I know you have a lot on your mind."

Mark picks up a twig from the rock beside him and fiddles with it absentmindedly. "I don't know," he says.

"If you did know, what would it be?" Dawn presses.

He smiles at her. She's good at getting information out of people. "Maybe you should have been a shrink instead of a cop," he says.

She laughs. "Believe it or not, you aren't far off. I was a psychology major in college. I thought about it, but I ended up transferring to the police academy instead."

"Huh."

"Now you're changing the subject to avoid answering my question," she continues. "Whatcha thinking about in that head of yours?"

"I guess I'm wondering what to do next."

"Like next, as in the trajectory of your life?" Dawn asks. "Or next, as in what to eat for dinner tonight?"

"Neither. Both."

They laugh together, but they both know he's serious. Something about just sitting together and being is enough. A true friend is an invaluable gift. They appreciate how lucky they are to have found each other.

"I'm glad we're friends," Dawn says softly.

"Me, too," Mark replies. "More than you know. I suspect I'm going to need your friendship as I face what's ahead."

She nods and smiles. "I'm here, Mark. You can count on me."

He does and he will, whether he likes it or not.

11

THE PATH

"I'm back," Michael announces as he approaches the flat rock where Dawn and Mark are stretched out, waiting. It's been over an hour since he left to find a phone signal and call Reya.

"What took you so long?" Dawn asks. She's growing hungry, too, and is getting frustrated with the way things are unfolding. It didn't take long for her to suspect that Michael was doing more than simply calling Reya to say that Mark had been found safe. She wonders what he's up to.

Michael smiles and the others attempt to read his expression. It's hard to tell where he stands. "I had to walk a ways up the creek before I got a signal, and then, well, they were forming a search party."

"The department?" Dawn asks.

"Yes," he replies. "Augmented by volunteers. They have a staging area set up at the high school and were about to start combing through these woods in teams."

"Holy shit," Mark says. "All because I was in the

woods for a night? Doesn't anyone go camping around here?"

Michael narrows his eyes. He doesn't think Mark is taking the situation seriously enough. "This is a far stretch from camping," he says under his breath.

Dawn tenses. She doesn't want to see these men pitted against each other. She's well aware that Mark needs all the friends he can get. She wants to see Michael counted as one of them. "So, you told them he is okay? To call it all off?"

"Yes," he says, "but it isn't that simple. There are a lot of people who now … know."

Dawn stands, apparently guessing what Michael is going to say next. She puts her hands on her hips. "Then explain," she says. "Make it simple for us."

Mark sits upright, alert to Dawn's concern and eager to learn what will happen to him once he emerges from the forest. Part of him thinks that maybe he doesn't want to leave. The safety and simplicity of the little cave has a certain appeal. "Please," he adds.

"Let's focus on getting out of here and back to civilization," Michael says. "It's a twenty-minute walk upstream to the closest exit point."

"But I heard voices nearby when I first woke up this morning," Mark says. "They were closer than a twenty-minute walk."

Michael nods. "That's right, you heard Jim Perkins on patrol. He had Reya with him." Mark nods in response, then Michael continues, "They were on a gravel road on the other side of the creek. It's too wide for us to cross here unless you're a strong swimmer and don't mind getting completely submerged. I don't mind the swim, but I'd rather not ruin my phone and my smartwatch. I don't have anything waterproof to put them in."

"Me neither," Dawn says. "I don't want to destroy my phone. So, we'll walk to a point where we can cross on foot, right? The creek is much narrower as you head east."

"Yes," Michael replies. "Or else we can climb up to the ridge where Thirsty Soul is—where we all came from last night. The walk alongside the creek will be much easier."

"Okay," Mark says. He's hesitant to say too much. He figures he'll let Dawn ask the questions. She's happy to take the lead.

"Before we head back, is there anything else we should know?" she asks Michael.

"Like what?"

"Like why the police department was willing to put together a search party less than twenty-four hours after Mark was last seen at the football game? That's unusual, wouldn't you say?"

Michael clasps his hands together and holds them in front of his waist as if he's at a TV press conference and carefully measuring his response. "Do you really want to do this?" he asks Dawn. "Here and now?"

"He has a right to know," she says sternly.

They stand staring at each other, no one willing to fold.

"Is Reya mad at me? Did you talk to her?" Mark inserts.

Michael looks Mark's way. A gentle breeze moves through the trees. To a casual observer, the three of them probably appear like they're out for a laid-back Saturday hike on a beautiful day. No one would guess the issues they're being forced to grapple with as a result of Mark's behavior.

"I didn't speak with her directly, no," Michael replies. "I spoke to a woman in police dispatch who will relay the message. I'm sure Reya will be happy to hear that you're safe."

"Dispatch?" Dawn asks, growing angry.

Mark whips his head her way. "What's wrong with that? Does it mean something bad?"

Michael opens his palms. "Calm down. This will go more smoothly if everyone keeps a level head. Okay?"

"What's he talking about?" Mark whispers to Dawn. "Why do I feel like I'm about to be trapped … like an animal?"

Dawn leans over and puts an arm around Mark's shoulders. She turns them both to one side to allow a more private conversation.

"You're scaring me," Mark says. "What's coming?"

"I won't lie to you, Mark," she says. "It sounds like Michael reported your mental condition, and people in the police department will want you under control, if you know what I mean. They will see you as a threat to public safety."

"Under control? A risk to public safety?" Mark asks. "I'm not a risk to anyone. I wouldn't hurt a fly. I've never even been in a fight."

"I know, Mark. I promise, I do," she says.

Michael crosses his arms. He's willing to let them talk without being interrupted. He's done what he thought was right. He'll leave it to Dawn to explain that to Mark.

After a few minutes of reassuring conversation, Dawn leaves Mark and marches over to talk with Michael. She motions to a nearby tree a short distance away. "Really?" she says once they're out of Mark's earshot. "You didn't even talk to him about what happened. You're jumping the gun, and he and his family will pay the price."

"Come on, Dawn," Michael says. "You may be upset right now, but you know this is what's best. There are procedures for this sort of situation. Those procedures were created for the safety of everyone involved. Mark ran into the woods like a wild animal and spent the night in a cave. If he were in even half of his right mind, he'd realize how insane that is."

"So, what?" she asks. "Did you tell them he's a threat? Are they going to greet him with raised guns and handcuffs? Put him on an involuntary psych hold?"

"I'll leave that for the authorities to decide," Michael says. "But he needs to be checked out. What you told me last night was scary. He could have hurt someone."

"He wouldn't do that."

"Not on purpose," he replies.

"Not at all," Dawn insists. "He's going through something, okay? He needs our support—our friendship—not the heavy hand of the law."

Michael shakes his head. "This is the way we show our friendship, Dawn. Friends get friends help when they clearly need it. I should have called for the ambulance at the game last night. I didn't do it—against my better judgment, I might add—but if I had, Mark would have been in the hospital last night instead of running through the woods like a wild man. What if he had ended up in the creek and drowned? It's deep in these parts. What would we have said to his pregnant girlfriend? To his son? The kid would definitely come asking one day."

Dawn doubles over and props her hands on her

knees. Michael has a valid point. He's doing what they've been trained to do. What makes logical sense. "Look," she says through gritted teeth, "I get it. I don't disagree with anything you've said. But Mark doesn't think a traditional doctor can fix what's wrong with him. My gut tells me he's right."

"Because a bird led him to the safety of the cave?" Michael asks. "Do you even hear yourself right now?" He's exasperated, and he's losing patience with what he perceives as a lack of professionalism on Dawn's part. She's a cop, and he wishes she'd start acting like one.

"How did you know about the bird?" she asks. "Were you eavesdropping on us?"

Michael inhales sharply. "You didn't leave me much choice. He clearly wasn't going to open up to me, and I needed to report his condition accurately. It's my duty. It's yours, too."

"You asshole," Dawn spits. She turns, then stomps back toward Mark. Michael stops her.

"Wait," he says as he grabs her arm. "Not so fast. Maybe I deserved that."

"You think?" she asks, incredulous. "We have a real problem here. We can't keep Mark in the woods, yet I don't want to see him taken away and locked up. Are you going to be part of the problem, Michael, or part of the solution? I would *really* like you to be part of the solution."

Mark's been waiting patiently but decides he's too hungry and thirsty to continue. Besides, he's tired of being talked about like he isn't here. He can hear pieces and parts of what they're discussing. He gets the gist. "Hey," he says to the others as he walks their way. "I'm ready to go. I need some food and water, and a hot shower. We'll figure the rest out when we get back to town."

Dawn sighs, looking from one man to the other. "Mark," she says, "I want you to be aware. What you did —running into the woods last night, in the storm—looks bad. Not everyone will understand."

"You think I don't know that?" he asks.

"We need to get you checked out," Michael tries. "We should have done that last night at the football game."

Mark shrugs. "Maybe we should."

Dawn's mouth falls open. "You're okay with that? Because knowing what I know about how these things work, I'm not so sure I'm okay with it."

"Let him speak for himself," Michael snaps.

"Whatever," Mark says. "Let's just get out of here. You said we walk along the creek, right? I'm ready when you are."

He figures he might as well let medics check him out. He's surely fine, but what can it hurt? And if they want to do a psych exam, maybe that's okay, too. He's weary from the events of the past few weeks and wants a reprieve. He'd like the odd visions to stop, if that's possible. He'd like to go back to normal life, like it was before the accident. Maybe someone can give him something to make him better. Maybe someone can pry these bizarre scenes out of his mind so he can be rid of them.

Michael seems encouraged. "Okay, then. Follow me."

Dawn asks again if Mark is sure, telling him that whatever awaits might not be pretty. She explains that letting reports of this incident get out could affect his job, which they all know how much he needs. Mark thinks back to Misty and her promise that she'd make Principal Heinman understand.

"I made a friend at the high school who promised to help me," Mark says as the three of them follow a trail down to the creek and then head east along its banks. "She's the receptionist or secretary or whatever. For the principal, who is my boss. She's worked with him a long time. I think I can trust her."

Dawn sighs. "I'm glad to hear it, but I'm not sure she'll have the power to do anything if this comes out. You don't seem to realize how bad this looks."

They walk in silence for a while, all considering the implications and pondering what the rest of the day will bring. The twenty minutes feel like they go by quickly. Before they know it, they're almost to the high school where police have set up the staging area. The noise from the crowd wafts through the edge of the forest and reaches them just as they're ready to set foot on a paved walking path that leads to the main parking lot at the back of the building.

"We're almost there," Michael says. "You can do this, Mark. I believe in you."

Dawn tenses when she sees the size of the crowd that's gathered. "So many people," she mumbles. An ambulance is parked near the crowd, along with at least four police cruisers.

"It's okay," Michael says, shooting her a look that says she had better not back out now. From his perspective, there isn't an alternative. "Come on. Keep going."

"Did you know there would be so many people?" she asks him.

He stops and turns to face her. "I didn't have a number of people in mind. Why does it matter?"

"Because this is his *life*," she says emphatically. "If you told them he was okay, that means they should have called off the search, right?"

"I'd assume so, yes," Michael replies.

"Then why are there so many people here?" she asks again.

Mark knows exactly why. "They're here to gawk," he says. "Someone spread the word, and now I'm about to be the laughing stock of Thirsty Creek."

Dawn's face crumples at his words. "No, Mark, don't say—"

"You might want to think about how this looks for you," Michael interrupts, his posture defensive. "You're so wrapped up in Mark's plight that I'm not sure you've considered your own."

"What do you mean by that?" she replies.

Michael purses his lips. "Let's see. Mark isn't a married man but lives with a woman who is having his baby. While she's working and preparing for the baby's arrival, he's out here gallivanting with you."

"Gallivanting?" she asks, clearly offended.

"Dawn and I are just friends," Mark says. "There's nothing romantic between us."

"That's true," Dawn says.

"Tell that to the people who are about to observe exactly how protective you are of him," Michael says. "As you emerge from the woods together. And as he's— well, he isn't in his right mind. The whole thing has a strange feel to it. Kind of like that lady astronaut in the news some years ago who drove across the country in an adult diaper to see a married colleague. It's weird. You should know better, Dawn."

Now Dawn's had it. Her face turns red with anger. "The *lady* astronaut?" she blurts. "As opposed to all the *man* astronauts who don't need the extra word when you refer to them? I think that tells me all I need to know about you, Michael Zhang. I'm disappointed. And that story isn't remotely close to what's happening here."

"Sure," Michael retorts. "Tell that to them." He tips his head toward the crowd. They've now apparently noticed Mark and are pouring his way like a swarm of bees.

Mark freezes. He pats the pocket of the sweatpants he's wearing, hoping those three little pills somehow made their way inside. No such luck. He's never been the subject of public attention and scrutiny. Not unless you count the fascination people have with his birthmarks. "What do we do?" he asks.

Michael drops his arms to his side and walks toward the crowd. He doesn't seem fazed by the clamor. "We go to the police, and we let them file a report," he says. "They'll want to speak to all three of us."

Mark looks at Dawn. "Should we go back into the forest?" he asks. "To the cave? I think we'd be safe there. I want to be safe there. I think we should—"

She places both hands on Mark's shoulders and looks him in the eye. "That wouldn't be the right thing to do," she says softly. "Normal people wouldn't think that way. Michael's correct that we need to think about how this looks. I'm not saying I'm going to throw you under the bus. I wouldn't. I *won't*. I'll be here by your side as long as you need me."

"But they seem angry, or something. I don't know," Mark stammers. "It's like they smell blood."

"If that's true, they'd just follow you into the forest, anyway," she says.

He nods his understanding. "I guess you have a point." He glances at the crowd and gestures. "Do you think Reya is up there? Is she waiting on me?"

"I don't know," Dawn says, dropping her hands. "Probably. Do you want her to be?"

"I do," he replies as some people in the crowd begin to run toward him. They're moving at a quick clip and will reach him soon. "I just don't want her to be mad. I wish I could do and be everything she wants me to. I'm such a failure in her eyes."

With the fastest among the crowd nearly there, Dawn slaps Mark on the back, hard. "We're out of time for pep talks," she says. "Do your best. Let's walk toward the building together."

They lock arms and begin to walk, eyes straight ahead, as people congregate around them. Shouted questions turn into a loud hum as more and more people arrive and everyone talks at once. Some words carry above the din and can be heard, even though they're probably out of context. Mark tries not to actively listen but gets the idea that his situation has been dramatized. He hears the word wolfman and something about animal instincts. If that isn't surprising enough, someone else asks if he's an alien here to warn townspeople about impending doom.

He glances at Dawn. "Are they serious?" he asks, leaning close to her ear so she can hear him.

"Seems so," she replies.

"Huh," he says. "And they think I'm the one who's

crazy." They laugh together at the absurdity of it all. It's all they know to do in the moment. Neither of them ever expected to find themselves in a situation like this.

As they near the parking lot of the high school gymnasium, Mark suddenly stops in his tracks. The sun shines down on him and he squints as he looks up at it. The crowd gets quiet as they wait to learn what's happening. Dawn already knows. She recognizes the look on her friend's face. He's seeing something again. She hopes he won't take off this time.

"What is it?" she asks. "What do you see?"

As a new vision comes into focus for Mark, hundreds of small birthmarks on his body begin to tingle. They're everywhere, some so small that they could be confused for moles or freckles. They're united now. The tingling turns to soreness as they're activated. Instinctively, Mark grabs for them, brushing and pulling on his skin, first on his arms, then his legs, and finally his torso and neck. "They're all over me," he mumbles. He tries to speak only to Dawn but the others can hear. A few pull out phones and begin to film. Mark is too engrossed to care. Too wrapped up. Too immersed. He couldn't do anything to stop the gawkers from filming him if he wanted to.

His consciousness slides to a new time and place. It happens against his will. If he could control the vision, he'd push it away until he could find privacy. He tries to push back against the scene, but he can't. It's upon him now. Overwhelming him.

"Easy does it," he hears from somewhere far away. It's Dawn's voice. "I've got you, Mark. You're okay." He thinks he feels her support him as he collapses to the ground. He thinks he feels green grass underneath his legs as they sprawl out to one side. And then, he leaves the present reality altogether.

"Who's there?" he asks as he stares upward. He sees someone. A human body dangles from some sort of hook, high above a platform. The person is in a metal device. The sky is a gloomy gray, fitting the mood. A crowd is gathered around him, watching. "Who is in that contraption?"

An answer comes into his mind. It's Mark himself, hanging in chains on the public square. It's thirteenth century York, England, and he's in a gibbet. He's watching himself from a distance but he knows it's him up there. He's still alive, although barely. Crows are pecking at his flesh through the cage.

Oh, my God, Mark thinks. *How horrific. What could I possibly have done to deserve this?*

He recognizes the gibbet because he was teaching the students in his history class about it a few days prior. He distinctly remembers explaining to them that placing someone in a gibbet cage causes a grotesque, slow death. Throughout history, human beings have devised a disturbing number of torture devices, mostly to discourage bad behavior and keep the masses in line. But the gibbet is one of the cruelest Mark has ever heard of. To think that he experienced death by such a device makes him physically ill. He heaves, the bile that remains in his empty stomach spilling onto the ground. He isn't sure if his retching is limited to the thirteenth-century vision or whether he is actually retching in front of the crowd on the grass outside Thirsty Creek High School. Either way, it's miserable. It feels like his insides are coming out through his mouth, twisting and knotting as they move.

Make it stop, he thinks. *Please! If I'm to learn a lesson, then show me what I've done. What is this barbarous punishment for?*

As if some consciousness—perhaps his own—is listening and ready to demonstrate what happened, the scene changes. In a flash, Mark is walking on a country dirt road. It's evening and the sun has almost gone down for the day. The air has a hint of a chill, and it feels like early fall. Neatly tended farmland stretches as far as the eye can see across gently rolling hills. Harvest time is nearly here, and the land knows it. The tired soil and the hefty trees are ready to give of their fruits then take a much-needed rest until spring.

This isn't so bad, he thinks. *What's next?*

He looks left and sees two other men walking alongside him. They have sinister grins on their faces, and they appear rowdy. Instinctively, Mark sniffs the air and smells alcohol on their breath. Maybe it's on his own breath, too. The men are disheveled. Shoes with holes in them and tattered clothing lead upward to grimy cheeks and oily hair. They look like they're up to no good.

Remembering how he could converse with people in the Peloponnesian War scene, Mark decides to ask a few questions.

"Where are we going?" he begins.

One of the men groans as crooked, yellow teeth peek from his lips. "Why would you ask that? You know good and well where we're going. It took us the past few hours to convince you to come along. Don't tell me that time spent was for nothing."

Mark is beginning to relax into the way things work in these visions. Like a dreamer becoming lucid and able to control some parts of the experience, he relishes the freedom. He even allows himself to marvel at the sensation of being in England in an entirely foreign time and place. As a history buff, he finds this remarkable. Like a fanboy at a Comic-Con, Mark wouldn't mind spending a long while in the village to observe firsthand what he's read about. At the same time, though, a sense of impending doom fills every fiber of his being. He knows that what he's about to experience will be unpleasant, to say the least. And he doesn't know how to make the vision stop. He does what he can and asks another question.

"I guess it wasn't easy to convince me, yeah?" he says. These men are familiar. He feels like he knows them, much more so than he did the soldiers in the ancient war.

"It wasn't easy at all," the other guy says. "We needed a third person, you know? It's a three-man job. But don't worry, I told you no one would be home, and I'm certain they won't."

"Yeah, it'll be quick," the first man adds. "In and out. We'll grab the valuables and be on our way. We'll slip away. When the family returns home and finds things missing, no one will suspect us."

Mark's heart sinks. A robbery. He doesn't want to be part of a robbery. He gets a strange sensation that seems like knowing and remembering and learning something new all at once. The house they're on the way to rob won't be empty.

Tears sting at his eyes. He chokes them back. He doesn't want to let these men know that he's upset. He also fears interfering with the course of events. He isn't sure what cosmic law he might violate if he tries to alter the course of history, but it seems like some space-time continuum could be disrupted. Gathering his wits, he asks another question of the men.

"What do we do if someone is home?" he asks.

In unison, the men say, "What we must." It's a simple statement that holds so much potential for violence and despair.

Mark can intuit some basic facts about his life in England. The spooky part is the way his birthmarks light up when he's about to have a vision. That phenomenon is beginning to feel like a curse.

Focusing back on the York country scene in front of him, Mark reviews the English man's station in life. He isn't a criminal at this point, but he's fallen in with some men who are. He's young—no more than thirty—and he has a bright future ahead. It would be a shame to throw that away for a robbery he didn't want to participate in and a resulting horrific death by gibbet. Unfortunately, Mark gets the distinct impression that he has no choice. What's done is done. And now he must relive it, for some heart-wrenching reason.

As if someone pressed the fast-forward button on a movie, the scene unfolds at a rapid speed. The next thing Mark knows, the three men are at the farmhouse, forcing their way through a wooden door. It's completely dark outside now, and no lanterns burn inside. They bound into the family's private space, pillaging their personal belongings and tossing things around.

Mark hates to admit it but he feels a rush. Being where he isn't supposed to be and having his hands on someone else's riches is strangely alluring. He didn't want to come, but now that he's here, he can see the appeal. The English version of himself beckons from a lowly family with meager financial means. He wouldn't mind having more riches. More riches would have afforded his English little sister a doctor before she died. She might still be alive if he'd had these jewels, silver, and linens then.

Mark is both awed and terrified by his uncanny ability to know about this English man's life in such detail, and to feel ownership of it, like it's his own. He allows himself to be fully immersed in the scene. To fully experience it.

Smiling with delight, he shoves one valuable piece after another into a brown cloth sack he has brought with him for the job. Deciding that the main living area has been exhausted, Mark turns a corner and finds himself in a long hall. At the other end, a light appears from a previously dark room. Someone has a torch. The men he came with are still behind him, which means that someone *is* home, after all. His body stiffens and beads of perspiration form heavy on his brow.

He hears a commotion in the direction of the light. Whoever is there must have heard Mark's crew. He freezes. To his horror, he turns left to see a young boy standing in front of him, mouth agape, ready to scream. The boy's lips quiver. He can't be more than seven or eight, and he's frightened. The boy takes in a sharp breath, and Mark knows that his vocalization is seconds away. Once he screams, the others will hear and come to defend their home.

Acting fast and without considering the consequences, Mark reaches out and covers the child's mouth with his big, grimy hand. He presses the boy against a stone wall, eager to gain enough leverage to keep any potential sound from coming out. The boy's eyes go wide. His brows raise so high they nearly reach the hairline above his milky forehead. His little body flails below Mark's hand, his limbs bouncing as if he's a marionette. Unable to stomach the horror of what he's doing, he turns away from the boy's gaze to watch down the hall and make sure no one else is coming. To make sure no one else will see him. To make sure no one bears witness to his harsh treatment of this innocent child. Only, someone does.

A second boy, not much taller than the first and with the same pale, milky skin, emerges from a room mid-way down the hall. A brother. When he lays eyes on Mark and processes the intrusion, he drops a candle and a book that he's carrying and collapses into a ball on the floor. Holding onto his knees and shaking, the brother points, aghast.

Mark whips his head around to gaze back at the small boy beneath his strong hand. In what now feels like slow, excruciating motion, he intuits the child's death before he feels his lifeless body and before he sees the vacant look in his innocent eyes. Not realizing his own strength, Mark has choked the life out of the boy while his sibling looked on. Mark is gutted. Monumentally so. He never knew he could feel so much emotional and spiritual pain. So much regret. Devastation pours over him like caustic acid. His negligence led to the death of a wide-eyed, guileless child.

Suddenly, Mark hears a ringing sound and feels sucked out of the scene at the farmhouse. He's back in the town of York, and this time he's inside the gibbet instead of watching from a distance. He's being punished for the robbery and murder. He looks to his right and sees his accomplices, both being hoisted to hang in chains alongside him. An old, graying priest wearing a crimson robe and holding a wooden cross says a prayer as the three men are raised high above the gallows.

The scene fast forwards one final time to the hours before Mark's fated death. Crows with silky black feathers sit on the metal bars that surround him. They peer at him with beady eyes as they peck at his decaying body. These crows aren't friendly like the one who led him to the safety of the cave. These crows are cold, calculating, and savage.

Peck. Peck. Peck. Peck.

In sync, the birthmarks on Mark's modern-day form bubble and sear under his skin until finally, he escapes the misery, and everything goes utterly black.

12

A PROPOSAL

Mark hears them while his eyes are still closed. He's groggy, as if he has the biggest hangover of his life. His thinking is sluggish. Multiple people are discussing him and offering opinions on how his condition should be managed. Some of the voices are recognizable. Others are unfamiliar. His head is swimming, but he suspects that what he smells is the distinctive odor of a hospital.

Figures, he thinks. He doesn't remember getting here. *There must have been an ambulance ride. Someone must have lifted me from the grass.* After the gibbet and the crows, it's all a blank. He shudders as he recalls the horrible experience in England … the boy.

Mark decides to pretend that he's sleeping for a while longer so he can listen to the debate raging around him. It's getting intense. Reya's voice stands out.

"I'm telling you," she says forcefully, "he needs psychiatric help. He isn't right. He's been acting strange for weeks now, and I'm beginning to fear for my safety."

Her words are hard for Mark to hear, which makes

pretending to be asleep a challenge. He forms a fist with one hand and squeezes a blanket on his bed. It helps a little. It's a release for the building tension. There's a dull ringing in his ears that doesn't seem normal. It isn't loud enough to hurt, exactly. Just loud enough to be annoying.

"If you really believe he's that bad off, we could place him under a seventy-two-hour involuntary mental health hold," a man says.

It sounds to Mark like Dr. Tipton's voice, although that doesn't make much sense. Dr. Tipton is the surgeon who repaired the injury to his shoulder after the accident. Why would a surgeon be discussing a mental health hold?

It takes a beat for Mark to process the fact that he might be held against his will. *Wait. What?*

His brows raise. He has to fight to keep his eyes from shooting open. Panic sets in, deep in the pit of his stomach. He realizes that he might need psychiatric help —he admitted as much to Dawn and Michael in the forest—but he doesn't feel safe right now. He doesn't know whom he can trust.

"I think it's a good idea," Reya replies. "Would that be enough time to get him on medication that can put a stop to his erratic behavior?"

"Maybe," the man says. "The primary purpose of a psych hold is observation. Medication management is a long-term proposition. But we're getting ahead of ourselves. There are criteria his behavior must meet before it's even an option."

"What's the criteria?"

"The patient's behavior must be one of three things: a danger to himself, a danger to others, or what's often called grave disability, meaning he is unable to provide for his own basic needs," the man explains. His voice is deep and mellow. The longer Mark hears him, the more he thinks that this man is someone new. His voice seems lower than Dr. Tipton's.

"These holds aren't placed very often," a woman says. "It's a big deal. It has to be serious … and absolutely necessary. I'm not sure it is necessary in Mark's case." He immediately recognizes the woman as Dawn. He's happy to hear his friend's voice. He suspects she'll be a better advocate than Reya will, based on what he's learned so far. He wishes Reya would be more understanding. More open-minded.

"You're not the one having his baby any day now," Reya snaps. "Excuse my bluntness, Officer, but you don't have a dog in this fight. Assuming you aren't going to press charges, of course."

What charges? Mark wonders.

"He's my friend," Dawn returns. Her voice is steady. She sounds sincere.

"Yeah, we've heard … for all of what, two and a half, three weeks now?" Reya asks. She's being rude to Dawn, and Mark doesn't like it.

"Let's stay on track, ladies," the man says. "I know you each have extenuating circumstances that make this situation a challenge—"

Reya cuts him off. "I'm due to give birth to a baby soon, and his father has gone stark raving mad. What's her extenuating circumstance? That she has a little bruise on her throat? So, what?"

Mark stirs, but not enough to be detected. *What happened to Dawn's throat?* He wonders if she had a run-in with the saber-toothed tiger. At this point, he wouldn't be surprised.

Dawn remains calm and collected. Bless her. It's a tall order the way Reya is lashing out. "It's not a competition," she says. "You're his girlfriend. You're the mother of his child. No one wants to interfere with your relationship. Certainly not me."

"Good," the man says, clearly hoping to move things along and avoid a catfight. "Many people care about Mr. Simbas. He's a lucky man to have so many good people rooting for him."

"I agree," another male says. It's Michael. Mark recognizes his voice, and he doesn't feel mad at him anymore. He's glad that Michael is here.

"You would," Reya says. "You're on *her* side." She hisses the words, like a coiled snake preparing to strike. She's talking about Dawn.

Mark hasn't had an opportunity to introduce Reya to his new friends yet. Although, he could have found time if he'd really wanted to. He's been avoiding it, assuming Reya wouldn't like them. Not that he thinks there's anything wrong with his friends. They're good people. It's just that Reya wants him home preparing for the baby instead of spending time out. He had assumed she would resent him if he took time for himself, and it sounds like he was right.

At the moment, Reya seems to be targeting Dawn and taking her own frustrations out on Dawn. Mark wishes she wouldn't.

"There aren't any sides here," Michael says. "Except for Mark's. We're all here to help him. Dr. Aberdeen just wants to do that the best way he knows how. Why don't we stop bickering and let him do his job?"

Mark can hear Reya fuming. He knows the signs. Her breathing becomes shallower and she taps one toe on the floor with increasing tempo until finally, she collects her thoughts and is ready to unleash them with a thinly veiled vengeance. "Why, I ought to—" she begins.

Michael cuts her off. "Look, ma'am," he says. "To be blunt, you don't have any real power here. Dr. Aberdeen is being nice to you. You aren't Mark's wife. Unless he signed legal documents naming you as his proxy for healthcare decisions, I'm afraid you aren't calling the shots."

There's silence for a moment. Mark is tempted to open just one eye to take a look, but he doesn't. He's learning more this way than he would otherwise. He assumes Reya is furious, though. He doesn't want the others to antagonize her. Yet he doesn't want her getting him tossed into a psych ward where they'll throw away the key, either.

"It seems emotions are running high today," a third man says. "I trust we can find a way to let cool heads prevail. Mark would want it that way. Not to mention, that baby doesn't need all the stress hormones that are probably coursing through his mom's body right now." It takes Mark a minute, but he realizes that the voice belongs to Al. He's happy to know that Al has shown up for him. He isn't used to having this much support from friends.

"Is he right?" Reya asks the doctor. "Am I not the decision maker?"

Dr. Aberdeen sighs. "Does Mark have an advanced healthcare directive or a living will?"

"Not to my knowledge," Reya says. "We never talked about any of that. I just thought—"

"Then no," the doctor says. "Not necessarily. There's a hospital policy for determining next of kin when decisions need to be made and a patient has not filed legal papers to appoint anyone to do so in his place. It's a lot of 'if this, then that' type of legalese. You might end up as decision maker. Or you might not."

"That hardly seems fair," Reya fumes. "We live together and are expecting a baby. What happens to him directly impacts the baby and me, whether I like it or not."

"Then perhaps you should have gotten married," Michael says.

"Or filed legal papers," Dawn adds.

This is turning into a mess. Mark inwardly cringes as he listens to the strife. He wants them to get on with it. He wants to know his fate. If he's sentenced to an involuntary hold, he'll deal with it. He won't like it, but he'll deal with it. It can't be worse than what he's been through recently. If they can give him something to make the visions stop, he'd welcome that. And if they aren't going to hold him, then he needs to get out of the hospital and on with his life. He must find Butch and score more Oxy. Then there's work on Monday. And perhaps searching for a therapist who can help him begin to sort things out. Or someone like Dawn's Gigi.

Mark doesn't realize the scope of what happened on the high school lawn when he was inwardly experiencing the scene from England. He's missing pieces of the puzzle and doesn't even know it.

"Let's talk some more about what we could be looking at here," Dr. Aberdeen says, redirecting the conversation. "Okay?"

Reluctantly, Reya agrees. "Okay," she says. Once she speaks, a chorus of agreements sound behind her.

"Are you folks familiar with a mental disorder called schizophrenia?" the doctor asks.

The word cuts Mark like a knife. He knows the disorder well.

His oldest sister, Bella, was schizophrenic. The disorder destroyed her life. It took years of fiddling with medications and dosages before she achieved any semblance of a normal existence, but even then, it wasn't enough. She died by suicide at the age of thirty-five, just three weeks shy of her planned wedding. It was heartbreaking for everyone who knew her, which made it all the more tragic when their middle sister, Lindsey, was diagnosed as schizophrenic a short time later. She lasted longer—nearly seven years in total after diagnosis—but she, too, eventually took her own life. Both of his sisters were tortured by the cruelty of a disorder that is cold and unforgiving. They fought valiantly against it. Mark never blamed them for doing what they did, often thinking he would probably make the same choice if the darkness ever came for him.

It runs in my family, Mark thinks reluctantly.

Mark hasn't told anyone about what happened to his sisters. They were quite a bit older than him, and Reya didn't know them. He figures it's better to keep that kind of information private. With both of his parents dead, it's easy to simply eliminate his family of origin from the equation and keep any stories he tells about them vague. He does his best not to talk about them at all.

"I've heard of it," Reya says, "but I don't know much about it, really. Is that what you think is wrong with him?"

Mark hears Dawn, Michael, and Al whispering to

each other. They've heard of it, apparently. Perhaps they've even suspected it in Mark's case.

Is that what Michael was implying in the forest? Mark wonders. *Is one minor episode enough to get a person committed?*

"It's a disorder that affects thinking and behavior," the doctor explains. "Hallmarks are hallucinations, delusions, and highly disordered thinking and behavior."

"He has all of that, all right," Reya remarks. "Highly disordered seems to be putting it mildly."

How does she know? Mark wonders. He hasn't told her about any of his visions. *Michael must have shared what he overheard. Damn him.*

"I'm not sure I agree," Dawn speaks up and says. Her voice is a little unsteady but still calm. "He's going through something. I don't know that we should jump to conclusions. My grandmother used to talk about people who see things differently … like Mark has been seeing them lately. She made it sound like more of a spiritual condition than a medical one."

Dr. Aberdeen sighs, and Mark thinks he hears the man shift his weight in his chair. "I'm no expert in those matters," he muses. "And I won't challenge your grandmother's beliefs. I will say, however, that the video footage I saw from this afternoon looks similar to what we typically see in schizophrenics. They aren't usually aggressive, per se, but they can hurt other people without even realizing it. It's like they go somewhere else in their minds and lose a grip on reality. He's about the right age for it, too."

"Really?" Reya asks.

"Yes. In males, symptoms typically manifest by the late twenties or early thirties."

"Aren't there other symptoms that he *doesn't* have?"

Dawn tries. "Seems like I've heard of schizophrenics stringing together random words that come out sounding like gobbledygook. Also making weird postures or not responding when people talk to them. He isn't doing any of that, to my knowledge."

"You're right, based on what's been reported to me about his behavior. Bear in mind, though, that he need not have all of the possible symptoms to be diagnosed," Dr. Aberdeen says. "We'd watch for those things during the seventy-two-hour hold, if we decide to move forward."

Dawn's restless. Mark can hear her sliding her fingers across the buttons on her shirt. He's seen her finger seams and small objects when she's nervous. He's sure she's doing it now. He wants her to speak up more. To ask the questions that need to be answered. "What about medications?" she asks. "I'd hate to see him bogged down under heavy psychiatric drugs. What would you give him if he's on a psych hold?"

"I would like to know that, too," Reya adds. Perhaps she's trying to find common ground. Mark hopes so.

"There are several drugs we can try," he replies. "I'd need to thoroughly evaluate him before making a recommendation as to which we'd begin with."

"But you would drug him right away?" Dawn asks.

"Most likely, yes," the doctor replies. "Schizophrenia is a complex disorder. It's lifelong. It can't be cured, but it can be controlled with proper management. Medication is a key component of that management. It's important that we get started with that treatment as soon as possible. Early treatment has been shown to improve long-term outlook."

"Sounds reasonable to me," Michael says.

"It does to me as well," Reya says. "I don't want him to be embarrassed by this. Though, I guess, that ship has already sailed. Video footage from this afternoon is probably all over the internet by now. I received a phone call from a TV reporter out of Nashville. It sounded like she plans to show some of it on tonight's broadcast. It seems like the sooner Mark can start getting well, the better it will be for everyone involved. And if we can report that he's under the care of a psychiatrist for a serious mental disorder, maybe people will cut him some slack."

The legs of a chair creak as someone stands. "I'm sorry," Dawn says. "I don't mean to disagree. I'm not trying to be difficult or disrespectful. I think we should give this a little more time, though. I suggest we watch and wait, but not under a psych hold. I think that's overkill at this juncture. And I don't think Mark would want to be locked up against his will."

"Then how will he get better?" Reya asks. She's calmed down a bit and sounds genuinely curious about Dawn's opinion. She's still on edge, though, and Mark is well aware that she could ramp up again at any time. The ringing in his ears seems to be intensifying. He hopes Reya will keep her voice down.

"Like I said, my grandmother—" Dawn tries to explain once again.

"Really?" Michael blurts. "This again? Your grandmother wasn't a medical professional, was she?"

"No—" Dawn says, unable to form a sentence before Michael jumps in once more.

"Mark needs medical care. *Based on science*," he continues. "He does not need some woo-woo foolishness based on superstition or New Age nonsense."

"Respectfully, Michael," Dawn says, "medical science doesn't know everything. Many experiences fall outside the realm of what can be tested and proved. If Mark needs some kind of spiritual or psychic guidance, I believe we should help him find it. At least, we should try to do so before we let him get doped up on God knows what in a mental institution."

"No one is suggesting that we go from A to Z with schizophrenia," Dr. Aberdeen inserts. "I'm not even asserting that he definitely has it. I am simply saying that parts of his story suggest schizophrenia. I'd need to do a full work-up and observe him over the course of a few days to know for sure. It could be something else entirely."

"He has schizophrenia," Michael says, matter-of-factly.

"Or it could be nothing, right?" Dawn asks. "I mean, nothing medical, anyway."

"Dr. Aberdeen?" Reya asks.

The doctor doesn't answer right away. He isn't sure how to respond.

Mark is growing anxious. He doesn't think he can pretend to be asleep much longer, and he wants to join the conversation about his condition. He stirs, as if he is just waking up. "Who's there?" he asks as he opens his eyes. The lights in the room are dim, and the color of things seems a bit off. The ringing in his ears seems to grow louder now that visual input has been added.

Everyone in the room turns his direction and offers a welcoming smile.

"Good to have you back," Al says gently, then moves out of the way for others to offer their greeting.

"There you are," Michael says. "We're at the hospital

to have you checked out, like we promised. You're going to get the help you need." He pats Mark's forearm like he has several times before. He means to be a comfort.

"Hey, there, stranger," Dawn says. She doesn't step close, but Mark thinks he sees a bandage covering her throat. His pulse quickens. Before he has a chance to ask about the bandage, Reya walks to the side of his bed.

"Hey, honey," she says sweetly. Her tone is strained. She doesn't sound like her usual self. She keeps a distance. She doesn't touch him, which prompts Mark to consider when she last put her hands on him. She's been keeping him at arm's length … since the accident. He tries to make a mental note, but his faculties fail him. He knows that he probably won't remember.

Mark feels disoriented. His head swims as he tries to process everything. He raises a hand to block some of the light.

"He isn't looking so good," a woman's voice says. "I'll check his vitals." Mark looks up to see Abby there, smiling her pity at him as she pushes buttons on a machine. He wants to greet her, and to ask how she's doing. He can't seem to form coherent sentences in his mind, let alone speak them.

"I'm …" he says.

"It's okay, Mark," Abby assures him. "You don't have to talk. Just rest. We'll take care of you."

"That's right," Michael says as he slides an arm around Abby's waist. "You're where you belong now. Where professionals can take care of you. They'll get you straightened out." He smiles. He means to reassure Mark, but it doesn't work. Not completely.

Abby leans into Michael. "Thanks for the vote of confidence, babe."

Mark had practically forgotten that the two of them were dating. He eyes Dr. Aberdeen, wondering if it's okay for the couple to show affection when Abby is on the job. The doc doesn't seem to mind, so Mark relaxes a bit. He's still too disoriented to speak coherently. He decides to focus on the happiness between Michael and Abby. They seem like a perfect match, and along with Abby's boys, a perfect family. That gets him thinking.

Reya would probably be happier if I asked her to marry me, he muses.

It's a random tangent, given the circumstances, but one that Mark latches onto. His mind wants something to focus on. Like the positive-thinking gurus say, he wonders if he'd be better off married. That would be positive. It would keep him from ever losing Reya. Hopefully, it would provide a better start for their son in this crazy world. Reya has been so mad at him. So frustrated. She's wanted him to step up and prioritize her and the baby. Maybe asking her to marry him would put all of that to rest.

Suddenly, determined to do what's right, Mark flings himself out of bed. He's wobbly, and he nearly falls when he puts weight on his legs, but they find the strength to hold him. There's a collective gasp in the room when he stands. Abby and Michael are standing closest. They both reach to steady him, but he pushes them away.

"No," he says. Then, "I mean—no, thank you."

They step back, concerned. Abby's eyes glance at the hospital gown Mark is wearing. She knows from her experience helping patients that it hangs wide open in the back. Mark feels the breeze on his naked buttocks. He reaches a hand back to pull the gown closed. When he does, a tangle of cords and tubes move with him. He tries gripping the IV pole, but notices that his injured arm is bound to his body again. Looking down, he sees that they've put on a new sling.

"Dammit!" he shouts.

The others startle. Perhaps his voice was louder than he realized. At least he's finding it again.

"Mark," Michael says, "why don't you get back in bed?"

He shakes his head. Clamoring around beside the bed, he searches for Reya. His gaze is laser focused, and it doesn't take him long to recognize her form standing at the foot of his bed. He purposely avoids making eye contact with anyone else. He wants Reya to know that she is the most important person to him. In a shaky succession that seems almost like a dream to Mark's fractured consciousness, Dr. Aberdeen and Al move out of the way and Reya appears in tighter focus. Mark stumbles as he walks, one tedious step at a time, the IV pole dragging behind him. When he reaches his love, he drops down hard on one knee.

Michael moves to help Mark onto his feet, then Abby puts an arm out to stop him. She realizes what's happening and doesn't want to interfere. Reya's eyes grow wide as Mark lets his hospital gown fall open in favor of reaching his hand out to her. Another collective gasp echoes throughout the room.

"Reya," he begins. "I don't have a ring …"

"Oh, my God," she blurts. "Mark, don't—"

"Let me finish," he implores. "This isn't how I envisioned asking you to marry me. I thought we'd be out at a romantic dinner or something. Not that we can afford romantic dinners out … but you know what I mean." Mark's words are slurred. The difference isn't perceptible to him, yet the others can tell.

"Please," Reya says, "don't do this. I don't—"

He cuts her off again. He draws a deep, cleansing breath and takes his shot. "Reya Hughes, will you marry me?"

There's silence for what feels like a very long time. Reya looks from Mark to the others, making eye contact with them, one by one. It's as if she's waiting for someone to tell her what she should do. She doesn't smile. She doesn't jump up and down with glee. She doesn't cover her mouth in shock and happy awe. She doesn't say yes.

"Mark, I tried to stop you," she says quietly. "This isn't … we don't …" She frowns, then puts a protective hand over her pregnant belly. It's huge, and to Mark, it seems to be growing larger by the minute. The baby could come any day now. Finally, she finds the courage to say what she feels. "I'm sorry. I don't want to marry you."

The words reach Mark like a punch to the gut. He never considered that she might refuse him. He thought a proposal was what she wanted. He thought it would make her happy. That she'd calm down and settle into a life with him and their baby. That they'd be a real family. That he could be a good father to his son. That it might make up for his mistakes in England. Maybe that last part wasn't a conscious realization, but it was there nonetheless.

Suddenly, Mark becomes angry. "How did you know?" he snaps. Every birthmark on his body seems to come alive. The marks tingle and begin to burn.

"Know what?" Reya asks.

"About the boy," Mark replies. Spittle forms at the corners of his mouth. He's humiliated and defensive. He's also confused.

"Our baby?" Reya asks. "You *know* he's a boy. I told you about the appointment where the ultrasound tech let it slip. Are you feeling okay?"

Mark stands, then staggers. His gown hangs wide open. His private parts are exposed. He doesn't seem to care. "You know what I'm talking about. Don't try to pretend. Someone told you, didn't they?"

Reya shakes her head. "What in the world?"

"I'm talking about the boy in England," Mark says loudly. "You found out that I killed him, *didn't you*?" His voice rises, antagonizing the woman he supposedly loves. Al steps forward and in between Mark and Reya. He stands up straight, his body language indicating his allegiance. He might be Mark's friend, but he doesn't intend to leave Reya vulnerable.

Mark lurches sideways, his good arm wrapping around the footboard of the bed. Lights flicker around the edges of his vision as Abby pushes a button attached to the wall then rushes out of the room. He figures she's going to get someone else, but he can't imagine whom. The room is already full of people who purport to be capable of managing him. *Let them try*, he thinks.

"I have no idea what you're talking about," Reya says. "You're scaring me."

There's an ominous quiet in the room, and Mark gets the distinct feeling that something bad is about to happen. A chill runs up his spine, and his birthmarks light up even more intensely. They ache now, a scourge on his poor body. He considers trying to get out of there, but thinks better of it. He wouldn't make it far in his current condition. He must get himself disconnected from the wires and tubes, at least.

His gaze is drawn to the area at the head of the bed where the medical equipment is located. As he studies the machines and tries to determine how to untangle himself, he sees a pair of bright eyes and long, glimmering fangs looking back at him. He immediately recognizes the saber-toothed tiger from his front yard. The beast snarls, and fear courses through Mark's body. He trembles, his teeth chattering so loudly that he hears them knocking against each other like rows of tiny jackhammers.

He stumbles, this time falling backward onto a chair. The IV gets caught on something, forcing the needle in his hand to twist under his skin. He hears thunder and looks up at the ceiling to find that storm clouds are gathering overhead. A fine mist is settling around them, just like it did when the storm began in the ancient war. Out of the corner of his eye, he sees the shape of the big Spartan standing by the window. Mark recoils, desperate to find safety. He doesn't know where to turn.

"Mark, it's okay," Dawn says. "You're all right."

"Stay back," Michael says to her. "He almost choked the life out of you when he was hallucinating at the high school. Don't tempt a repeat performance. He's seeing things again. Look at him!"

Mark hears this and tries to process it as best he can. It hurts him to know that he injured his friend. The bandage on her neck makes more sense now. *Poor Dawn,* he thinks, but he can't dwell on it for long. His mind is alive with tricks. He looks in Dawn's direction, then—as if on cue—the English boy appears. The child steps forward, his pale skin glistening in the misty air. His eyes are hollow. His expression is one of complete and utter devastation. Thunder sounds, and a bolt of lightning illuminates the haunting figures.

Mark's hands fly to his head. He throws off the sling, freeing his arm. He just wants to make it all stop. He rocks back and forth, shuddering. Then there's a knock at the door.

"Come in," Dr. Aberdeen says, apparently taking on the role of welcome committee. Or a traffic controller.

The door opens, and a man in a hooded sweatshirt steps inside. His expression is sheepish. In one hand, he holds a crisp white envelope. "I have news to deliver," he says softly. His voice sounds to Mark like it's very far away. Like it's coming from a great distance. The sound echoes, bouncing around the room haphazardly.

"Come closer," the doctor says. "Don't be shy. What is your news?"

Mark glances around the room, sparks of light continuing to pop around the edges of his vision. The boy is still there. So are the Spartan, the storm clouds, and the eyes and fangs of the tiger in the shadows. *What if they all come after me at once?* he thinks. *I'll never make it. There's no place to hide.*

"I have a message for Mark Simbas," the hooded man says. "It's from Thirsty Creek High School Principal Marty Heinman." He extends an arm, hoisting the envelope in the air.

"Go ahead," Michael says. "Read it, Mark. It's from your employer. You should find out what the letter says."

Mark squints, the lights suddenly growing brighter. An aura of white light forms around the envelope in the man's outstretched hand. "I can't read it," he says.

The others seem to become disembodied, all floating

a few inches off the ground. Mark shakes his head, hoping normal perspective will return. It doesn't. Things are getting more and more bizarre. His fear is off the charts. Every cell in his body is amped up, convinced the end is near. *His* end is near.

"I'll read the letter to you," the hooded figure says. Mark nods reluctantly as the man opens the glowing envelope and unfolds the paper located inside. He tips his head slightly upward as he reads. His face is obscured. Mark can't make out his features. "It's from Principal Marty Heinmann," the man repeats. He begins to read incredibly quickly, as if someone pushed a fast-forward button and placed him on maximum speed.

"I can't understand what you're saying!" Mark shouts. "Slow down. Read it at normal speed." The fast-forward effect continues. Mark thinks he hears the word regret. Then the word termination. "Slow yourself down!" he yells. "Does he know, too? Did someone tell Principal Heinman about the boy?"

Dr. Aberdeen takes the letter from the man's hand. "It says you've been terminated from your position as history teacher at Thirsty Creek High School, effective immediately."

"No!" Mark shouts. "My wife and I have a baby on the way. I can't lose my job. I can't—"

"I'm not your wife," Reya inserts. "I said no. I refused your proposal. And plus, I knew you'd get yourself fired. You're such a disappointment."

"What?" Mark asks, his distress increasing to levels he didn't think possible. "Is it because of Jim? Jim Perkins is your lover, isn't he?"

"I don't know what you're talking about," Reya insists.

The saber-toothed tiger growls from the shadows. The Spartan's huge shoulders heave. The boy sniffles as he begins to cry. All the while, his birthmarks crawl on his skin and the storm swirls inside the hospital room. A part of Mark knows that it isn't possible to have a storm indoors. He knows that his mind is deceiving him. Yet his fear is very real. He is petrified.

Just when Mark is certain things can't get any worse, the hooded figure steps forward, exposing his face. Mark immediately recognizes him as the ghost of the man who helped him out of the car the day of his accident. He now sees the green color of the hoodie, the dirty boots, and the gold tooth glimmering from his open mouth, shining against his brown skin. Visions of the man's dismembered body flash in Mark's mind.

"Hey, buddy," the man says. "We have to get you out. No time to wait."

"What?" Mark says, his head spinning.

"Pay attention!" the man shouts. He gestures for Mark to follow him.

Mark lowers his brow, considering the situation like he did the day of the accident. "Why are you helping me?" he asks.

The man's face falls, apparently frustrated with the delay. He seems to be thinking about how to make Mark listen.

For his part, Mark is overwhelmed. Out of the corner of his eye, he sees Abby return. She's followed by a trio of orderlies in white scrubs. Mark searches the room for Dawn's face. She's his true friend. His most ardent supporter. He wants her approval before he leaves with this man. He wants her to come along. "Dawn?" he asks. "Dawn, where are you?" He feels a tugging on his arms. Someone is trying to restrain him. He resists, even though he can't seem to tune in to what's happening. He sees a flash of silver. It's long and shiny. Maybe it's a needle. Or the fangs of the prehistoric tiger.

"You'll feel better in a minute," a man says. "Almost there."

Mark looks up at the ceiling—the sky—for answers. Any answers. Then, the storm clouds part and a crow appears. He recognizes the bird from the Peloponnesian War. The one who led him to the safety of the cave. "You?" he asks.

The crow moves its head up and down in a nodding motion, then flies toward the door, near the ghost of the man in the hoodie. "Come with us," Mark thinks he hears the bird say.

He pauses a moment more, then finally, he gives in. He sets the intention to follow, wherever the hooded man and the crow want to take him. With a whooshing sound, he's sucked through time and space. At least, it feels that way.

Once again, everything goes black. Mark's predictable return to a deep, dark silence has become the only constant in his wretched, miserable life.

PART III

NO ESCAPE

13

NO RULES

Thirty-Six Hours Later

"**H**ow's the coffee?" the waitress asks.

It's nearly dawn, and early-bird types are beginning to trickle into the diner. It's raining. Again.

"Coffee's fine," Mark says as he stares at the menu on the table in front of him. The words are out of focus, as if he needs reading glasses. He finds that awfully strange. He's never needed reading glasses before.

"Glad we could exceed your expectations," the waitress says sarcastically. She rolls her eyes, disgusted. She's young. Not young enough to be in school, necessarily, but young enough to have better options than working at a run-down diner in the wee hours of the morning.

Mark jerks his gaze to her. He knows the irritated, impatient look she wears on her face all too well. "Sorry," he says. "It's good." He takes a big sip as proof.

The coffee is hot, and it burns his mouth. Unable to help himself, he spits scalding liquid all over the place.

"Sure," the waitress says, unconvinced. "Looks like the coffee is fabulous. I'll get you some napkins."

Mark nods, then begins to blot at his damp clothes, wringing the front of his white T-shirt out. He's wearing faded blue jeans with holes in the knees, black cowboy boots, and a black leather jacket. It strikes him as odd that he doesn't remember putting these clothes on. In fact, they aren't really his style. He squints, begging his brain to produce something useful. *How did I get here?* he wonders. *Who put these clothes on me?* Nothing comes to mind.

His attention is drawn to something in his pants pocket. His brows raise expectantly as his hand makes contact and he recognizes the size and shape of the object. It's a soft packet with little round pills. Lots of them. *Oxy*, he thinks. *Thank God.*

"Here you go," the waitress says as she shoves a stack of white napkins toward Mark.

Her nametag reads Taja. She's a pretty girl, and Mark can't help but notice the way the morning light accentuates her brown skin and feminine curves. This, too, seems odd to Mark. Not odd that Taja is attractive but odd that he noticed. He isn't the type to ogle women. That's partly because he's in a mostly happy relationship with Reya. It's also because his numerous birthmarks have left him perpetually lacking in self-confidence.

"Aren't you going to say thank you?" she asks when he doesn't respond right away.

"Sorry," he mumbles.

"It's okay. Seems like you apologize a lot," Taja says. Breaking the imaginary wall between them, she hikes her apron and sits down on the bench across the table from him. "What are you so sorry about?"

Mark is caught off guard. He doesn't remember what he was doing before this. The harder he tries, the more unnerved he becomes. Maybe he's lost. Or maybe he truly is losing his mind. He'd like to slip into the bathroom and get a few pills into his mouth. He isn't exactly in the mood to chat with an overly friendly stranger.

"It's just a word," he replies. "It doesn't have any deeper meaning." The innocent boy from England enters his mind, and he knows that his apologies do, in fact, have a much deeper meaning. He shrinks as he remembers. *Dammit*, he thinks. He'd rather forget that whole episode.

Taja scoffs, clearly not accepting his answer. "You're sorry for something big. I know that much. Your eyes give it away."

"Really?" he asks, caught off guard once again. "How so?"

She thumbs her teeth as she chuckles. It's an unusual mannerism. One Mark doesn't think he's seen before. "Have you looked in a mirror lately?" she asks him. "Your eyes are a gorgeous, piercing blue. Pretty nice. They're the color I imagine glacier water is, up in the Arctic Circle. But they're sad. *So* sad. Looks to me like those eyes have seen things. More things than a person should."

He shrugs, attempting to stay calm even though his pulse is racing. "Can I place an order for food?" he asks, ignoring her inquiry. "I'm starving." He isn't exaggerating in that regard. His stomach is in knots as it twists and turns inside of him. Mark's ravenous, as if he hasn't eaten in weeks.

Taja narrows her eyes and peers at him. After a moment, she gives in. She seems to want to ask more questions about his personal life, but she settles for sticking to the matter at hand. Standing, she asks "What can I get you?"

Mark sighs with relief. "What's good?"

"Cherry pie's good, but that doesn't mean you should eat it on an empty stomach. Not before you have something substantial. You need to ask better questions."

He purses his lips. She's right. "Good point. How about some bacon? Eggs?"

"Now you're talking," she says. "Want me to make it a meal deal?" She gestures to the laminated menu on the table. "With OJ and toast? Cheaper that way."

Mark tilts his head to one side as he realizes that he doesn't know what's on the menu, despite staring at it for a good while. He also realizes that he never mentioned having an empty stomach. "How do you know?" he asks.

Taja exhales heavily. She's growing tired of this conversation. "How do I know what? That a meal is cheaper than ordering a la carte? Because I work here. They pay me the big bucks to know these things."

Mark laughs, suddenly finding the woman's demeanor and comments hilarious. If he doesn't laugh, he might cry. "Good one," he says. "Get me whatever you think I'd like. You're right. I do have an empty stomach, so something substantial first. Then pie." She nods her agreement and heads off to the kitchen to ring in his order.

He turns and looks out the window. The sun is nearly above the horizon. It appears that it won't matter much on this rainy September day, though. The cloud cover overhead makes everything look dim. It's the kind of depressing weather that drives those prone to depression back under the covers to spend extended periods of time in bed.

That thought prompts Mark to consider what day it is. It still feels like the weekend. Except the crowd in the diner doesn't seem like a weekend crowd. He glances around, appraising the clientele. Mostly men occupy the booths and counter stools, save for one elderly couple, presumably retirees. He figures the men are working types. They're probably having breakfast before their shifts. They seem blue collar because many are in uniforms. "Hey," he says to a trio of men in the booth next to him, "what day is it?"

An oily man with pale skin and dark black stubble turns around. "You mean the date?"

"The day of the week," Mark clarifies. "Is it still Sunday?"

The guy glances at his buddies before answering. When he turns back to Mark, he says, "It's Monday. Where have you been? Living under a rock?" The men laugh, and Mark is reminded that bullies come in all ages and walks of life.

"Thanks," Mark says simply. "Good to know." He's growing agitated, although he can't fully explain why. His skin becomes clammy as beads of perspiration gather on his brow.

Bullies are nothing new. Neither are irritated waitresses. Or irritated people in general, for that matter. He's never sure whether he's at fault. Maybe he provokes their irritation. Either way, he's growing concerned about how he got to this diner, in these clothes, and with

Oxy in his pocket. He doesn't remember anything since being at the hospital. Even that is fuzzy, perhaps because he doesn't actually *want* to remember.

His life is in the shitter. That much is undeniably true.

"I don't know, guys, what do you think?" the man asks loudly. His accent is thick, backwoods Tennessee. He's the kind of stereotypical, aggressive redneck that countless movies have been made about. "Sure enough, this asswipe *does* look like he's been living under a rock," he continues. "All those marks on him. Hoo-wee! He looks like one of those slimy, spotted things. What are they called?"

"Salamanders," another guy adds helpfully in between bites of bacon.

"That's it!" the bully shouts with delight, pointing at Mark. "A spotted salamander, all slimy and nasty, crawling around under rocks. I'll bet he doesn't get much pussy looking like that. I mean, would you fuck him?"

Mark's eyes grow as wide as saucers. That escalated quickly. This is more harassment and vulgarity than he's used to. Lowering his head, he stays quiet, hoping they'll leave him alone. "Okay, that's enough," he says softly. "I get the idea. Good day to you, now."

The men laugh raucously, clearly not finished with Mark but allowing a reprieve, for the moment. They plow food into their faces as if it's a competition to see who can clean their plate first. Maybe it is.

Glancing out at the rain again, Mark slides a hand into his pants pocket and maneuvers the baggie that contains the round pills. Using his thumb and index finger, he works it open. It takes a few tries, but he gets it. He practically salivates as his body reacts to what's incoming. He thinks that perhaps he can wash a few pills down without anyone noticing. That way, he won't have to go to the bathroom. He lifts his coffee mug, blowing on the contents to help it cool faster. Deciding to brave the hotness, he pops three pills into his mouth and takes a swig. The smooth, little white pills feel heavenly as they move to the back of his tongue and then down his throat. He closes his eyes, savoring the sensation and waiting for the high. *Here it comes*, he thinks.

Mark remembers the feeling of craving from the pot-smoking years of his youth. As a teenager, he smoked an awful lot of marijuana in his parents' basement. He wonders if maybe that has something to do with whatever is ailing his brain now.

Ugh, he thinks as memories from his last hospital visit come flooding back. They're spotty. He can't quite recall everyone who was in the room. He definitely can't recall how he got out of the place. His heart thumps in his chest as he considers the possibility of having broken out. *Will they come after me?* he wonders. *Am I … a fugitive? More importantly, do they know what I've done?*

"Whatcha doing?" Taja asks as she sets a glass of orange juice on the table in front of him.

"Huh?" He hadn't realized his eyes were still closed. It will take about twenty minutes for the Oxy to kick in. Mark wants that time to pass as quickly as possible.

"Don't try to tell me you weren't doing anything," she insists. "I wasn't born yesterday." She sits across from him again. Apparently, she's determined to make friends. If not that, she's determined to do *something* or another. She's latched onto Mark like a dog with a bone.

"Just relaxing for a minute," he tries. "Thanks for the juice."

She nods as she appraises him. Her head is tilted back. She looks down her nose. "Um hmm," she replies.

Mark shakes his head. His heart is pounding now. He's beginning to feel genuinely panicked. He isn't sure why, but his body is well on its way to full alert. He can't sustain under this level of distress. Maybe he settled down after leaving the hospital and had time to recharge. If so, he doesn't remember that. As far as he knows, he was in distress at the hospital, and now he's woken up—or come back to waking consciousness, or whatever this is—in the diner. And again, he's in distress.

Scanning the table in front of him for a diversion, his eyes land on a little black book of matches. Printed in white cursive lettering on the front is the phrase "Thank You." He grabs the book and tucks it into his pocket, next to the Oxy. "There. I was looking for those."

"You smoke?" Taja asks.

"I used to."

She doesn't reply, instead opting to give Mark some space.

He looks out the window once more. His gaze is pulled there, as if he knows someone is coming. He thinks about Reya and wonders where she is. He vaguely remembers asking her to marry him. "Did I really propose?" he asks out loud.

Taja leans forward, her interest piqued. "You have a girlfriend?" she asks. "Or a boyfriend?"

Mark wrinkles his nose. "Do I look like I have a boyfriend?"

"I don't judge," she replies.

He shrugs. "No boyfriend. I *had* a girlfriend. I'm not sure if I do anymore."

A sympathetic expression settles over Taja's face. "Oh, no. What makes you think you don't?"

Mark exhales a long, deep breath he didn't realize he was holding. "I think I made an ass of myself. I don't know. Why do you care?"

"I guess I—" A bell dings from somewhere in the kitchen, and she stands quickly. "Be right back. Your plate's ready."

She leaves to retrieve Mark's meal, and the guys at the next table take the opportunity to chaff him some more. Mark tenses when the ringleader turns his way again. "Please," he says, "I'd like to eat my breakfast in peace, as soon as Taja brings it to me. Can we do this another time, maybe?"

The bully laughs, and Mark is struck by how much the guy reminds him of Butch. He's almost like a middle-aged version. Butch became easier to deal with once he got what he wanted. In Mark's case, that was someone to sell drugs to.

"No dice," the man says with a smug grin.

"What do you want with me?" Mark asks.

"Nothin' at all," the man replies. "You think you're smart or somethin'? You tryin' to get in my head? Because I don't like people trying to get in my head."

Before Mark can reply, Taja returns with his breakfast. Scrambled eggs, bacon, toast, and hashbrown casserole are situated on a plain white plate. She places his meal on the table carefully, then pulls a roll of silverware out of her apron pocket and sets it down alongside the plate. "There," she says. "Eat up."

The rednecks are still shoveling food in. Taja gives them a look of warning and they turn back to mind their own business.

"Thanks," Mark says, holding eye contact with her and noticing how pretty her long dark eyelashes are. When she spots him noticing her, she blushes. Embarrassed, he looks down at his food. "I'm sorry," he adds.

"There it is again," Taja scolds. "Don't be sorry. Seriously. Don't do it. You don't need to apologize."

"Okay," he agrees. "I'll try." The eggs are fluffy, just the way he likes them. He's ravenous. The food tastes amazing going in.

"I'm sorry. So sorry," the man in the next booth mocks without turning around. His buddies laugh. They're a perfect peanut gallery for their ringleader's bad humor.

"Ignore them," Taja says. "Just because you came here with them doesn't mean you have to leave—"

Mark practically chokes on his food. "I did what?" he asks, cutting her off.

Taja leans back, confused. "I was going to say that you don't have to leave with them. You can call someone else to pick you up."

"No phone," Mark says quickly. "What do you mean I came here with them?"

She scowls. "Stop playing."

Mark pauses between bites of bacon to slather strawberry jam on a piece of toast. "Are you saying I arrived …? That doesn't make any sense. I don't know these guys. Do you mean that we walked in the front door at the same time? Because that was probably just a coincidence."

She leans forward, her elbows spread wide on the table. "Are you kidding me? Do you not remember? You rode with the loudmouth one back there. I saw you get out of his truck."

"That's impossible," Mark replies, sure of himself.

Taja laces her fingers together and taps one index finger. She tilts her head toward the parking lot. "Fine. Point to the car you came here in. And don't tell me you walked. We're too high up on the ridge for that. You would have been run down on that narrow two-lane road. No shoulder."

Mark takes a bite of toast, then stops chewing when he realizes that he has zero memory of arriving at the diner. He squints, trying to pry something from his failing brain. Nothing comes. Taja could be right. Her memory is surely more reliable than his is right now. "Well …" he begins. "I …"

"You don't remember, do you?" she asks. She already knows the answer. She knows what she saw.

"I guess not," Mark says softly. "Something is really wrong with me. I don't know what, and I don't know what to do about it."

Taja closes her eyes and exhales. She takes one of Mark's hands in both of hers. "Oh, honey."

Tears spring to Mark's eyes. He doesn't want to go there, though. He needs to eat. Not become a weepy mess in front of the bully who, apparently, brought him here. "Wait," he says, thinking of alternate explanations. "Is this a prank? Am I being punked?"

"Punked?" Taja asks. Now she's confused.

"You know, Ashton Kutcher," Mark clarifies. "The show. He played pranks on people and called it being punked."

"No, honey," she replies. "You're not being punked."

Mark exhales again. He wishes he was being punked.

He'd like nothing more than to see Ashton jump out from behind the counter and tell him this was one big joke. "Okay," he says simply.

Taja sits with him as he finishes eating. Two other waitresses buzz around, taking orders and delivering plates. They must be covering for Taja. Mark figures she's probably done the same for them at some point. They don't seem to mind picking up the slack.

"What can I do to help you?" she asks as she stares deeply into Mark's eyes. "You look like you could use a friend."

Mark smiles, then takes a drink of juice. "You aren't the first person to say that to me recently," he explains. "I must look like a piping hot mess, huh?" She doesn't acknowledge the self-deprecation. "Anyway, yeah, something is wrong with me. But I have friends. New friends, actually. They've been really good to me."

"Can I call them for you?" she asks. "You said you don't have a phone."

Finishing the last bites of his food, Mark thinks about how to take Taja up on her offer. He would like to see Reya, although she might not want to see him. "Could you call my girlfriend?" he asks. "She probably won't answer a number she doesn't recognize, but we could try."

"Of course," she replies. "I've got you." She slides a mobile phone with a purple case out of her apron, then opens up the keypad and hands it to Mark.

The rowdy men are finished eating, too, but they've quieted down now. *Did something I said make them decide to give me a break?* Mark wonders. He doesn't complain. "Okay," he says to his new friend as he types in Reya's mobile phone number and pushes the green button to connect the call.

"Good," Taja says softly. "This is your chance. Make it count."

His palms sweat as it rings. Each second is excruciating. The waiting is almost too much. When she answers, his chest rises.

"Hello?" Reya says.

"It's Reya! She answered!" Mark says to Taja, who then excuses herself to give him some privacy. She takes his empty plate back to the kitchen with her.

"Mark?" Reya replies. "Is that you?" Then, "Where are you right now? What are you doing calling me from this number?"

Marks sits up straight and tall in the booth, brimming with excitement over hearing Reya's voice. He knows she refused his marriage proposal the last time they saw each other, but he thinks that maybe she'd reconsider if he proposed somewhere else. Somewhere more private than a crowded hospital room. "I'm at a diner. Up on the ridge," he says. "The waitress let me borrow her phone." He covers the mic and shouts to anyone who might answer. "What's the name of this place?" he asks.

The loudmouthed man gives him an assist without turning around. "Glenmore Ridge Diner," he says. "On Route 41."

Mark relays the location to Reya, his voice teeming with anticipation. "Will you come pick me up?" he asks.

"Stay put," she says. "Someone will be there."

"Someone? Not you?" he asks. The call ends before she replies. He tries to call her back, but there's no answer.

When the man in the next booth hears that Mark's done with his telephone call, he turns and says, "So, you do get some pussy, eh? You went and proved me wrong."

Mark laughs, the discomfort in his body easing thanks to a square meal, a dose of OxyContin, and the knowledge that his love is coming to get him. He assumes she'll be the one who shows up. Who else would she send? "I guess so," he replies. "Hopefully, I'll get some tonight." It's a bold statement. One Mark wouldn't typically say out loud. For some reason, he feels emboldened. He knows he'll have work to do to get back in Reya's good graces, but he'd like to try. Any chance is worth taking.

"Maybe you aren't so bad, after all," the man mutters. "I reckon you deserve a fair shot." He shoves a hand out for Mark to shake. "Truce?"

Mark nods his agreement, feeling like things might finally be going his way. "Truce."

They look at each other a moment as Mark wonders about what Taja said. "Did you really bring me here?" he asks, although he still can't wrap his mind around that reality.

"That's right," the man says. "In my Chevy Silverado, parked right there in the front spot. You didn't think you walked, did you? Your waitress is right about that road. A walker'd never make it up here in one piece."

"You're probably right. Did you listen to everything we said?" Mark asks. He thinks back to Michael eavesdropping on his and Dawn's conversation in the woods. He doesn't like not having privacy, and he remembers how Michael took the liberty of reporting his mental status to the authorities. That didn't turn out well.

"Not everything," the man says. "I'm just the hired help here. No need to read too much into it. I was told to drop you off with clean clothes and a fresh supply in your pocket, if you know what I mean."

Mark's eyes narrow. "Hired by who?"

"Not at liberty to say," he replies. "Don't worry about it."

"Are these your clothes that I'm wearing?" Mark asks.

"Not mine, but I got them for you, down at the Goodwill," he explains.

Mark's puzzled by this. "So, you had enough time to go to Goodwill for these clothes? They aren't even open yet. I don't think so, anyway."

"Got 'em yesterday," the man says. He glances into the parking lot and something seems to catch his attention. He stands, then tosses some cash onto the table. "Look," he says to Mark, "I'm sorry for the things I said. I shouldn't have given you a hard time like that. You want a word of advice?"

"Yeah. Why not?"

"Be careful who you trust," the man says in a hushed voice. "Those doctors down at the county hospital thought my sister was mental. They locked her up and threw away the key. One day, she clawed her own eyes out and bled to death. Don't let that happen to you, okay? You don't want that. I'm tellin' you, you don't."

Horrified, Mark nods. "No, I definitely don't. I'm okay, though. Really."

The man looks at the parking lot again, then hurries

out the door with his buddies trailing behind. "Take care of yourself," he calls.

"You, too!" Mark says.

Right on cue, Taja returns with the cherry pie Mark ordered. She has two plates—one in each hand—and both are topped with a scoop of smooth vanilla ice cream. She puts one slice of pie down in front of him, then sits and begins to dig into the second piece herself. A shiny silver fork clinks against her teeth as she takes her first bite. "Now, that's good," she says.

Mark's head is full of questions, namely, who that man was and who hired him. He takes a bite of pie, which tastes as delicious as it looks. "Who was that?" he asks.

Taja shrugs. "I don't know his name. He comes in here from time to time. I could ask when I see him again."

"I don't remember him bringing me here," he muses. "I guess I don't remember a lot of things."

She smiles. "Will you remember me?"

He smiles in return. "How could I forget a face as pretty as yours?" His words surprise him as they tumble out of his mouth. He isn't the kind of man to say things like that to a pretty young woman. He takes another bite of pie to cover his bashfulness. It's such good pie.

"You done with your call?" she asks, gesturing to her phone on the table.

"I guess," Mark says as he chews. "My girlfriend didn't sound happy to hear from me. She says someone is coming. I don't know who."

Taja raises a brow. "Sounds like you had better call someone else."

Mark thinks for a moment and quickly agrees that

she's right. "I could call my friend, Dawn. She'd come get me."

Taja nods. "I would, if I were you. Always good to have a back-up plan." She pushes the phone toward Mark.

He lets his fork rest on the plate long enough to key in Dawn's phone number. He's glad he remembers it. His memory has been hit or miss lately. "I remember her number," he says proudly. "I'll call her as soon as I finish this tasty pie."

Taja looks pleased. She's still smiling sweetly when a man wearing a full-body white fencing suit walks in the front door. He has a long sword sheathed at his side. His face is barely visible under a metal mesh mask which has a bib attached and is tucked loosely around his neck. He looks entirely out of place in the diner. In fact, the details of his suit—the brown leather belt with gold adornments and the red metal rim around the edges of the mask—suggest that this garb is of the historical variety.

Mark thinks he recognizes them as French. Specifically, seventeenth-century France. Mark has taught history classes about just such attire.

"That's weird," he remarks. "What is that guy doing in here, dressed like that? Is there a historical reenactment going on? Because you'd think I would've heard about it … being a history teacher and all."

Taja turns to follow Mark's gaze. "Who? Officer Perkins?"

Perkins. Mark knows that name. "How do you know he's a police officer?" he asks.

She chuckles. "One, because he's wearing a police officer uniform, silly. And two, because he comes in here a lot. I've served him plenty of times. He always orders a Diet Coke with no ice and a ham and cheese omelet."

Mark closes his eyes, shakes his head, then opens his eyes to look again. Tiny, sparkly lights pop around the edges of his vision. There, plain as day, stands Officer Jim Perkins in his Thirsty Creek Police Department uniform. Jim is scanning the room, apparently looking for someone. Mark blinks and looks once more to find the man in the white fencing suit. The view switches back and forth each time Mark opens and closes his eyes, like a glitch on a computer screen. It's alarming, to say the least.

"Oh, no," Mark says. "It's happening again."

"*What's* happening?" Taja asks.

"It's hard to explain," he replies, ducking his head to avoid being seen. He isn't sure where his mind might take him, and he doesn't want to make a spectacle of himself like he did at the high school when the scene from England emerged.

Jim sees Mark and heads his way to say hello. All the while, Mark's vision flips from the present reality to Renaissance France. It's one of the strangest things he's ever experienced, even more so than his other visions of late. It's as if he can see Jim, both now and back then. *Was it Jim, back then?* he wonders. *Could we have … known each other before?*

"Mark, hi there," Jim says when he reaches the table. "How's it going?"

"Your name is Mark," Taja mumbles. "Good to know." Mark hadn't thought to tell her his name. He figures she might as well hear it, though, since he knows hers. He nods briefly to acknowledge the exchange. "And you're a history teacher," she adds. Mark nods again, but his attention is on Jim.

"Yeah, it's going okay," he replies to Jim. He doesn't dare tell him that he has no memory of getting there or that he's seeing him in the body of a seventeenth-century French fencer. The French vision is beginning to overwhelm Mark. He tells himself to focus. "How are things going for you?"

Jim pulls back his jacket and places a hand on his thick, black police officer's belt. "I'm good. Thanks for asking. I have to tell you, however, that I'm here because Reya called me. You have some serious explaining to do."

14

WORDS OF REGRET

It only takes Mark a split second to make the decision. He feels like a cornered animal, and he decides to react like one. Although, maybe the decision comes from a more primitive part of his brain than he'd like to admit. That's what happens when you're pushed to your limits and have little hope left to cling to. Mark's world has erupted into total chaos. Why pretend to be civilized and demure? It's time to leave false pretense behind.

"Gotta go," Mark mumbles as he stands and walks toward the front door.

He passes Jim as he makes his way between the row of booths and the breakfast counter. His urge is to move fast, swinging both arms. His shoulder is still sore from the injury, but adrenaline is pumping and a little shoulder pain is the least of his worries. He knows he can take more Oxy to make it go away, thanks to the generous soul who replenished his supply. But seeing the officer there in uniform, Mark realizes he must slow things down and keep his cool.

"Wait!" Taja calls. "You need to close out your check." When he doesn't respond, she adds, "You didn't pay!"

Mark grunts. He isn't sure if he has money with him. He realizes he should have checked on that little detail sooner. To his credit, though, he wasn't even consciously aware of entering the diner. Who could expect him to have all the details sorted out, given his confusion? He reaches into both pants pockets. No wallet. Just the Oxy. He considers leaving some to cover his tab, but decides against it. "I'll come back to pay," he says. "I must have forgotten my wallet."

Taja's face falls. Not because Mark stiffed her and she'll have to cover his bill, but because she was becoming fond of him and hates to see him go. "Please come back sometime," she says, her voice barely reaching his ears as he pushes hard on the glass door. "I'd like to see you again."

Without acknowledging her plea, Mark is gone. Once in the open air, he feels as free as he possibly can at this juncture. He doesn't care that the rain immediately soaks him or that thunder sounds a warning boom overhead. His entire life seems like one massive thunderstorm lately. All bad news with little reprieve in between crushing blows.

He sees the tiny flickers around the edges of his vision and knows that the French scene isn't finished with him yet. "Dammit!" he shouts as he pauses midway through the parking lot. "Won't you leave me be? I'm going out of my mind. It's ruining my life."

He slides into a squatting position and leans his hands on his knees. He feels woozy, like he could either collapse into a ball like a preyed-upon animal waiting for a predator to end its life, or sprint away with the speed and grace of a powerful lion. He truly isn't sure which one his body would prefer at the moment. Anger rises in his throat. He's felt it flare multiple times, but it's more insistent now. More powerful. He knows he won't be able to hold it at bay much longer.

Mark raises his head and spots a treeline in the distance, across Route 41. Beyond it are woods so thick a person could disappear into them and not be found. He's tempted to do just that. Maybe the crow will show up and lead him to another cave. That doesn't sound too bad right now. He looks up into the sky in search of the bird. "Bird, are you there?" he asks. "Will you guide me?"

"Who are you talking to?" a deep voice asks from somewhere behind him.

It's Jim. Mark recognizes his voice right away. He shakes his head. "No one," he says stubbornly. "Don't try to ask me again. I know the drill. You'll say I'm out of my mind because I'm talking to a bird and you'll try to take me back to the hospital."

Mark doesn't turn around, but instead, continues to eye the treeline. He hopes that maybe the glitch in his vision can be held at bay if he doesn't look directly at Officer Perkins. Maybe he won't see the man in the fencing suit if he averts his gaze.

"Are you talking to a bird? Actually, never mind. No need to get ahead of ourselves," Jim says slowly. "I wanted to ask you a few questions. That's all. How about we go back inside, out of the rain? I'll cover the cost of your breakfast. No worries."

It's obvious to Mark that Jim has had training in de-escalation methods. Jim is using them, following the guidelines that someone, somewhere decided should work. It pisses Mark off. He doesn't like being handled. He's sick and tired of it. "No," he says. "Go back inside. I'm leaving. We'll talk another time. I'm not ready."

"Where will you go?" Jim asks.

Mark scratches an itch behind one ear with gusto, and he feels like a wild animal as he does it. Something is awakening inside of him. "None of your concern," he says.

He can hear the pitter-patter of rain on a plastic surface. Jim must be wearing a raincoat or a poncho. He'd like one that could keep him dry, too, but he tells himself that wild animals don't need rain gear. They simply get out of the storm. By taking shelter in a cave, for instance.

"I'd like to know your plan," Jim adds. "So that I can tell Reya. She's worried about you, you know?" His voice is too calm. Too measured. Something about it makes Mark want to fight him. It doesn't seem fair that Jim would be so calm and centered. Besides that, Mark hates the way Jim talks about Reya, as if they're close. As if he knows her as well as Mark does. As if he has any right to speak on her behalf at all.

Mark stares at the tree line, considering how things might play out if he flees into the woods again. He'd be wet and exhausted after a run through the mud. He doesn't know if there's any shelter to be had. He doesn't have a phone. Although, the knowledge that he's flush with Oxy lands in the column of reasons to disappear into the wilderness. The food in his belly and the pills in his pocket should last quite a while. A couple of days, maybe. "Where's Dawn?" he asks.

Jim hesitates. "The mother of your child is due to give birth any day now. Don't you want to be there when the baby makes his entrance into this world?"

Anger flares hot on Mark's face. "Leave Reya out of this," he says. "I know how she feels about me right now. Tell me where Dawn is. Please."

A bright flash explodes in front of Mark's vision. He drops to a seated position on the ground as the French scene creeps in. He sees himself readying for a duel. A white fencing uniform is spread out on a bed near him. There's a gold adornment on his belt, exactly like the one he saw Jim wearing. He can smell the scent of metal polish that has been used to shine the gold. Searching the scene for his head piece, he quickly finds it. It, too, has a bright-red edge on the metal face mask. A pang of knowing hits him. He's going up against a formidable opponent, and only one of them will walk away with their life.

Mark rubs his eyes with his palms and silently begs the vision to go away. He doesn't want Jim to see him like this. He doesn't want anyone to see him like this. He knows that if this vision is anything like the others, he'll lose all connection with the here and now.

Mark forces his eyes to focus on the present-day reality in front of him. He raises his head and eyes the forest again. Fog and a dense mist fill the space between the trees. It appears so tempting. So safe and secure. He wants to get away from Jim's pressing questions. He wants to let himself be wild. To commune with the earth and its beasts. He wouldn't even mind seeing the saber-toothed tiger again. He thinks he'd rather go up against the big cat than be stuck in a hospital.

He hears a bell as the diner door swings open. His senses are heightened. He knows it's Taja without turning to look. "Go back inside, Taja," he calls. "This doesn't concern you."

There's a pause. Mark suspects that Jim and Taja are communicating through facial expressions and gestures he can't see. Finally, "Is this officer being good to you?" she asks.

For that, Mark turns around. He's surprised Taja has the courage to challenge Jim right in front of his face. Mark wonders how he's been so lucky to come across so many friendly people who seem to genuinely care about him. Taja is the latest in a string of truly good people. "I'm okay," he says. "I appreciate your concern. Now go back inside, please." She obliges, and Mark hears the bell ring once more.

The French scene feels heavy. It's still waiting to fully emerge. Thank God, it's waiting. Mark knows it won't wait much longer.

Suddenly, right on cue, a set of short, thin birthmarks on his lower abdomen become excruciatingly painful. They burn and sear, as if someone poured salt into an open wound. Mark hasn't ever felt salt in a wound—as far as he knows—but he imagines this is what it feels like. He cries out in anguish, gripping his gut.

"What's wrong with you now?" Jim asks.

Mark honestly doesn't know. He's too preoccupied with the pain tearing through him. It tugs in a ripping motion. "It hurts," he mumbles.

"Should I call for an ambulance?"

Mark certainly doesn't plan to take a ride in an

ambulance any time soon. Or ever again, if he can help it. "No!" he shouts through gritted teeth. "I'm fine."

"You don't sound fine," Jim says. "You haven't sounded fine for a while now, truth be told. If I were you, I'd let the ambulance get me."

"No!" Mark emphasizes again. "You don't know all I've been through. They don't believe me. They think I'm crazy."

"Are you crazy?" he asks, but Mark is too preoccupied to reply. Mark isn't concerned with the details of this conversation at the moment. He's simply trying to get through the day. Through the hours. Through the minutes. Meanwhile, Jim's growing impatient. "Look, Mr. Simbas, I'd like you to come down to the station with me for questioning. As a preemptive measure."

The birthmarks on Mark's belly are burning even more intensely. He can hardly stand the pain. "I … I can't," he manages to say. "I haven't done anything wrong. I won't go with you."

"You better go somewhere," Jim says. "Away from here. Go somewhere else. Somewhere you can fix whatever needs fixing."

Mark grunts as he writhes in pain. He inhales sharply, then glances at the misty forest again. He could still make it. If he focuses every ounce of his energy, he should be able to get himself across the road and into the woods before the French scene takes over completely. It isn't only the desire for privacy that compels him. He's overwhelmed by the growing awareness of rage directed at Jim. It's so intense, it scares him. He feels like he could tear the man limb from limb. That wouldn't be a good move. They'd lock him up for sure.

He still doesn't turn around. Instead, he looks harder at the woods. It seems like his only real option. If he stays here—close to Jim—he'll beat the guy to a bloody pulp. The birthmarks on his lower abdomen are on fire. The pain alone would make a lesser man flee into the forest. Mark thinks he's handling all of this pretty damn well. But he's got to move. The scene is pressing its way into his consciousness. He can't stay. He *has* to go.

Lights flicker around the edge of Mark's vision. Within seconds, the scene switches to the Frenchman in the white fencing uniform. Mark shakes his head in an effort to shake it off, but the birthmarks won't let him move on. They flare, seeming to wriggle and move on his skin. Instead of holding the French scene at bay, he tells himself to embrace it. He closes his eyes and lets the imagery flow freely, and it does just that.

In an instant, he's in the seventeenth-century room where his clothes have been set out in preparation for the duel. The white jacket, knee socks, and knickers are spread out on a bed with a wooden frame that is positioned against a stone wall. The room is small, with scarcely enough room to both sleep and dress in. His fencing shoes, chest protector, and mask are situated on a wooden nightstand beside the bed. There are no weapons in sight. Mark assumes his épée—or saber, maybe—will be waiting for him outside. He isn't as familiar with this particular time and place in history as he is with some others. He racks his brain, hoping it will fill in gaps and remember what he has learned.

What am I doing here? he wonders. *Am I here to face a real opponent? Or is this further evidence of my descent into madness.*

In response, a flood of knowing washes over him. Mark realizes that he is, in fact, here to face another man in a deadly duel. And that's not the only unsettling piece of information he receives. The two of them are fighting over a woman. He has a vague sense of lying down in the parking lot of the diner and covering his head with his hands, but that reality is distant now. His focus is what's happening in France.

A knock at the door of Mark's French bedroom startles him.

"Hello," a young man's voice says as he opens the door a crack and peeks in. He's here to escort Mark to the garden where the duel is to take place.

Oh, God, no, Mark thinks, remembering the boy in England. A wave of nausea washes over him as the gravity of that situation comes rushing back. He hopes against hope that this vision will be more pleasant.

"Hello, there," Mark replies.

"How are you doing?" the young man asks sheepishly. He knows exactly how Mark is doing. He's facing near-certain death in a duel. His opponent is bigger and stronger than he is. Mark has little chance of walking away the victor.

"Fine, thank you," Mark lies. He isn't doing well at all. It's common courtesy to reply politely, though. This poor boy isn't to blame for what's happening.

In a new wave of knowing, additional information makes its way into Mark's awareness. It's as if a tiny package of knowledge has been dropped into his brain. He receives the package and mentally opens it, revealing weighty contents. "Oh, no," he mumbles as new realizations settle over him.

Intuitively, Mark knows that—in this time and place—he is a low-born noble from a family down on its luck. They don't have money any more, and their reputation has suffered as a result. The Renaissance is in full swing, but it takes money that Mark doesn't have to truly thrive in this age. He also knows that he is the one who challenged his opponent to the duel. He could have made a different choice, and lived to tell about it. He could have spared his pride. The woman in question caused him to be impulsive. To issue the challenge before thinking it through.

Who is she? Mark thinks. He can sense that she's someone special. Someone he cares deeply for. Perhaps even someone he knows in the present.

The young man in front of him looks puzzled when Mark hesitates. He opens his mouth but doesn't speak. He closes his mouth, dumbfounded. "Sir?" he manages. He wants to be kind. He's duty-bound to meet Mark's needs, yet he doesn't know how to handle his subject's apparent confusion about the very serious situation he finds himself in.

Realizing he should speed up the discovery process, Mark restates the question silently. His mind obliges, shifting the scene to just moments before the duel begins. The next thing he knows, he's in the garden of a picturesque mansion. He can smell the fragrant flowers and hear their leaves rustling in the breeze. He intuitively understands that the lush property belongs to his opponent's family. He also knows that his adversary is an officer in the military. He's well-liked and respected. A worthy suitor for the woman they both wish to court.

Mark looks down at his uniform. He's fully outfitted and ready for the fight. His pulse quickens as he waits, realizing that the critical moment when the duel starts is but a short time away. *Who is she?* he asks again, in his mind. He wants to know. He feels compelled to know. *Whom am I doing this for?*

A small crowd in front of him parts and a beautiful woman emerges, meeting his gaze. She's demure, wearing a fancy pink dress that accentuates an ample bosom. In one hand, she holds a paper fan bearing an intricate lattice design. In the other, a single stem white rose. Her hair is long and dark. It's pinned at the back. When she smiles, Mark feels himself go weak in the knees.

"My love," Mark's adversary says as he wraps one arm around the woman's waist and pulls her in for a kiss. A sharp pang of jealousy practically knocks the wind out of Mark, and he's sure this woman is what all the fuss is about.

She turns, exposing a different angle of her face, and something in Mark clicks. He recognizes her. She looks different, but he can tell from the eyes. It's Reya. *His* Reya. And another man has his hands all over her.

In a whirlwind of feelings and imagery, the scene fast forwards. Mark watches helplessly as the duel begins. Weapons clank and clash as each man moves to protect himself and strike the other. Mark puts up a valiant fight, but it doesn't take long for the bigger man to end Mark's life with a few expert twists of his blade. In the end, Mark succumbs to his injuries while crumpled in a heap on the grass in the middle of the manicured garden, rich red blood pouring from his wounds.

He feels Thirsty Creek, Tennessee, coming back into focus.

"What do you mean?" Jim asks. He sounds exasperated. Mark must have been talking out loud without realizing it. Perhaps Jim has been asking questions that Mark didn't hear.

Mark feels nauseous as he arrives, fully alert and aware in his present body with this ugly new understanding of the relationship—and potentially, history—he shares with Reya. No wonder Mark felt so jealous of the chummy rapport between his girlfriend and Jim.

"I need help," Mark says. "Will you help me, please?" He knows how this looks, and he knows Jim will be quick to have him put away—one way or another.

"Yes," Jim says in response. He's wet from the rain now, too. He must have been leaning over Mark while he was out of it because his face is mostly dry, except for the tears streaming down his cheeks. "I'm calling this in."

"Don't!" Mark pleads. In the nick of time, tires slide on wet blacktop as a car pulls slowly into the parking lot and stops nearby. Mark looks puzzled at first, then recognizes the car. "Gigi?" he asks.

"What?" Jim replies. "No, that's Dawn Rollins. The waitress said you had her number keyed in, so she went ahead and called. Dawn came right away."

Mark smiles. "Her Mustang is named Gigi," he explains, "after her grandmother who gave her the money to buy it. Come to think of it, I need to talk to someone like her grandmother. That's what I've been missing. If I could just speak to someone who truly understands what I'm going through, maybe this will all make sense."

Dawn jumps out of the Mustang and rushes to Mark's side. She gives Jim little more than a passing glance. They're colleagues. They used to be friends, but Dawn is none too happy with the way Jim has treated

Mark of late. "Hey there, stranger," Dawn says as she helps Mark stand. "I hear you need a ride."

Mark nods. "I do. My friendly waitress, Taja, called you for me."

"Thanks for coming," Mark mouths. He's too choked up to speak. He appreciates these ladies so very much.

He climbs into Dawn's car, then the two of them speed away, leaving the diner—and Jim—in their dust.

15

RECKONING

"Do you feel comfortable in your skin?" the old woman asks as she settles into a cushioned chair. It's an odd question, and one that Mark has never fully considered.

The three of them are sitting on the patio outside Bernadette Lancaster's condo at Valley View retirement home. The rain has tapered off, but there's a chill in the air that prompted Bernadette to wear a sweater and a knit hat outdoors. She's all bundled up as if it's the dead of winter. Maybe September in Tennessee *is* the dead of winter, as far as she's concerned. Many people her age head south to places like Florida or Arizona around this time of year to spend the winter months in a warmer climate.

"I don't know," Mark says sheepishly. "I've never liked having all of these birthmarks, if that's what you mean."

"Why not?" she probes, her wise green eyes shining brightly behind her black-rimmed glasses. "They don't change who you are on the inside. You're still you. Am I wrong?"

Mark shakes his head as he and Dawn eat orange slices Bernadette has set out on the table in front of them. Dawn shoves a rind against her teeth, then smiles to expose the fruit's skin. She looks silly, and Mark chuckles. "You aren't wrong," he agrees. Dawn brought him here, explaining that Bernadette was a close friend of her grandmother's. She insists that—of everyone in Thirsty Creek—Bernadette will know what to do.

"I get the sense there's more to the story," the old lady says, her face determined.

Mark shifts nervously in his chair. "Are you … psychic?" he asks. "No offense, but you don't exactly look the part. I expected dim lighting and crystal balls. Tarot cards, maybe. You know? Like on TV. Yet you appear to be a perfectly normal and sane person."

Bernadette smiles with delight. "Then I have you fooled, young man." She throws her head back and lets out a raucous cackle. Something about it makes the hairs on the back of Mark's neck stand on end.

"Okay," he says simply.

Dawn leans forward. "Bernadette here played Bunko with Gigi for years. They soon became fast friends— once they realized all they had in common."

"Bunko?" Mark asks.

"It's a dice game," Dawn explains. "It's played in a large group, but Gigi and Bernadette paired up and got to know each other more closely. Right, Bee?"

Bernadette smiles, pleased to hear Dawn use her nickname. She seems lonely, like she craves human interaction. Mark knows the feeling. Even though he lives with Reya—or used to—he often feels alone. The feeling dates back to his childhood. "It must be nice to have a friend like that," he muses.

"Hey, now," Dawn says, shoving Mark's arm gently. "What am I? Chopped liver?" She grins as Mark shrugs timidly. "You have friends, Mark. By the looks of it, you're making new ones every day."

They all laugh, and it feels good. Mark senses that the conversation will turn deadly serious soon. He'll take the reprieve from all the heaviness while he can get it.

"Okay, okay," Dawn says. "We agree that it's good to have friends and to be friends. Mark knows that. Don't you?" She eyes him sympathetically.

"I do," he replies. "I've met some of the nicest people lately. Although, to be fair, I've also met some of the most irritating people as well."

"Yeah? Like who?" Dawn asks.

"Well, for starters, there was that asshole at the scene of the car accident. Theodore. Tell me you remember him," he says to Dawn.

"I do," she confirms. "But I didn't think he was a bad guy. A bit pretentious, perhaps."

Mark's face tenses. "Pretentious?" he asks. "That's all?"

Dawn nods as Bernadette looks on knowingly. "He didn't irritate me, for what it's worth. I'm not sure why he bothered you so much."

Mark shudders dramatically in response. "That prick makes my skin crawl," he says.

"Sounds like it's a good thing you ran into him," Bernadette muses.

Mark meets her gaze. "I'm sorry. A good thing? Why in the world would meeting someone who irritates me be a *good* thing?"

"Because it's part of your awakening," she says matter-of-factly. "People come into our lives and activate certain responses deep within us. That's when you know you're on the right path. The path of awakening."

Dawn chews her lip nervously. She's sitting with one leg crossed over the other, and she bounces the outstretched foot to the rhythm of salsa music that can be heard from the condo of Bernadette's next-door neighbor. "What's wrong?" Mark asks her when he notices.

She shakes her head dismissively. "Don't mind me. This stuff creeps me out. That's all. Go on. Get to the woo-woo part. We all know it's coming."

Mark nods. "I guess we do."

Taking the cue, Bernadette leans farther forward. "Who else has irritated you?" she asks, and Mark wonders how much Dawn has told the old woman. He hasn't had much chance to catch Dawn up on the vision of the French duel.

"Jim irritates me," Mark admits. "Even more than Theodore at this point. And it's funny because, at first, I thought he was a friend. I thought he was *your* friend, Dawn."

"We were friendly," Dawn says. "But I don't like the way he's treated you."

Mark smiles appreciatively. "Thank you," he says, his voice thin and breathy.

Bernadette glances down at an elegant silver watch on one wrist. It had been hidden under the sleeve of her sweater. The reflective surface on its face catches the light from the sun and redirects it. "I don't mean to be rude," she says, "but an old broad like me has earned the luxury of cutting to the chase."

"Are we keeping you from something?" Mark asks.

"Not yet," Bernadette says. "Though you will be if we don't move things along at a faster clip. Family Feud comes on in an hour. That Steve Harvey is a gas."

Mark looks confused. "I don't know what that means," he admits. He's probably too young to have heard the phrase before.

"It means that he's funny," Dawn clarifies. "Bee is saying Steve Harvey is funny."

Mark's brows raise in understanding. "Oh, okay," he says.

He and Dawn exchange knowing glances. *This is it,* he thinks. *The only remaining hope of making sense of what's happening to me lies with this old woman, and we're on the clock. The mysteries of my mind must be solved before Steve Harvey graces her television.*

After a pause, Bernadette says, "Are we ready to get down to business?"

"I might regret this," Mark replies, "but yes, let's do it."

"Good," Bernadette says, a knowing smile spreading across her face. "You get comfortable while I get into the zone. I'll close my eyes and will probably be silent for a few minutes. It takes time for the spirits to speak to me. When I have something to say, I will."

Mark nods. "You'll do this right here? On the patio?"

Bernadette chuckles. "You have a better place in mind?"

"I guess I envisioned a dark room or something. I don't know," Mark replies. "Forgive me. I'm new to this."

"You want a room with a crystal ball and tarot cards, yeah?"

"Something like that," he confirms. "But please, do your thing. I'll keep quiet."

Bernadette sighs, then nods her agreement. "Watch and learn, kid," she says as her eyes roll back in her head and she makes a circle out of the thumb and forefinger of each hand. It's the kind of posture monks and yogis assume during meditation. Bernadette looks like an odd bird, doing this psychic—*whatever* this is—right on the patio of her condo while salsa music continues in the background.

For what feels like a long time, the old woman is perfectly still. Her eyes flutter under their lids, but nothing else moves. Mark and Dawn watch her like a hawk, anxiously waiting for her to speak. Mark wonders if Dawn's grandmother did this, too, but he doesn't dare interrupt Bernadette to ask.

Mark is remarkably calm, given everything he's been through lately. He thought he might experience more visions while in the presence of the psychic woman, but that's not proving to be the case. His mind is clear. He's ready to face what he must. He feels like a sick patient willing to gratefully receive a grave diagnosis. A person reaches a point where they're simply relieved to know what's wrong. To put a name and a face to what ails them. He hopes Bernadette will help him do that here today. He wants to get on with whatever is next. It's time.

Suddenly, the lights flicker off and on inside Bernadette's condo. It reminds Mark of the lights he sees around the edges of his vision when a new scene enters his consciousness. A clank and then a hum can be heard as power turns back on. A few seconds later, a breeze whips around them, shaking the umbrella overhead. Bernadette doesn't stir.

Finally, moments later, the old woman opens her eyes wide and stares at Mark. "Get me a pen and paper," she says to Dawn without shifting her gaze. Dawn jumps up and goes into the condo to do as she's been told.

"What is it?" Mark asks eagerly. "What do you see?"

He purposely hasn't shared much of his story with Bernadette. He wants to be as sure as possible that her reactions are received from somewhere other than her own mind. It's the best way he knows to prove that her psychic abilities are legitimate.

"They think you have a mental disorder. That you should be medicated and locked up," she says. There's a hint of sadness in her voice. Mark appreciates her compassion.

"Did Dawn tell you about that?" he asks, immediately regretting it.

"No, I didn't," Dawn says as she returns with the pen and paper, then closes a sliding glass door behind her. "I didn't mention that, specifically."

"Let me guess. Schizophrenia?" Bernadette adds. "Because you see reality differently. I'm sorry."

Mark shakes his head. He inadvertently gave the truth away when he asked Dawn if she'd told Bernadette. The old woman could piece the mental disorder aspect together with some general knowledge and what she had been told. *Damn*, he thinks. *I need to know if this woman can actually help me.* He changes the subject. "What do you want the pen and paper for? Do you sketch things that you see in your mind's eye? Or do you draw lots of lines like that kid on TV does? He's a medium, right? Hollywood Medium, I believe they call him."

Bernadette chuckles. "Nothing like that. I want to take notes on what we discuss. That's all."

"Oh," Mark says, growing disappointed. Perhaps he should find someone with a crystal ball. This is turning out to be a huge letdown.

"Now, I suspect you're seeing things that aren't really there. Am I correct?" she asks.

Mark nods reluctantly. "Maybe. I don't know."

"Are you hearing things, too? Smelling things?"

He remembers the roar of the saber-toothed tiger, the sounds of stomping feet and crashing waves in Ancient Greece, and the smell of alcohol on the breath of the men in England. The answer is absolutely. Yes. He doesn't want to give it away, though.

"The look on your face tells me all I need to know," Bernadette says. "So, that's yes to hearing and smelling things that aren't there." She picks up the pen and makes a note on the paper in front of her.

"I thought you were supposed to be telling me things," Mark says. "Not the other way around."

"Patience," she says, holding up a hand. "We're getting there."

He jerks his gaze to one side, resting it on a trio of clay pots filled with colorful pansies. Dawn reaches out and squeezes his hand. "Don't get frustrated," she implores. "Give Bee a chance before you decide she can't help you."

Mark knows his friend might be right. It's just that he's so sick and tired of living like this. He wants this misery to end. "Right," he says. "I know."

For her part, Bernadette doesn't seem phased by Mark's doubt. She has more questions ready for him. "Do you meditate?" she asks. "If not, I could teach you how. I have a daily practice that really keeps my mind clear and in tip-top condition. It might—"

"Is that before or after Steve Harvey?" Mark quips, cutting her off.

Dawn smacks him on the knee. "Stop it," she says.

Mark shakes his head again. "Sorry, go on. Please. Tell me what you see … about my life … my future."

Bernadette hesitates, but is poised to resume. She seems largely oblivious to Mark's distress. He's beginning to think she simply wanted a way to pass the time this morning. *Doesn't she understand how serious my predicament is?* he wonders.

"How's your diet?" she asks. "Because vitamin D deficiency—or even B12 deficiency—can really mess a person up." She scribbles the name of both vitamins on her paper as Mark silently seethes.

He looks at Dawn, waiting for her to concede that this isn't working. She exhales a burst of air she's been holding, then slowly nods to acknowledge that this is a bust. "Could I talk to you privately for a moment?" Mark asks her.

"Sure," she replies.

"Bernadette, please excuse us," Mark says. "May Dawn and I step inside your condo for a brief chat? We'll be right back."

"You may," the old woman replies. "I'll close my eyes again and see what additional information I can get about your situation."

"Thank you for your efforts," Mark says. "I appreciate you trying to help me." He's being sincere. Even though he's disappointed in the results, he doesn't want to hurt Bernadette's feelings. She's a nice old lady, and she was a friend of Dawn's grandmother.

"I'll keep at it," she replies. "When you come back out, I'll have something else for you."

Mark smiles, but he knows nothing useful is coming. He feels deflated, like a sad balloon. He follows Dawn's lead as she steps inside the condo.

"It was worth a try," Dawn says when the glass door is closed and they're alone.

"Yeah," he replies.

Dawn shrugs. "I've heard some people say that intuition or psychic powers, or whatever you want to call it, shows up when it shows up. They can't summon it on demand. Maybe that's how it is for Bee."

"Maybe."

"Hey, don't look so blue," she says as she elbows Mark playfully. "We can find someone in Nashville, right? There's plenty more to try. We're just beginning to investigate."

"If you say so," he mutters.

They stand silently for a moment, letting the gravity of the situation sink in. Mark needs a job, a place to stay, a car, and a phone. He hates to ask Dawn for help with any of those things, but he doesn't have much choice. He's going to be a huge disappointment to his son. He figures he might as well face that fact, as much as it hurts to do so.

Remembering the Oxy in his pocket, Mark decides it's a good time to let the drug give him a desperately needed boost. He lifts his head, searching for the bathroom. His eyes land on what looks like a powder room across from the kitchen. "Excuse me for a minute, will you? I need to use the restroom."

"Okay," Dawn replies. "It's over there, by the kitchen."

Mark nods, then makes his way to the privacy of the little room and locks the door tightly behind him. It feels like the entire world is crashing down on him. The deluge is relentless.

He turns on the water in the sink, then takes the plastic baggie of pills from his pocket and pops a few into his mouth. He moves them to the back of his throat, then swallows with the help of a swig of water. He remembers doing the same in the bathroom at the high school football game just a few days prior. He still had a job then, and Reya was still talking to him. He shudders to think what his life might be like in another few weeks. If the descent continues at the same rate, it won't be good. *Fuck it*, he thinks, then pops a few more pills into his mouth. *What do I have to lose?*

He's leaning against the bathroom door and waiting for the drugs to take effect when he's jolted by a sharp knock on the other side. "Mark?" Dawn asks. Her tone is urgent.

"Yeah?"

"Are you okay in there?"

"Fine," he replies. "I'll be out in a few minutes."

"Mark, I need to tell you something," she says. "Please, come out right away."

He purses his lips, wondering what has Dawn worked up. She isn't the type to get alarmed unnecessarily. He checks to be sure the Oxy has been returned securely to his pants pocket, then turns and flings the door open. "What is it?" he asks.

Dawn's expression is tense. "Maybe you should sit down," she says. "You've been through a lot lately."

"I'm fine. Tell me."

She shakes her head, but decides to go ahead. "I got a text from Michael. Reya's in labor."

"What?" Mark asks, excited. A smile spreads across his face. "That's great news! But wait. How does Michael know?"

Dawn takes a breath to steady herself. "He picked Reya up in his rig. There may be a complication. Her water broke and the fluid was blood-tinged. She hasn't felt the baby move in hours."

"Oh, God," Mark mumbles, shoving a hand through his hair. "I have to get to the hospital."

"Slow down," Dawn says. "She didn't call you, remember."

"I don't have a phone for her to call!" Mark shouts. "If you think I'm going to miss the birth of my son, you're out of your mind. Reya can't keep me away, even if she wanted to. I've got to go to them."

After a beat, Dawn says, "I think we should wait a while. I asked Michael to text again once she's admitted. They don't know anything yet."

Mark closes his eyes, wondering what to do. When he opens them, his gaze lands on Dawn's car keys. She placed them in a wooden bowl on the sofa table when they arrived at Bernadette's condo. He knows exactly what he has to do. There's no time for discussion or debate. "Okay," he says to his friend. "Go ahead out on the patio with Bernadette. We've kept her waiting long enough. I'll wash my hands and join you. I'll only be a minute."

"I can wait—" she says.

"No need. We don't want to be rude. Just keep your phone next to you in case Michael texts an update from the hospital," he says.

Dawn nods, then turns to join Bernadette, as promised. Mark makes a show of dutifully washing his hands while he waits for his friend to reach the patio and sit down. Once she does, he leaps into action, grabbing her car keys and scooting out the front door. *I'm sorry, Dawn*, he thinks. *I have to go. Now. I hope you can forgive me.*

The car's alarm system beeps when Mark presses the key fob to unlock the driver's door. Dawn and Bernadette will probably hear it around back, so he has to move fast. He jumps into the vehicle and starts up the ignition. The engine purrs, ready to take him to his love and their newborn son. He backs out of the parking space, then speeds as he turns onto the open road.

It's a short drive from Valley View to the hospital. Mark estimates that he'll arrive in less than ten minutes. Maybe less, if traffic is thin. As he drives, he works to process what's happening. It's a lot. Deciding he needs a little music in the background, he turns on the radio and cranks it up. "Once Bitten Twice Shy" blares through the speakers, its familiar "my, my, my" lyrics stirring Mark's emotions.

The song is immediately familiar, but it takes Mark a few beats to remember that it was playing on the radio the day of his car accident. So much has transpired since then. In fact—looking back—that day was a demarcation. There was life before, and now there's life after. Nothing is the same as it was. Mark wonders if he would have changed his route that morning to avoid the crash, had he known. If feels dangerous to cheat fate, yet he wishes he could return to the more peaceful and predictable existence he once had.

Was I really living, though? he thinks. *Shouldn't life be more than what it was? My existence was small. Shallow. It's as if I was waiting for something to happen that would open me up and show me that there's more than a stifling job and tiptoeing around my girlfriend, hoping she'd eventually come to love me as much as I love her.*

Tears prick at the corners of his eyes. Although he doesn't want to be petty or immature, he can't help but think how unfair this all is. His life is in shambles, and now his son could be in danger.

Mark doesn't have to be a medical professional to know that blood-tinged amniotic fluid and lack of fetal movement doesn't sound good. He once knew a colleague who didn't feel her baby move for several hours. As it turned out, the placenta had separated from the wall of her uterus and the baby was dead in there. A full-term baby, suffocated from having his oxygen supply cut off. It was devastating to everyone who knew her. That woman never fully recovered.

Let him be okay, Mark thinks. *I can't handle that kind of loss right now. Or ever. I need my son to be okay.*

Overwhelmed by emotion, Mark turns the music up even louder to meet his mood. As the beat pounds and the voices wail, he realizes just how hard he's tried to hold everything together.

He's tired of feeling desperate to do the impossible. Desperate to hide his birthmarks from a world ready to scorn him for the pigment in his skin. Desperate to cope with the dysfunction of his parents that had nothing to do with him or his poor sisters. As an adult, desperate to hold onto jobs that were keeping him small. Desperate to earn enough money to survive and support a family. Desperate to keep his bizarre visions at bay so the people around him wouldn't think he's crazy. Desperate to make friends who would have his best interests at heart. And most of all, desperate to keep Reya happy. To keep Reya *with him*. Desperate, desperate, desperate.

"Dammit!" he yells as he pounds the steering wheel.

Mark's vision begins to blur. He isn't certain whether that's because his eyes are filled with tears or it's a result of the Oxy kicking in. He swerves, nearly missing a metal mailbox on the side of the road. He then overcorrects, careening into a lane of oncoming traffic. A car honks its horn at him, narrowly missing a collision. He waves an apology, then keeps going. He must get to the hospital. To Reya and the baby.

Am I cursed? he thinks. *Do I have to pay for the things I've done? I don't think I'm a bad guy, but I've made mistakes. Sure. So, maybe this living hell won't be over until I take some necessary action. But what?*

Feeling a wetness on his leg, Mark's attention is drawn to a sticky liquid that appears to be all over the console and part of his lap. He looks more closely and finds Dawn's cup of diet soda on the floorboard. It must have been knocked out of the cup holder when he swerved to miss the mailbox. The lid is off, and the cup looks empty now. *Oh, no,* he thinks. *Dawn's going to kill me. She loves this car.*

Something about the spilled soda feels like a metaphor. It isn't spilled milk, but there's a case to be made for not crying over it. *There's a life lesson here*, he thinks. He presses on, picking up even more speed as he barrels toward the hospital.

It takes him a minute, but suddenly, he has an epiphany. *Maybe,* he thinks, *I'm not in control. Maybe fate is real. Maybe I should stop trying to control what happens in my life.*

His vision is tunneling now, and he's feeling woozy. The Oxy is taking over. Mark wishes he hadn't swallowed those extra few pills beyond what his body had become used to. He's never tested this much at once.

That thought causes him to consider the flip side again more seriously and wonders if his life actually *is* within his control. *If I'd made different choices, my life would be different. And whoa,* he thinks, his mind blown by the enormity of the realization. *Both things are true. I'm in control of nothing and everything—all at once.*

With that realization in mind, glass shatters and metal crunches in on Mark from the side. It happens so fast, he doesn't have time to see the truck as it barrels over him and crumples Dawn's car to pieces.

In an instant, everything goes black.

EPILOGUE

"He's beautiful!" the overjoyed new mother says as her pink, wriggling baby boy takes his first gulp of air and lets out a vigorous cry. Forgotten are the torturous pains and discomforts she endured just moments before. This moment is pure bliss. Pure love.

"You have a perfect little boy," the doctor says as he smiles proudly. He hands the baby to an attendant, happy to have helped bring another healthy child into the world.

The mother and the doctor look on as a young nurse wraps the infant in a receiving blanket and holds him up like the prize they know he is. When the baby cries once more, delighted coos erupt from everyone present in the labor and delivery room.

His lungs are strong. His body is capable. This child will thrive.

"You did good, mama," an old, wise nurse says as she gives the mother's arm a gentle squeeze.

"Would you like to hold your son?" the doctor asks.

"Yes!" the mother exclaims, propping herself up and making her arms a cradle. Under the doctor's watchful gaze, the young nurse lowers the baby into his mother's waiting arms.

When mother's and baby's eyes meet, everything else falls away. Born out of unconditional love, this baby is blessed with a positive new beginning.

Noticing a small, strawberry-colored spot on the baby's forehead, the mother grows concerned. The spot looks different from the rest of the infant's skin. "Is that a birthmark?" she asks.

The doctor leans in to take a closer look. "That pink patch?" he asks.

The mother nods. "Should I be worried?"

"It's harmless," he says. "It will probably go away on its own. It might be more visible when he cries. But don't worry. Most of these marks fade and disappear completely."

"What if this one doesn't go away?"

The doctor and the old, wise nurse glance at each other, then at the anxious new mother. They've seen this time and again. New mothers are prone to worry about the tiniest things.

"Don't worry, mama," the nurse reaffirms.

With a reassuring smile, the doctor moves on to more important matters. "Tell us, what is the baby's name?" he asks.

The new mother's face lights up. Beaming with pride, she says, "Mark. My baby's name is Mark."

THE END.

Get Christopher Kelly's next book:

Counting Sheep
A Supernatural Thriller

ENJOY THIS BOOK?

ABOUT THE AUTHOR

Standards of Starlight Books
Christopher Kelly

Christopher Kelly is the combined pen name of Kelly Utt and her son, Christopher. Together, they write pulse-pounding supernatural thrillers.

Their novels are inspired by the works of some of their favorite writers and filmmakers, including Dean Koontz, Jeff VanderMeer, H. P. Lovecraft, Stephen King, Guillermo del Toro, and M. Night Shyamalan.

They live in Nashville, Tennessee, USA.

Connect at christopherkellybooks.com, and on Instagram, Facebook, and TikTok at @authorchristopherkelly.

www.ingramcontent.com/pod-product-compliance
Lightning Source LLC
Chambersburg PA
CBHW050829190726
48286CB00007B/2018